D1550557

THE CASE OF THE CARELESS KITTEN

ERLE STANLEY GARDNER (1889-1970) was the best-selling American author of the 20th century, mainly due to the enormous success of his Perry Mason series, which numbered more than 80 novels and inspired a half-dozen motion pictures, radio programs, and a long-running television series that starred Raymond Burr. Having begun his career as a pulp writer, Gardner brought a hard-boiled style and sensibility to the early Mason books, but gradually developed into a more classic detective story novelist, showing enough clues to allow the astute reader to solve the mystery. For more than a quarter of a century he wrote more than a million words a year under his own name and numerous pseudonyms, the most famous being A.A. Fair.

OTTO PENZLER, the creator of American Mystery Classics, is also the founder of the Mysterious Press (1975), a literary crime imprint now associated with Grove/Atlantic; MysteriousPress.com (2011), an electronic-book publishing company; and New York City's Mysterious Bookshop (1979). He has won a Raven, the Ellery Queen Award, two Edgars (for the *Encyclopedia of Mystery and Detection*, 1977, and *The Lineup*, 2010), and lifetime achievement awards from NoirCon and *The Strand Magazine*. He has edited more than 70 anthologies and written extensively about mystery fiction.

THE CASE OF THE CARELESS KITTEN

ERLE STANLEY GARDNER

Introduction by
OTTO PENZLER

**AMERICAN
MYSTERY
CLASSICS**

Penzler Publishers
New York

Published in 2019 by Penzler Publishers
58 Warren Street, New York, NY 10007
penzlerpublishers.com

Distributed by W. W. Norton

Cover image: Andy Ross
Cover design: Mauricio Diaz

Paperback ISBN 9781613161166
Hardcover ISBN 9781613161159
eBook ISBN 9781613161197

Library of Congress Control Number: 2018963378

Printed in the United States of America

9 8 7 6 5 4 3 2 1

THE CASE OF THE CARELESS KITTEN

INTRODUCTION

To TALK about Erle Stanley Gardner, it is inevitable that large numbers come into play. Here are a few:

*86—Number of Perry Mason books; eighty-two novels, four short story collections.

*130—Number of mystery novels written by Gardner.

*1,200,000—The number of words that Gardner wrote annually during most of the 1920s and 1930s. That is a novel a month, plus a stack of short stories, for a fifteen-year stretch.

*2,400,000—The number of words Gardner wrote in his most productive year, 1932.

*300,000,000—The number of books Gardner has sold in the United States alone, making him the best-selling writer in the history of American literature.

What cannot be quantified is what magic resided in that indefatigable brain that made so many millions of readers come back, book after book, for more of the same. Not that it was the same.

The Perry Mason series had a template, a model, a formula, if you like. But the series changed dramatically over the years. Gardner started his career as a writer for the pulp magazines that flourished in the 1920s and 1930s. Authors were famously paid a penny a word by most of the pulps, but the top writers in the top magazines managed to get all the way up to three cents a word. This munificent fee was reserved for the best of the best of their time, some of whom remain popular and successful to the present day (Dashiell Hammett, Raymond Chandler, Cornell Woolrich), some of whom are remembered and read mostly by the modest coterie that avidly reads and collects pulp fiction (Carroll John Daly, Arthur Leo Zagat, Arthur J. Burks). One who earned the big bucks regularly, especially when he wrote for *Black Mask*, the greatest of the pulps, was Erle Stanley Gardner.

Gardner had learned and honed his craft in the pulps, so it is not surprising that the earliest Perry Mason novels were hard-boiled, tough-guy books, with Mason as a fearless, two-fisted battler, rather than the calm self-possessed figure that most readers remember today. Reading the first Mason novels, *The Case of the Velvet Claws*, published in 1933, and *The Case of the Careless Kitten*, published twenty years later, it is difficult to remember that they were written by the same author. Both styles, by the way, were first-rate, just different.

Gardner was born in Malden, Massachusetts, in 1889. Because his father was a mining engineer, he traveled often as a child. As a teenager, he participated in professional boxing as well as promoting unlicensed matches, placing himself at risk of criminal prosecution, which gave him an interest in the law. He took a job as a typist at a California law firm and after reading law for fifty hours a week for three years, he was admitted to the California bar. He practiced in Oxnard from 1911 to 1918, gaining a reputation as a champion of the underdog through his defense of poor Mexican and Chinese clients.

He left to become a tire salesman in order to earn more money but he missed the courtroom and joined another law firm in 1921. It is then that he started to write fiction, hoping that he could augment his modest income. He worked a full day at court, followed that with several hours of research in the law library, then went home to write fiction into the small hours, setting a goal of at least 4,000 words a day. He sold two stories in 1921, none in 1922, and only one in 1923, but it was to the prestigious *Black Mask*. The following year, thirteen of his stories saw print, five of them in *Black Mask*. Over the next decade he wrote nearly fifteen million words and sold hundreds of stories, many pseudonymously so that he could have multiple stories in a single magazine, each under a different name.

In 1932, he finally took a vacation, an extended trip to China, since he had become so financially successful. That is also the year in which he began to submit his first novel, *The Case of the Velvet Claws*. It was rejected by several publishers before William Morrow took it, and Gardner published every mystery with that house for the rest of his life. Thayer Hobson, then the president of Morrow, suggested that the protagonist of that book, Perry Mason, should become a series character and Gardner agreed.

The Mason novels became an immediate success so Gardner resigned from his law practice to devote full time to writing. He was eager to have privacy so acquired parcels of land in the Southwest and eventually settled into the "Gardner Fiction Factory" on a thousand-acre ranch in Temecula, California. The ranch had a dozen guest cottages and trailers to house his support staff of twenty employees, all of whom are reported to have called him "Uncle Erle." Among them were six secretaries, all working full time, transcribing his dictated novels, non-fiction books and articles, and correspondence.

He was intensely interested in prison conditions and was a strong advocate of reform. In 1948, he formed the Court of Last Resort, a private organization dedicated to helping those believed to have been unfairly incarcerated. The group succeeded in freeing many unjustly convicted men and Gardner wrote a book, *The Court of Last Resort*, describing the group's work; it won an Edgar for the best fact crime book of the year.

In the 1960s, Gardner became alarmed at some changes in American literature. He told the *New York Times*, "I have always aimed my fiction at the masses who constitute the solid backbone of America, I have tried to keep faith with the American family. In a day when the prevailing mystery story trends are towards sex, sadism, and seduction, I try to base my stories on speed, situation, and suspense."

While Gardner wrote prolifically about a wide variety of characters under many pseudonyms, most notably thirty novels about Bertha Cook and Donald Lam under the nom de plume A.A. Fair, all his books give evidence of clearly identifiable characteristics. There is a minimum of description and a maximum of dialogue. This was carried to a logical conclusion in the lengthy courtroom interrogations of the Perry Mason series. Mason and Gardner's other heroes are not averse to breaking the exact letter of the law in order to secure what they consider to be justice. They share contempt for pomposity. Villains or deserving victims are often self-important, wealthy individuals who can usually be identified because Gardner has given them two last names (such as Harrington Faulkner).

Mason's clients usually have something to hide and, although they are ultimately proven innocent, their secretiveness makes them appear suspect.

Clues often take a back seat in the Perry Mason books, with crisp dialogue and hectic action taking the forefront—a structure clearly adopted from his days as a pulp writer. Crime and motivation are not paragons of originality as Gardner wanted readers to identify with his characters.

Much like the Sherlock Holmes and Nero Wolfe stories, the Perry Mason novels also feature certain other characters on a regular basis. The most prominent is Della Street, Mason's secretary and the love of his life. Knowing that Mason would not allow her to work, she has refused his marriage proposals on five separate occasions. She has, however, remained steadfastly loyal, risking her life and freedom on his behalf; she has been arrested five times while performing her job.

Also present at all times is Paul Drake, the private detective who handles the lawyer's investigative work. He is invariably at Mason's side in times of stress, though he frequently complains that the work is bad for his digestion.

Hamilton Burger is the district attorney whose office has never successfully prosecuted one of Mason's clients. In a large percentage of those cases, the client was arrested through the efforts of the attorney's implacable (albeit friendly) foe, Lieutenant Arthur Tragg.

Although Mason is invariably well-prepared, he is so skilled at courtroom procedure that he can think on his feet and ask just the right question to befuddle a witness, embarrass a prosecutor, and exonerate a client.

The staggering popularity of the Perry Mason novels inevitably led to him being portrayed in other media, including six motion pictures in the 1930s, a successful radio series in the 1940s, and a top-rated television series starring Raymond Burr that began in 1957 and ran for a decade. More than a half-century later, it is still a staple of late-night television re-runs.

—OTTO PENZLER

1

THE KITTEN'S eyes, weaving back and forth, followed the ball of crumpled paper that Helen Kendal was waving high above the arm of the chair. The kitten was named Amber Eyes because of those yellow eyes.

Helen liked to watch them. Their black pupils were always changing, narrowing to ominous slits, widening to opaque pools of onyx. Those black and amber eyes had an almost hypnotic effect on Helen. After she had watched them a little while her thoughts seemed to slip. She would forget the near things, like today, and this room, and the kitten; she could even forget about Jerry Templar and Aunt Matilda's eccentric domineerings, and find herself suddenly thinking about things that were far away or long ago.

It was one of the long-ago things this time. Years and years ago. When Helen Kendal was ten, and there was another kitten, a gray-and-white one, up on the roof. So high up that it was afraid to come down. And a tall man with kind gray eyes had fetched a long ladder and was standing up at the wobbly tip of it, patiently coaxing the kitten toward his outstretched hand.

Uncle Franklin. Helen was thinking about him now as she had thought about him then. Not as she had learned to think about him afterward, from other people. Not as Aunt Matilda's runaway husband, not as Franklin Shore, the Missing Banker, in the big headlines, not as the man who had inexplicably thrown away success and wealth and power and family and lifelong friends, to lose himself, moneyless, among strangers. Helen was thinking of him, now, only as the Uncle Franklin who had risked his life to rescue a scared kitten for a sorrowful little girl, as the only father whom that little girl had ever known, a gentle, understanding, friendly father, remembered, after all these years, with a love that knew and would keep on knowing, against all seeming proofs to the contrary, that it had been returned.

That knowledge, suddenly rediscovered, made Helen Kendal absolutely sure that Franklin Shore was dead. He must be. He must have died long ago, soon after he had run away. He'd loved her. He must have loved her, or he wouldn't have risked sending her that picture post card from Florida soon after he disappeared, just when Aunt Matilda was trying so hard to find him and he must have been trying even harder to keep her from doing it. He couldn't have lived very long after that or there'd have been another message for Helen. He'd have known how she'd be hoping for one. He wouldn't have disappointed her. He was dead. He'd been dead for almost ten years.

He was dead, and Helen had a right to the twenty thousand dollars he had left her in his will. And that much money now, with Jerry Templar home on a week's leave—

Helen's thoughts slipped again. The Army had made a difference in Jerry. His blue eyes were steadier, his mouth grimmer. But the change in him only made Helen surer that she loved him, and surer than ever, for all his tight-lipped silence on the subject, that he'd kept on loving her. He wasn't going to marry her, though. Not when it might mean that Aunt Matilda would turn her out of the house, to live on his Army pay. But if she had money, money of her own, money enough to let Jerry feel perfectly sure that no matter what happened to him, she'd never be homeless or hungry—

There was no use in thinking about it. Aunt Matilda wasn't going to change her mind. It wasn't that kind of a mind. Once it was made up, even Aunt Matilda herself couldn't change it. And it was made up permanently to believe that Franklin Shore was alive, and just as permanently and immovably made up not to take the steps at law that would declare him legally dead and allow his will to be probated. Aunt Matilda didn't need her share of the estate. As Franklin Shore's wife, she controlled the property he had left behind him almost as completely as she could hope to control it as his widow and executrix. She controlled Helen, penniless and dependent, far more completely than she would control her after that twenty-thousand-dollar legacy was paid.

And Aunt Matilda enjoyed controlling people. She'd never willingly give up her purse-string power over Helen, especially not while Jerry Templar was here. Aunt Matilda had never liked him nor approved of Helen's liking him, and the change the Army had made in him only seemed to make her dislike more explicit than ever. There wasn't a chance on earth of her letting go of that legacy before Jerry's leave was up. Unless Uncle Gerald—

Helen's thoughts shifted again. Uncle Gerald, three days ago, telling her he was going to force Aunt Matilda's hand. His brother's will left him the same sum it bequeathed to Helen. Sixty-two and looking older, still practicing law for his living, he could use his money and felt he'd waited for it long enough.

"I can make Matilda act, and I'm going to do it," he'd said. "We all know Franklin's dead. He's been legally dead for three years. I want my legacy and I want you to have yours."

His eyes had softened and warmed as they studied her, Helen remembered, and his voice had been warmer, too, and gentler.

"You're more like your mother every time I see you, Helen.

Even when you were little you had her eyes, with the violets in them, and her hair, with the red just showing under the gold. And you've grown up to have her tall, slim, lovely body and her long, lovely hands, and even her quiet, lovely voice. I liked your father, but I never quite forgave him for taking her away from us."

He had stopped. And there had been something different about his voice when he went on. "You're going to need your twenty thousand dollars before long, Helen."

"I need it now," Helen had said.

"Jerry Templar?" Her face must have been answer enough, because he hadn't waited for her to speak. He'd nodded slowly. "All right. I'll try to get you that money." He'd sounded as if he meant to do more than just try. And it had been three days ago. Maybe—

Amber Eyes had stood it as long as he could. He flashed up in a leap toward that maddening ball of paper, clutching with teeth and claws; then, starting to fall, struck instinctively for Helen's wrist, clinging with needle-sharp claws trying to save himself from a fall to the carpeted floor.

Violently startled, Helen screamed.

Aunt Matilda called sharply from her room, "What's the matter, Helen?"

"Nothing," Helen said, laughing nervously as she grasped the kitten's paw with her free hand, disengaging the clutching claws. "Amber Eyes scratched me, that's all."

"What's the matter with Amber Eyes?"

"Nothing. We were just playing."

"Stop playing with that kitten. You're spoiling it."

"Yes, Aunt Matilda," Helen said dutifully, stroking the kitten and regarding the scratches on the back of her hand.

"I suppose," she said to Amber Eyes, "you don't know that your little claws are sharp. Now I've got to go put something on my hand."

She was in the bathroom at the medicine cabinet when she heard the sound of Matilda's cane; then the door of the bedroom opened, and Matilda stood frowning at her.

Matilda Shore, at sixty-four, had a full ten years of deferred vengeance behind her. Sciatica had not improved her disposition. She was a big-boned woman. In her youth, she must have had a certain Amazon type of beauty, but now she had lost all regard for personal appearance. Flesh had wrapped itself around her frame. Her shoulders were stooped. She habitually carried her head pushed forward and down. There were deep, sagging pouches under her eyes. Her mouth had taken on a sharp, downward curve. But none of the encroachments of time had been able to eradicate from her features the grim determination of a woman of indomitable will who lived with a single, definite purpose in mind.

"Let me see where the cat scratched you," she demanded.

"It wasn't the kitten's fault, Aunt Matilda. I was playing with it, and holding out a piece of paper for it to jump at. I didn't realize that I was holding it so far from the floor. Amber Eyes just tried to hang on, that's all."

Aunt Matilda glared at the scratched hand.

"I heard somebody talking a while ago. Who was it?"

"Jerry." Helen tried her best not to say it defensively, but Aunt Matilda's eyes were too much for her. "He only stayed a few minutes."

"So I noticed." It was clear that Aunt Matilda took a grim pleasure in the brevity of the visit. "You might as well make up your mind to it, Helen. It's quite plain that he's made up his. He has sense enough to see he can't possibly marry you. And it's a good thing for you that he can't. You're just fool enough to do it if he asked you to."

"Just exactly fool enough," Helen said.

"Meaning you aren't a fool at all." Aunt Matilda sniffed. "That's what fools always think. It's lucky for you that what you think doesn't matter. He's the worst possible type for a girl like you. He's a man's man. He'll never be any good to a woman. That padlocked, shut-mouthed repression of his would drive you mad. You've got enough of it for two, yourself. I've been married twice and I know what I'm talking about. The only sort of man you'll ever be happy with is somebody like George Alber, who—"

"Who leaves me absolutely cold," Helen said.

"He wouldn't if you saw more of him. If you'd get rid of this ridiculous idea that you're in love with Jerry Templar and mustn't be even civil to any other man. When even you can't possibly be fool enough not to see that he can't marry you on his private's pay. When—"

"Jerry won't be a private much longer," Helen said. "They're sending him to an officers' training camp."

"What of it? When he gets his commission—if he gets it—he'll only be shipped off to the ends of the earth and—"

"He'll be at the camp first." Helen spoke quickly, before Aunt Matilda could say anything about what would happen afterward. Helen wasn't letting herself think about that. "He'll be there for months, and I could be there, too, or somewhere near by. Near enough for us to see each other sometimes."

"I see." Aunt Matilda's voice was heavily ironic. "You've thought it all out, haven't you? Except, of course, for the trivial matter of what you'll live on while all this is happening. Or—" She stopped. "I see. Gerald's been talking to you. He's made you think he can make me give you the money Franklin left you. Well, you can put that idea out of your head. That money isn't due you till Franklin's dead. And he's no more dead than I am. He's alive. One of these days he'll come crawling back, begging me to forgive him."

She laughed, as if the word were comic. Helen suddenly understood, for the first time, why Aunt Matilda clung so fiercely to her belief that Franklin Shore was alive. She hated him too bitterly to bear the thought of his having gone beyond hatred's power to follow. She had one dream left and she lived on it, and in it—the dream of his coming back. Coming back for the only reasons that could drive him back. Old, alone, beaten, in want. For her to take payment from him in kind and in full for what he had done to her.

Komo, the houseboy, appearing silently from nowhere, stood in the doorway. "Excuse pleassse," he said.

Matilda said, "What is it now, Komo? The door's open. Come in. And don't be so damned pussyfooting when you walk."

The houseboy's dark glittering eyes surveyed Matilda Shore. "Party on telephone, pleassse," he said. "Statement made that call is most important."

"All right. I'll be there in a minute."

"Receiver is left down on extension in your bedroom," Komo announced, and turned to walk back down the corridor with quick, light steps.

Helen said, "Aunt Matilda, *why* don't you get rid of that houseboy? I don't trust him."

"Perhaps *you* don't. *I* do."

"He's Japanese."

"Nonsense. He's Korean. He hates the Japanese."

"He may *say* he's Korean, but that's just . . ."

"He's been saying so for twelve years."

"Well, he doesn't look like a Korean to me. He looks like a Japanese, he acts like a Japanese, and . . ."

"Ever know any Koreans?" Aunt Matilda interrupted.

"Well, no—not exactly, but . . ."

"Komo is a Korean," Matilda said positively, and turning, walked back to her bedroom, pulling the door closed behind her.

Helen returned to the living room. Her hand smarted from the scratches and the sting of the disinfectant. The kitten was nowhere in evidence. Helen sat down and tried to read, but her mind refused to concentrate on the printed page.

After some fifteen minutes, she tossed the magazine to one side, sat back and closed her eyes. The kitten, appearing from nowhere, seemed properly apologetic as it rubbed, purring, against her ankles. At length it jumped up on the arm of her chair. Its rough tongue scraped against the skin of her arm.

Helen heard the telephone ringing, heard Komo's light steps as he went to answer it, then he was standing beside her chair as though he had silently materialized from thin air.

"Excussse, please. This time, call for Missy."

Helen walked out to the reception hallway where the telephone was located. She picked up the receiver, wondering if this might not be Jerry calling to . . . "Hello," she said, her voice eager.

The voice which came over the telephone wire was quavering with some emotion. "Is this Helen Kendal?"

"Yes, of course."

"You don't know who this is?"

"No," Helen almost snapped. People who rang up and asked her to guess who was calling irritated her.

The voice seemed a little stronger now, more steady. "Be very careful what you say that might be overheard. You remember your Uncle Franklin?"

Helen's mouth was suddenly very dry. "Yes, yes, but . . ."

"This is your Uncle Franklin."

"I don't believe it. He's . . ."

"No, Helen, I'm not dead." The voice broke with emotion. "I'm very much alive."

"But . . ."

"I don't blame you for not believing it. You'd know me if you saw me again, wouldn't you?"

"Why, I . . . why, yes—of course."

The man's voice went on more firmly now. "You remember the time the dog chased the kitten up on the roof of the house? You begged me to get him down, and I took a ladder and climbed up. Remember the New Year's party when you wanted to try the punch and your Aunt Matilda told you you couldn't, and you sneaked some in the pantry, anyway? Remember how I followed you up to your room and talked to you until you developed a laughing jag— and how I never told anyone—not even your Aunt Matilda—about it?"

Helen felt a peculiar tingling sensation around the hair at the back of her neck. "Yes," she said in a voice which was hardly more than a whisper.

"Now do you believe me, Helen?"

"Uncle Frank . . ."

"Careful! Don't mention my name. Is your aunt at home?"

"Yes."

"She mustn't know that I've called. No one must know. Do you understand?"

"Why, I . . . why . . . No, I don't understand."

"There is only one way to straighten things out. You'll have to help me."

"I?"

"Yes."

"What can I do?"

"You can do something that no one else can do. Have you ever heard of a lawyer named Perry Mason?"

"I've heard of him."

"I want you to see him this afternoon, tell him the entire story so he'll know the facts. Tonight at nine o'clock I want you to bring him to the Castle Gate Hotel. You know where that is?"

"No."

"You can look it up. It's a cheap hotel. Don't be frightened.

Bring Mason to that hotel, ask for Henry Leech. He'll take you to me. Don't let anyone else know about this conversation or what's happening. Be sure you aren't followed. Tell Mason everything, but swear him to secrecy. I'll . . ."

She heard a quick, gasping intake of breath. Abruptly, the receiver clicked at the other end of the line, and there was only that peculiar singing of an open telephone line. She jiggled the receiver hook several times. "Operator," she called. "*Operator!*"

Through the partially opened door, Helen heard the unmistakable sounds of her aunt's approach, the slow, labored steps, the steady *thump . . . thump . . . thump* of the cane, the dragging shuffle of the right foot.

Hastily, she hung up the receiver.

"Who is it?" Aunt Matilda asked, entering the hall as Helen turned away from the telephone.

"I think it's a date," Helen said, trying to sound casual.

Aunt Matilda lowered her eyes to Helen's right hand. "How did that cat happen to scratch you?" she asked. "You're lying to protect it. I'm not going to keep it if it's becoming vicious."

"Don't be silly," Helen said. "I tell you, I was teasing it with a piece of paper."

"Well, it had no business scratching you. Was that your soldier boy on the telephone?"

Helen laughed evasively.

"What are you so excited about? You're all flushed." She shrugged her heavy shoulders contemptuously. "It would be just like that fool, Jerry Templar, to propose to a girl over the telephone. It wouldn't surprise me at that. . . . Helen, what in heaven's name is the matter with that kitten?"

Helen sighed wearily. "I told you it was my fault. I . . ."

"No, no! Look at him!"

Helen moved over, impelled by her aunt's fixed stare.

"He's just playing," she said. "Kittens play that way."

"It doesn't look like he's playing to me."

"Kittens do that when they're stretching. They have to flex their little muscles. They . . ."

Helen felt the words fading from her tongue as she lost assurance. The kitten was acting most peculiarly, its motions very different from the stretches by which kittens coax their immature muscles into growth. The little spine arched backwards. The paws were stretched out to the fullest extent. Little spasms sent tremors through the body. But what arrested Helen's attention and filled her with apprehension was the expression in the amber eyes, the manner in which the kitten's jaws were clamped together, bits of froth oozing from beneath curled, pale lips.

"Oh, dear, something's wrong! Amber Eyes is sick!" she exclaimed.

Matilda Shore said, "Don't go near it. The cat's gone mad. Cats do that just the same as dogs. You'd better go see a doctor at once about that hand."

"Nonsense!" Helen said. "The kitten's sick. . . . Poor little Amber Eyes. What's the matter? Did you hurt your self some way?"

Helen reached down to the rigid little body. As soon as her fingers touched the fur, the cat went into a very definite convulsion.

"I'm going to take that cat to a veterinary right away," Helen said.

"You watch out. You'll get hurt," Aunt Matilda warned.

"I'll take care of that," Helen promised, dashing to the closet and struggling into her coat.

"You get something to wrap that cat in," Aunt Matilda said, "so it can't scratch you. . . . Komo. . . . Oh, Komo."

The swarthy little man materialized almost at once in the doorway. "Yes, ma'am."

Helen said, "Get an old blanket or a quilt out of the closet. Something to wrap the cat in."

Komo regarded the kitten with a peculiar expression in his lacquered eyes. "Kitten sick?" he asked.

"Don't stand there asking foolish questions," Matilda said impatiently. "Of course the kitten's sick. Do what Miss Helen told you. Get that blanket."

"Yes, ma'am."

Helen hastily adjusted her hat in front of the mirror, then stooped to bend over the kitten.

"Keep away from him," Matilda warned. "I don't like the way he's acting."

"What is it, Amber Eyes?" Helen asked, her voice soothing.

The cat's eyes were staring fixedly, but at the sound of Helen's voice, he made a slight motion as though to turn his head. That little motion brought on another of those swift spasms, this time more violent.

Just as Komo brought the blanket, Helen heard steps on the outer porch. The door opened. Her uncle, Gerald Shore, crossed the reception hallway to the living room, taking off his hat and light coat as he moved. "Hello, everybody," he said cheerfully. "What seems to be the trouble?"

There was reassurance in Gerald Shore's deeply resonant voice. It never seemed necessary for him to raise that voice, yet he could be plainly heard, no matter how large the room.

"It's Amber Eyes," Helen said. "He's sick."

"What's wrong with him?"

"We don't know. He's having spasms. I'm taking him to a veterinary," Helen said. "I'm . . . Here, Komo, help me get the blanket around the cat. Watch out he doesn't bite now."

They wrapped the blanket around the kitten. Helen clasped the tense little body to her and could feel another spasm tighten the muscles as she started for the door.

"Come on," Gerald Shore said. "I'll drive the car. You can hold the cat."

"The cat's already scratched Helen," Matilda said.

"I washed it with alcohol," Helen explained.

"Cats can go mad just the same as dogs do," Matilda insisted.

Komo, smiling and nodding, said, "Fits. Excussse, please. All cats have fits. This very typical cat fit."

Helen turned to her Uncle Gerald. "Come on. *Please* let's get started."

Matilda Shore said to the houseboy, "Komo, you've let me run out of stout again. Now you go all the way uptown to the market and get me six bottles. Don't disturb me when you come back. I'll lie down until dinner. Helen, don't take on so over that kitten. Find a better outlet for your affections. Now get started, all of you."

She entered her bedroom, slamming the door shut behind her.

"Come on, Helen," Uncle Gerald said sympathetically.

Suddenly Helen remembered the telephone call. Curiously, she had forgotten it completely in the excitement over Amber Eyes. In a way it seemed unreal, like something that had never happened. Uncle Franklin! As soon as she took care of Amber Eyes, she would try to reach this Perry Mason.

2

GERALD SHORE had never had his brother's flair for making money, or rather, for keeping money. Where Franklin had watched his ever-growing fortune with the tight-lipped determination of a man who knows how to say no, Gerald had spent money recklessly on the "easy come, easy go" theory. Prior to 1929, Gerald had considered himself a wealthy man. Within a few short weeks, he not only had been completely stripped of his property, but had found himself dependent upon his law practice to give him even a living.

This period of transition had been most embarrassing. Having adjusted his practice on the theory that he would not waste his time with small cases, that he would see clients by appointment only, and would take only such cases as interested him, Gerald suddenly found himself eager to accept any honorable employment where there was even a fair possibility of a fee.

Holding the kitten close, feeling the convulsive waves that racked its little body, Helen thought gratefully that Uncle Gerald was more sympathetic, more understanding, than any man she knew. She wondered if he had always been like this. Certainly his difficulties and his trouble had not hardened him. It seemed even that since the crash he had been more gentle, more tolerant, than before. Whereas Aunt Matilda's idea was for Komo to put the

THE CASE OF THE CARELESS KITTEN · 15

kitten out of the way, Uncle Gerald obviously recognized a major emergency that relegated traffic laws to the background. It was but a matter of minutes before they had Amber Eyes in the hands of a competent veterinary.

Dr. Blakely, making a quick: diagnosis, reached for a hypodermic needle.

"It isn't—isn't rabies, is it?" Helen asked.

"Probably poison," he said. "Here, hold the cat's head. Hold him tightly by the neck and shoulders. Hold firmly now. Don't let go if he starts fighting."

He inserted the hypodermic needle, carefully regulated the amount of fluid which he injected, withdrew the needle, and said, "Temporarily, we'll put him in this cage. The kitten's going to eject the contents of its stomach. In that way, we'll get rid of any poison which remains. How long ago was it when you first observed any symptoms?"

"I don't think it could possibly have been over five or ten minutes," Helen said. "It didn't take us over three minutes to get here, and . . . well, perhaps ten minutes ago."

"We stand a good chance," Dr. Blakely said. "Nice little kitten. Hope we can save it."

"You think it's poison?"

"I think so. The treatment isn't going to be particularly pleasant. You'll think the animal is suffering even more than it is. You two had better wait out in the office. If I need any more help, I'll call you."

He drew on a pair of thick leather gloves.

"You're sure there's nothing we can do?" Helen asked.

He shook his head. "I can let you know more in a few minutes. It had been playing out in the yard, hadn't it?"

"No, I don't think so. I don't remember distinctly, but I *think* the kitten had been in the living room all the time."

"Well, we'll find out more about it after a while. Go sit down and wait."

Out in the waiting room, Gerald Shore settled himself in a chair, fished a cigar from his waistcoat pocket, bit off the end and struck a match. The flame, which was held in his cupped hands, illuminated the sensitive outlines of his features, the sweep of a high, contemplative forehead, kindly, tolerant eyes, about which were little crow's-feet of humor, a mouth which was uncompromising and determined without being too stern.

"Nothing we can do now, Helen. May as well sit down and take it easy. We've done everything we can."

They sat silently for several minutes, Helen's mind tumbling around between that strange telephone call and Amber Eyes and poison, and what she should do about her Uncle Franklin. In spite of what he had said, she wanted to confide in Uncle Gerald but she hesitated. Gerald Shore was quite evidently lost in thought, his mind occupied with a problem that plainly required concentration.

Abruptly he said, "Helen, as I told you a few days ago, we're going to do something about Franklin's will immediately. Matilda has been hanging on to what belongs to us long enough."

"Perhaps we ought to wait—just a little," Helen murmured uncertainly.

"We've waited long enough."

He saw that Helen was hesitating, trying to make up her mind to speak or to keep silent.

"Well," he asked, "what is it?"

Helen suddenly made up her mind with a rush. "I . . . I had a queer experience today," she blurted out.

"What?"

"A man telephoned."

Gerald chuckled. "I'd say it was queerer if any man who knew your number *hadn't* telephoned you. If I weren't your uncle and . . ."

"Don't be ridiculous! This man said— Oh, it just doesn't sound plausible. It *can't* be true!"

"If you'd be just a *little* more explicit," Gerald murmured encouragingly.

Helen's voice dropped almost to a whisper. "He said he was Franklin Shore. He seemed to recognize my voice, wanted to know if I recognized his."

Gerald Shore's face showed baffled, incredulous surprise. "Nonsense!" he exclaimed.

"It's true."

"Helen, you're excited. You . . ."

"Uncle Gerald, I swear it."

There was a long pause.

"When did the call come in?" Gerald asked finally.

"Just a few minutes before you came to the house."

"Some impostor, of course, trying to . . ."

"No. It was Uncle Franklin."

"Look here, Helen, did you—that is, was there anything familiar about his voice?"

"I don't know. I couldn't be sure of the voice—but it was Uncle Franklin, all right."

Her Uncle Gerald frowned at the tip of his cigar. "It's impossible! What did he say?"

"He wants me to meet him tonight at the Castle Gate Hotel— that is, I'm to see a man named Henry Leech there, and Henry Leech will take me to Uncle Franklin."

Gerald Shore relaxed. "That settles it. Obviously an impostor after money. We'll go to the police and set a trap for your friend."

Helen shook her head. "Uncle Franklin told me to see that

well-known lawyer, Perry Mason, tell him the whole story and bring him to the meeting tonight."

Gerald Shore stared at her blankly. "It's the damnedest thing I ever heard. What does he want with Perry Mason?"

"I don't know."

"Look here," Gerald said somewhat sternly, "you don't *know* that was Franklin talking, do you, Helen?"

"Well—"

"Then stop referring to that person as Franklin. That might affect the legal situation. All you know is, you heard a man's voice over the telephone. That man *told* you he was Franklin Shore."

"He said things that proved it."

"What?"

"A lot of things out of my childhood that only Uncle Franklin would know about: the time the kitten got up on the roof of the house and couldn't get down, and he rescued it; all about the New Year's party when I was thirteen and sneaked the punch and got tipsy. No one ever knew about that except Uncle Franklin. He followed me up to my room, and was so perfect about it. He just sat down and started talking. Even when I developed a laughing jag, he pretended not to notice. He told me that he didn't agree with Matilda's idea of bringing me up, that I was getting to be a big girl, and would have to experiment about life myself, but that it would be better if I learned how dangerous drink was—and learned to gauge just how much I could take. And maybe for a few years it would be better if I didn't drink at all. And then he got up and walked out."

Gerald's brows were level with thought. "And this person told you all about that when he called?"

Helen nodded.

Gerald Shore got up from the chair, walked over toward the window, stood with his hands in his pockets. Outwardly he seemed calm and thoughtful. Only the rapid little puffs of cigar smoke which emerged from his mouth showed nervousness.

"What happened after that?" he asked.

"Then Uncle Franklin—this man, whoever he was—asked me to get Perry Mason and be at the Castle Gate Hotel at nine o'clock and to ask for Henry Leech."

"But, good heavens, Helen, if it was Franklin who was talking over the telephone, why in the world didn't he come home and . . ."

"That's what I kept wondering about, and then I thought perhaps—well, you know, if he'd gone away with some other woman . . . I guess he wants to pave the way for coming back and probably wants someone to sound out Aunt Matilda on how she'll feel."

"But why didn't he call *me*? I'm his brother. I'm a lawyer. Why did he call *you*?"

"I don't know. He said I was the only one who could help him. Perhaps he tried to reach you and couldn't."

"And what happened after that? How did the conversation terminate?"

"He acted as though something had surprised him, as though someone had come in the room or something. He gave a quick little exclamation and hung up the telephone very abruptly."

"He asked you not to tell anyone?"

"Yes. But I—well, I thought I should tell you—under the circumstances."

"You didn't tell Matilda?"

"No."

"Sure she hasn't any suspicion?"

"No. I'm sure she thought I was talking to Jerry. And right after that she noticed the kitten was having spasms. Poor Amber Eyes! How could he possibly have got poison?"

"I don't know," Gerald said somewhat shortly. "Let's quit thinking about the kitten for a moment and think about Franklin. This doesn't make sense. Ten years' silence, and then this fantastic stage play of a return! Personally I always thought he'd run away with that woman. I felt sure he'd left Matilda some note that she'd suppressed. I thought as time passed without any word except that card from Miami that things probably hadn't gone so well. I always considered the possibility that he might have committed suicide. He'd have preferred that way out rather than face the humiliation of an ignominious return."

Gerald pushed his hands down more deeply into his pockets, stared out of the window. After a time he turned around and said to Helen, "When Franklin left, Matilda had a lot of the property in her name. If Franklin should show up he's not going to have much left for himself. You and I will have nothing. Franklin's my brother. He's your uncle. We both hope he's alive, but he is going to have to prove it."

Dr. Blakely came out from the operating room. "Your kitten was poisoned," he said to Helen.

"You're certain?"

"Absolutely."

Gerald turned again from the window to regard the doctor gravely. "What did you find?"

"Some poisoned meat had been administered but a very short time before the kitten was brought here. There were tablets of poison in the meat—perhaps more than one. I recovered a part of one tablet which hadn't as yet fully dissolved. It had probably been embedded in a piece of meat, and the kitten's digestive juices hadn't thoroughly dissolved it."

"Will—will he live?" Helen asked.

"Yes. He's going to be all right now. You can come back and get him in an hour or two, but you'd better let him either stay here for a few days, or let some friend keep him. Someone very deliberately tried to poison your kitten. You probably have some neighbor who doesn't like animals, or has some particular reason for disliking you."

"Why, I can't believe such a thing's possible," Helen said.

Dr. Blakely shrugged his shoulders. "Poisoned tablets packed in small wads of meat such as was given this kitten indicate the work of a deliberate poisoner. We have trouble with poisoners in various parts of the city; usually they're after dogs. They prepare little balls of meat and toss them into a yard. The dog grabs them eagerly. It's rather unusual that a kitten as young as this one gets such a big dose of poison."

Gerald said abruptly, "You want the kitten to stay away from the house for a few days, Doctor?"

"Yes."

"Is he out of danger now?"

"Yes. But I want to give him some further treatment—an hour or so."

Helen said, "Let's come back right after dinner and get him, Uncle Gerald. Then we can take him down to Tom Lunk—the gardener. He has a little bachelor shack that's out of the neighborhood. Amber Eyes loves him and will be happy there."

"That sounds like an excellent plan," Dr. Blakely said.

Gerald Shore nodded. "All right. Come on, Helen, you've got a lot to do."

Four or five blocks from the veterinary's Gerald Shore pulled into the curb in front of a drugstore.

"That appointment with Perry Mason," he explained. "I know him slightly, so I'll telephone for you. It will be a miracle if we can catch him now. He's a law unto himself as far as office hours go—and a lot of other things."

A few minutes later he emerged. "In an hour at his office. That all right?"

Helen nodded. "Hadn't you better come with me?"

"No. You'll tell him the story better if you do it in your own way without having me there. I'm particularly anxious to see how he reacts to it—if he gets the same impression I do. I told him I'd meet you somewhere in front of the Castle Gate Hotel at nine."

"What's your impression, Uncle Gerald?"

He smiled affectionately, but shook his head. He concentrated on his driving for a moment, then turned to Helen. "You really don't know whether that kitten was outdoors late this afternoon?"

"I've been trying to think, Uncle Gerald. I remember he was out in the back yard about three o'clock, but I can't remember that he was out after that."

"Who was at the house this afternoon?"

"Komo and Aunt Matilda and the cook."

"Who else?"

Under the direct impact of his eyes, she felt herself coloring. "Jerry Templar."

"How long before the kitten developed those spasms?"

"Not very long."

"Was George Alber there?"

"Yes, only for a few minutes. He came to see Aunt Matilda and then kept hanging around—until Jerry came—then I got rid of him in a hurry. Why?"

A muscle flickered in Gerald's cheek, as if his jaws had tightened. "How much do you know about this—this devotion of Matilda's to George Alber?"

"I know she likes him," Helen said. "She's always—"

"You don't know what's behind it, then? You don't know that she almost married his father?"

"I never knew that. It—it's hard to imagine Aunt Matilda as ever having been—"

"She was, though. Along in 1920, when she was forty or so, she was an attractive widow. And Stephen Alber was a good-looking widower. George is a lot like him. It wasn't any wonder to us that they fell for each other. It was a good deal more of a wonder when they had a quarrel and Matilda married Franklin. I always thought she did that mainly to hurt Stephen. It did hurt him, too, but he got over it. Married, two or three years afterwards. You probably remember when he was divorced, along about 1930."

Helen shook her head. "It's hard to believe anybody could ever have been in love with Aunt Matilda. And it's even harder to imagine her being in love."

"But she was. So much in love that I don't think she ever got over it. I think she's still in love with Stephen Alber. I think the biggest of her reasons for hating Franklin isn't that he walked out on her. She knew he'd always hated Steve Alber, and I'm pretty sure that the thing she can't forgive him for is what he did to Steve."

"What did he do?" Helen said.

"Nothing, really. The bank did it after Franklin disappeared. But I shouldn't wonder if he'd been getting ready to do it before he left. The big smash in '29 hit Alber pretty hard, along with everybody else, but he managed to save some of the pieces. He hung on to them till along in '32, just after Franklin left. Then the bank put on the screws. I shouldn't wonder if Franklin had been intending to do it himself. He certainly didn't like Alber. Anyway, Alber went under and never came up. Perhaps that wasn't what killed him, but I guess it helped. And Matilda—" He stopped. They were almost home. "I'm going with you tonight. I'll be outside of the Castle Gate at nine."

Helen hesitated. "Uncle Franklin said I mustn't bring anybody except Mr. Mason. He sounded terribly in earnest about it."

"No matter," Gerald said. "I'm going with you." His voice dropped a tone as he stopped in front of the house. "Be careful what you say. There's George Alber."

3

GEORGE ALBER was coming down the steps. If he looked as much like his father as Uncle Gerald said he did, Helen thought, it was easy enough to believe that twenty-odd years ago Aunt Matilda—and plenty of other women, probably—had fallen rather hard for Stephen Alber.

They would have had to be the kind of women, though, who lose their hearts to photographs of motion-picture actors. Retouched photographs, Helen told herself. There was something of that artificial quality about George Alber's handsomeness, as if some careful pencil had drawn the Greek straightness of the nose, given the eyebrows that precisely perfect line, sketched a little extra wave into the thick, brightly dark hair.

But the retoucher hadn't taken quite enough pains on the mouth. It was too full-lipped, and the jaw was too prominent. They marred the picture a little, that chin and mouth; they let coarseness into it, and vanity, and a kind of ruthlessness that might easily be cruel.

"What's this about the kitten's going mad?" His voice was something like his face, Helen told herself. Retouched, so that instead of being just right, it was just a little too right to be real. "The cook says it scratched you. Let's see that hand."

He reached for it. His fingers were long and strong and beautifully kept, but Helen didn't like their touch. She jerked her hand away.

"My hand's all right. And Amber Eyes wasn't mad. He—"

"You can't afford to take that for granted." He wagged his head. "From what the cook says—"

"The cook got her information second-hand from Aunt Matilda," Helen interrupted. "The kitten was poisoned."

"Poisoned!" Alber exclaimed.

"That's right."

"You're certain?"

"Absolutely."

"But I can't understand that."

Gerald Shore, opening the left-hand car door and sliding out from behind the steering wheel, said dryly, "There's no particular reason why you shouldn't be able to understand it. Pellets of poison were embedded in several particles of meat and fed to the animal by someone who wanted to make a very thorough job of killing the kitten. I don't know how I can explain it to you any more plainly."

George Alber apparently failed to notice the sarcasm. He said, smiling, "I didn't mean that I couldn't understand *what* had happened. I can't understand *why*."

Gerald said, "The answer is obvious. Someone wanted the kitten out of the way."

"But why?" George Alber persisted.

It was that question which suddenly impressed Helen. She turned to her uncle, her forehead puckered into a frown. "Yes, Uncle Gerald, *why* should anyone want to poison Amber Eyes?"

Gerald Shore dismissed the subject, rather brusquely Helen thought. "You can't account for the psychology of an animal-poisoner. People go along and drop poisoned bits of meat into yards. The veterinary says they're rather prevalent in certain sections of the city."

Helen watched George Alber's eyes lock with those of her uncle. There was, she realized, a certain innate combativeness about the younger man which made him advance under fire rather than retreat. "I doubt very much if the kitten could have been poisoned in that way," he said. "One scrap of meat, perhaps, yes. But several scraps—well, I doubt it."

Gerald Shore, on the defensive and somewhat nettled by finding himself in that position, said, "Several scraps of meat might have been tossed into the yard within a space of a few feet. I see no reason why a kitten couldn't pick them up."

George Alber turned back to Helen. "When was the kitten out last, Helen?"

She said, "I don't know, George. I can't *remember* that it went out after three o'clock."

"Could it have picked up the poison then?"

"The veterinary says that it must have been administered within a few minutes of the time of the first spasm, not very long before we got it to the hospital. That's all that saved the kitten's life."

Alber nodded slowly as though that merely confirmed some idea which he had had in mind all along, then said suddenly, "Well, I'll be on my way. I only dropped in. Be seeing you later. Sorry about Amber Eyes. Take good care of him."

"We will," Helen said. "We're going to let Tom Lunk keep him for a few days."

George Alber walked across to the curb where his car was parked, jumped in, and drove away.

Gerald Shore said with an intensity of feeling which came as somewhat of a surprise to his niece, "I definitely and distinctly dislike that man."

"Why, Uncle Gerald?"

"I don't know. He's too—too damned assured. You can take it in an older man, but what the devil has he ever done to warrant his assuming such a cocksure air? How does it happen he isn't in the Army?"

"Defective hearing in his left ear," Helen explained. "Haven't you ever noticed he always turns so his right side is toward you?"

Gerald snorted. "It's his profile. Notice the way he holds his head. Trying to ape the pose of some matinee idol in the pictures."

"No, he isn't, Uncle Gerald. That's unfair. It's on account of his hearing. I know that for a fact. He tried to enlist."

Gerald Shore asked abruptly, "When does Jerry Templar go back to camp?"

"Monday." Helen tried not to think how near Monday was.

"Does he know where they're sending him?"

"If he does, he isn't telling."

They were at the door of the house. Gerald pushed it open for her, but he didn't follow her in.

"I've got some things to see to uptown. You'll have to get down to Mason's office on your own." He glanced at his watch. "You'll have to start pretty soon, too, and you won't be back in time for dinner, so you'd better say you're having it with me. That'll satisfy Matilda and let you give Mason all the time he wants. He'll want plenty, unless I miss my guess. And I'll be waiting for you outside the Castle Gate at nine."

He shut the door before Helen could remind him again that Uncle Franklin had very positively told her that nobody except Perry Mason was even to know about that appointment at the Castle Gate.

4

PERRY MASON had that peculiar, confidence-inspiring magnetism which is so frequently found in tall men. In repose, his features and his manner had the weathered patience of hard granite. It was only in times of stress that his irrepressible personality flooded through. Before a jury, for instance, he could summon the skill and grace of a finished actor. His voice was a responsive instrument that accompanied and emphasized his words. His questions held a razor-edged sharpness which cut through the clumsy falsehoods of sullen, stubborn perjurers. In critical courtroom crises he was a fast-moving, quick-thinking force molding men's minds, playing on their emotions, out-thinking his antagonists; dramatic, persuasive, agile, yet never forsaking the fortress of deadly logic which buttressed every contention.

Della Street, Mason's secretary, unlocked the door of the lawyer's private office, and entered to find Mason seated in the swivel chair back of his desk, his long legs elevated, the ankles crossed on a corner of the big desk.

"Well, here I am," she announced, taking off her gloves and slipping out of her coat.

Mason said nothing until she emerged from the cloak closet having deposited her hat and coat. Then he said, "Della, virtue has been rewarded. I told you this morning that we shouldn't clutter up our minds with that equity case, even if there was money in it. Eight hours later we get *this*."

"There was a ten-thousand-dollar fee in that equity case," Della said frostily. "What's in this?"

Mason grinned. "It's an adventure that will make you feel ten years younger."

"Most of your cases make me feel ten years older!"

Mason ignored her. "This has none of the dull, routine angles that drive me to drink. It sparkles with bizarre mystery, adventure, romance. To put it another way, it's cockeyed crazy and doesn't make any sense at all—one hell of a swell case."

"So I gathered when you telephoned," she observed, crossing over to seat herself on the opposite corner of his desk, conscious of that peculiar gleam in his eyes which came only in moments of inner excitement.

Perry Mason had the rare ability so seldom found in professional men to derive enjoyment from his work. After a certain period, the doctor who has run the gamut of experiences with human illnesses acquires a certain impersonal efficiency. He regards the patients not so much as persons as depositories of various symptoms or anatomical structures which are to be coaxed or carved back to health. The lawyer, having acquired a sufficient background of experience, is apt to become imbued with the mechanics of procedure. But Perry Mason had a mind which was only content when it was detouring the technicalities of legal red tape. He not only regarded each case as a venture studded with excitement, but became impatient with the delays of routine procedure. More and more, as his practice developed, he became interested in personalities. More and more, his methods became dazzlingly brilliant, increasingly dangerous, and highly unorthodox. And Della Street knew that this peculiar light in his eye meant that in this new case he had found a tantalizing puzzle.

Perry was staring at her and automatically Della looked at herself through his eyes. Her brown suede pumps were good. Her legs were perfect. If the beige tailored suit didn't fit it was not because she hadn't been to a good tailor. Her face was all right, and she had a new shade of lipstick. Her hat was outrageous. She hoped he was satisfied.

"Della," Mason sighed, "sometimes I think you are getting blasé."

"Yes?" she drawled ominously. "Do tell me about it."

"You're getting conservative, mercenary, cautious. You're more interested in periods than you are in question marks."

Della relaxed. "Someone around this office has to be practical," she said. "But if it's not too much to ask, what's all the excitement about? I don't mind leaving half a good dinner uneaten and rushing over here, but I would like to know which missionary ate the cannibal."

"It was after you'd left the office," he said. "I was getting ready to leave—doing some work on that brief in the Johnson case. A lawyer whom I know slightly telephoned and wanted an appointment for his niece and a little later she came in and talked to me."

Della Street slipped from the desk to pick up a notebook from her desk. She drew up a chair, and her informal manner gave place to secretarial efficiency. "What were the names?" she asked.

"Gerald Shore's the lawyer, has an office in the Debenture Investment Building. As I remember it, he handles rather a specialized branch of practice—does a good deal with mining corporations. Think he's something of a gambler himself, does work largely for promoters, and takes fees partially in cash and partially in stocks in the companies he organizes."

"Any money in it?" Della Street asked.

"Don't be so damned mercenary," Mason said, grinning. "I think he makes more out of it than money."

"How do you mean?"

"He's always chasing mirages. Our realistic philosophers hold that as being poor economy. Simply because a mirage has no definite substance, they overlook the fact that it's such a lovely object to chase. They also lose sight of the fact that the mirage-chaser is getting great joy out of life. He's always interested in what he's chasing, which is more than you can say of many men who struggle toward more practical goals. Interest in life is the very best form of wealth."

"Any retainer?"

"Not yet," Mason admitted.

"I see. The niece's name?"

"Helen Kendal."

"Age?"

"About twenty-four. Very exciting violet eyes. On the blonde side. Nice chassis, nice assembly, nice accessories—definitely nice."

"*And* no retainer," Della Street muttered. "You say she's a niece of Gerald Shore?"

"Yes. I'll give you a brief sketch of the family history." He reached for some scrawled notes and began to dictate. Swiftly and compactly, the salient facts in the case went into Della Street's notebook.

On a January evening in 1932, Franklin Shore, then fifty-seven and in vigorous health, went into his study after dining with his wife. There he received a caller whom he must have admitted himself, since no servant had answered the door. A maid had seen somebody coming up the drive, and thought she recognized him as Gerald Shore, and Matilda Shore also thought that the voice she heard in the study was Gerald's, but she had not heard it clearly enough to be sure and Gerald himself denied having been there.

Whoever the visitor was, he wanted money. Matilda Shore distinctly heard her husband's voice, lifted in anger, refusing to lend it, saying something about the world's being crowded with jack-asses who only needed a few thousands to get back on Easy Street, when even a jackass ought to know that there was never going to be any such street again.

That was all of the talk Matilda Shore overheard. She went upstairs to read in bed and didn't hear the visitor leave. She did not find out until next morning that Franklin Shore had also left.

Those were the days when a whisper could break a bank, so that Shore's wife and business associates did not take the police into their confidence until Shore had been missing for some days. Every effort, official and private, was thereafter made to locate him, but no trace of him could be found. The bank's affairs proved to be in perfect order, so that, in spite of the headlines, the institution suffered no damage from its president's disappearance. His own affairs were also in order, and, instead of explaining his action, that made it more mysterious, because, except for a few hundred dollars he habitually carried with him, he had apparently left without funds. His checkbook was found on his desk, with the date on a blank check filled in and a broken line indicating that he had begun to write the name of a payee and then evidently either changed his mind or been interrupted. The book showed a balance of $58,941.13 in his joint account with his wife, and this balance was proved correct except for one check for $10,000, drawn on a blank taken from another checkbook, about which Shore had telephoned his secretary before the disappearance.

There were the usual whispers. Several times during the few months before he vanished, Shore had been seen with a woman, unknown to any of those who reported having seen the pair, but good-looking, noticeably well dressed and somewhere in the thirties. But there was nothing to suggest that she had left in Shore's company, except for a picture post card, from Miami, Florida, postmarked June 5, 1932, which his niece had received six months after the disappearance. The message, in handwriting identified by experts as unmistakably that of Franklin Shore, read:

No idea how much longer we shall be here, but we're en-joying the mild climate and, believe it or not, swimming.

With lots of love,

Your Uncle Franklin

The plural pronouns, of course, seemed to justify the whispers about the blonde unknown, but the investigators who were hur-ried to Miami found no trace of Franklin Shore. He had a number of acquaintances there, and the fact that none of them had seen him argued that he could not have made any long stay.

His will was found. It left the bulk of his estate to his wife, with twenty-thousand-dollar legacies to his niece and brother.

"How about them?" Della Street looked up hopefully from her book.

"They haven't been paid. The niece has been living with her aunt for years. Gerald Shore has, I think, had some indirect bene-fits. But the legacies are still payable—that is, they will be if Frank-lin Shore is dead."

"But nothing has been heard from him for . . ."

"That's just the point," Mason said. "Something has. He tele-phoned his niece today. She's to meet him tonight. He insisted that I be present at the interview. I'm going to take you along."

"Do I take a notebook?" she asked.

"By all means a notebook," Mason said. "We're going to have notes, so we'll know everything that's said, and be able to discuss the significance of the things that aren't said."

"But why doesn't he get in touch with his wife and come back home?"

"That's just the point. There was something mysterious about his disappearance, some talk at the time of his having run away with a younger woman. Apparently, he isn't too certain of the reception his wife will give him."

"She knows nothing about his being here now?"

"No. Franklin specifically instructed his niece to say nothing to anyone. She did confide in her Uncle Gerald, the one who telephoned me."

"Is Matilda Shore the forgiving kind?" Della Street asked.

Mason grinned. "Definitely not, and reading between the lines of Helen Kendal's story, I'd say she's a most objectionable, peculiar character. What's more, there's an old love affair involved, too. The man is dead, but his son, George Alber, is the spitting image of his father and Matilda is very much attached to him. I gather that Gerald Shore views that relationship with alarm."

"Why?"

"In young Alber," Mason said, "she sees the image of the man whom she once loved. Her only living relatives being Gerald Shore and Helen Kendal, ordinarily, they'd be the beneficiaries under her will. Sometime ago, before young Alber read 'Welcome' on the mat, she intimated that they were not only her heirs but would inherit the entire fortune."

"It is a fortune?"

"Yes."

"Enter Alber!"

Mason grinned. "Enter Alber. Gerald Shore thinks he's turning loose all his charm, and there's no question about the fact that he has become a frequent visitor at the house."

"Good heavens, you don't mean that this woman of sixty-four is going to marry this . . ."

"Probably not," Mason said. "But she wants her niece to marry him. And Alber seems to like that idea. Matilda Shore has become quite a despot, and she controls the purse strings. However, you haven't heard all the ramifications of the case yet. Not only was there this mysterious telephone call, but a kitten was poisoned this afternoon."

Della raised her eyebrows. "What has the poisoned kitten to do with the return of Franklin Shore?"

"Perhaps nothing, perhaps a lot."

"In what way?"

"It was probably an inside job."

"Why inside?"

"Because, checking up as best they can, the cat doesn't seem to have been out of the house after three o'clock in the afternoon. The symptoms of poisoning developed right around five o'clock. The veterinary says the poison was administered not over fifteen or twenty minutes before the cat was brought to him for treatment. That was about quarter past five."

"What kind of poison?" Della Street asked. "A kind that could have been administered to a human being?"

"That's the rub," Mason admitted. "Apparently, it was a strychnine poisoning. Strychnia has a bitter taste. An animal would swallow it if the poison were skillfully embedded in small balls of meat, because animals seldom chew. But a human being would have detected the bitter taste; particularly if the meat had been cooked."

"And you want me to go with you tonight?"

"Yes. A man by the name of Leech is going to escort us to the place where Franklin is hiding."

"Why's he hiding?"

Mason laughed. "Why did he disappear in the first place? I've often wondered about that, Della. Why a man who was enough of a realist to keep selling stocks short during the years which followed the crash of twenty-nine, who was making money hand over fist, who had everything that he wanted in life, should suddenly disappear *and take none of the money with him.*"

"Perhaps he'd been salting some away," Della Street said.

"Not in these days of income taxes," Mason pointed out.

"He might have falsified his books."

"An individual with a smaller income might have done that, but Franklin Shore's affairs were too complex. No, Della, we're in the way of solving an ancient mystery. The solution is going to be interesting and may be highly exciting. You want to get the picture of Matilda Shore as Helen Kendal painted it. A morose, strong-minded woman with over a million dollars locked in her grasping hands, approaching the end of life, something of a Tartar, addicted to chirping lovebirds, a servant who has always posed as a Korean, but who acts, looks, and talks like a Japanese. She's kept alive by one thing—the desire to be there waiting when her husband finally returns. Come on, Della, we're on the trail of another adventure in crime!"

Della grimaced. "There's no crime yet," she pointed out.

"Well," Mason said, walking over to the hat closet and whipping on his coat, "at least we have one attempted crime."

"What's that?"

"The kitten."

"The case of the poisoned kitten?" she asked.

She slipped a notebook and half a dozen pencils into her purse, and then stood by the desk as though worried about something.

"Coming?" demanded Perry impatiently.

"Chief, have you ever seen a kitten eat?"

"Does a duck swim? Why?"

"A cat usually picks at its food. That kitten must have been terribly hungry to gulp down those balls of meat."

"This kitten was just careless, I guess. Hurry up."

"Very careless," nodded Della. "I think when I open the file for this case I'll call it 'The Case of the Careless Kitten.'"

5

In Mason's car, driving toward the Castle Gate Hotel, Della Street asked, "Did Franklin Shore put *all* of his property in his wife's name?"

"Just about all, as I understand it. There were joint accounts in the bank."

"How long before the disappearance?"

"It had been going on for three or four years."

"Then if she wants to keep him from coming back, she could . . ."

"Couldn't keep him from coming back physically," Mason interrupted, "but she certainly could embarrass his come-back financially. Suppose the moment he showed up, she filed suit for divorce, asked for a property award, and all that out of what little property remains in his name? Get the sketch? She'd claim the other property was all hers."

"You think that's what she's planning?"

Mason said, "He certainly has *some* reason for wanting me there at the conference. I don't think he wants me to play tiddly-winks."

They were silent for several blocks, then Della Street asked, "Where do we meet the others?"

"A block from the Castle Gate Hotel."

"What kind of a place is it?"

"Second-rate, down-at-the-heel hotel, an outward front of respectability, but it's a thin veneer."

"And Henry Leech wanted Helen Kendal and you to come alone?"

"Yes."

"Think he'll object to the four of us?"

"I don't know. There are some peculiar angles, and I want notes taken so I'll know what is said, and what isn't said. . . . Up on the next corner is where we meet the others. Here's a good parking place."

Mason eased the car into the curb, switched off the lights and ignition, helped Della Street out, and locked the door. Two figures detached themselves from the shadows of a doorway. Gerald Shore came forward to shake hands. Introductions were performed in a low voice.

"Coast all clear?" Mason asked.

"I think so, yes."

"You haven't been followed?"

"Not as far as we can tell."

Helen Kendal said, "I'm quite certain no one has followed us."

Mason nodded toward the building in the middle of the next block where a section of blank wall rising above the top of the nearest house had been lettered "CASTLE GATE HOTEL. *Rooms One Dollar and Up.* MONTHLY RATES. TRANSIENTS. *Restaurant.*" The sign had been faded and sooted by the grime of a big city.

Mason took Helen Kendal's arm. "You and I will go first," he said. "Shore, you and Miss Street can follow, after an interval of twenty or thirty seconds. Don't appear to be with us until we start up in the elevator."

Gerald Shore hesitated. "After all," he said, "the person *I* want to see is my brother Franklin. I don't care about seeing this man

Leech. If my presence may frighten him, I'd prefer to sit and wait in the automobile."

Mason said, "Miss Street is going with me. That'll make three of us. You may as well make four."

Shore reached a sudden decision. "No, I'll wait here in the automobile, but the minute you meet my brother, I want you to tell him I'm here and that I simply *must* see him before he talks with anyone. Do you understand? Before he talks with *anyone.*"

Mason regarded the man quizzically. "Before he talks with me?"

"With anyone."

Mason shook his head. "If you want any such message delivered, deliver it yourself. The man has sent for me. He probably wants to consult me professionally."

Shore's bow was courtly. "My mistake, counselor. I'm sorry. But I'll wait here just the same. I doubt that my brother is in that hotel. When you come out with Leech, I'll join you."

He walked back to a place near the corner where he had parked his automobile, unlocked the door, got in, and sat down.

Mason smiled reassuringly at Helen Kendal. "We may as well go."

They walked along the echoing, all but deserted sidewalk to the drab entrance of the out-dated hotel. Mason held the door open for the two young women, followed them in.

The lobby was some twenty feet wide, running back to terminate in a U-shaped desk and counter behind which was a switchboard. A somewhat bored clerk sat, reading one of the more lurid "true" detective magazines. Across from the clerk were two automatic elevators. There were some fifteen or twenty chairs in the lobby, for the most part arranged in a row along one wall. Half a dozen individuals sprawling dispiritedly in these chairs raised their eyes to look, at first casually, then with sharpened interest at the two trim, slim-waisted young women followed by the tall figure of the lawyer.

The clerk at the desk glanced up from his magazine, and did them the honor of letting his attention remain on them.

"You have a Henry Leech registered here?" Mason asked, as he reached the desk.

"Yes."

"Been here long?" Mason asked.

"About a year."

"Indeed! What's his room?"

"Three-eighteen."

"Will you ring him please?"

The clerk, who apparently was also the telephone operator, moved over to the switchboard and plugged in a line. He pressed a button several times while holding an earpiece against his left ear. His eyes studied Della Street and Helen Kendal with an interest which he made no effort to conceal.

"I'm sorry. He isn't in."

Mason looked at his watch. "He was to meet me here at this time."

The clerk said, "I didn't think he was in. A man came to see him two or three hours ago. He was out. I haven't seen him come back. I . . ." He broke off as a special delivery messenger came up to the desk.

"Got a special delivery for the clerk at the Castle Gate," the boy said.

The clerk signed for the special delivery, opened the letter, read it, then looked up at Mason. "Are you Mr. Perry Mason?" he asked. "That's right."

"Well, I guess Leech was to meet you all right. It's really for you—but he addressed it to me."

THE CASE OF THE CARELESS KITTEN · 41

The clerk handed Mason a sheet of paper on which a message had been neatly typewritten:

To clerk at Castle Gate Hotel:

A gentleman will call for me tonight. He is Perry Mason, lawyer. Please tell him I cannot keep appointment, but he is to come at once to place indicated. Circumstances have necessitated a change in plans. This is unfortunate. Tell him to drive, please, to reservoir near top of road back of Hollywood according to course traced on map enclosed herewith. Once more excuse, please, change in plans. It is unavoidable.

Henry Leech

The signature as well as the message was typewritten. The map which was enclosed with the letter was an Auto Club map of Hollywood and vicinity. An ink line had been traced along Hollywood Boulevard, turning to the right on Ivar Street, then following a winding course to a spot on the map marked STORAGE RESERVOIR.

The clerk said, "I *thought* he went out—a couple of hours ago. I haven't seen him return."

Mason studied the special delivery letter, abruptly folded both letter and map, and shoved them down into the side pocket of his coat. "Let's go," he said.

6

THE HEADLIGHTS of the two automobiles twisted and turned, alternately showing dazzling circles against a cut bank, then swinging out to send parallel cones of light across dark canyons. The road snaked its way up the mountains, climbing steadily. Mason and Della Street drove the car in the lead, Gerald Shore and his niece following in their car.

"Did it strike you there was anything strange about that letter of instructions?" Mason asked Della, deftly spinning the wheel to follow the curves in the road.

Della Street, her eyes shifting alternately from the map to the road ahead, said, "It has a vaguely familiar sound as though I knew the person who had written it—sort of a style of expression, I guess you might call it."

Mason laughed. "If you heard it read aloud in the proper tone of voice, you'd recognize at once what it was."

"I don't get you."

Mason said, "Try bowing and smiling as you read the lines out loud. Read them without expression, in a monotone, and see what you get."

Della Street unfolded the letter from the envelope, started

reading. At the end of the fourth line, she said, "Good heavens, it's the way a Japanese would write."

Mason said, "You couldn't have made a letter sound more Japanese if you'd deliberately set out to do it. And notice that the signature is typewritten—also that the letter is addressed simply to the clerk at the Castle Gate Hotel. Leech has been staying there for a year. He'd almost certainly have known the clerk by name, and would have addressed the letter accordingly."

"Then you don't think we'll find Leech up here? You think this is a wild-goose chase?"

"I don't know. I noticed that peculiar style of expression and wondered if you'd noticed it, too."

"I hadn't at the time. I suppose I would have if I'd heard it read aloud. Now that you've pointed it out, it's perfectly plain."

Mason shifted the car into second, pushed the throttle well down, sent the big machine screaming around the curves. For the space of several minutes his hands and arms were busy with the steering wheel; then the road straightened somewhat and leveled off. All around them was a black rim of quiet mountains. Above this rim were the steady stars. Below and behind, a carpet of twinkling lights extended in a huge crescent for mile upon mile, marking the location of Los Angeles, Hollywood, and the suburban towns, an apparently unbroken cluster of myriad pin-pointed lights interspersed here and there with blobs of color from neon signs. Against this vast sea of illumination, the outlines of the mountains up which they had climbed were dark, patient silhouettes.

Mason slipped the car back into high gear, eased the pressure on the throttle, and the powerful silent motor in the big car became a mere whisper of synchronized power. Through the open windows the silence of the mountains seeped in, a silence that was broken only by the sound of tires gliding over the road, and the ominous *whooo whooo whooo* of an owl.

A moment later the lights of Gerald Shore's car were reflected back from windshield and rear-view mirror in Mason's car, partially blinding him by their glare, so that it was not until Mason was almost on top of the parked unlighted automobile that he saw it and swerved sharply to the right. A few yards ahead, the road curved abruptly, and a circular fringe of eucalypti marked the location of a reservoir.

"This is it," Della said.

Mason pulled his car to the side of the road and parked. Gerald Shore swung in behind the lawyer. Both drivers switched off headlights and motors.

Almost instantly, the silence of the mountain spaces engulfed them. From under the hood of Mason's car, the cooling motor block gave forth little cracks of sound which were magnified by the surrounding silence until they became as distinct explosions. The sound of Gerald Shore's feet coming up from behind seemed unusually loud.

Adjusting his voice to the quiet which surrounded them, Gerald Shore said, "That must be the car back there, but I didn't see anyone in it."

There was an uncertain note in Della Street's laugh. "It doesn't look like much of a party to me," she announced with nervous flippancy. "Are you sure they said Tuesday night?"

Helen Kendal's voice from behind Gerald Shore was sharp with apprehension. "There's someone in that automobile, sitting behind the steering wheel. He hasn't moved, just keeps sitting there, waiting."

"Got a flashlight?" Shore asked. "Somehow, I feel uneasy about this whole business. There's no reason why my brother should have decoyed us up here simply to meet him."

Mason said, "I'll get a flashlight." He opened the glove compartment of the car, pulled out a three-cell electric flashlight, and said, "Come on, let's go."

They formed a compact little group as they marched back along the road, the flashlight spraying a circular spot of white light on the ground.

The parked automobile remained dark, silent, and motionless. There was no sign of life from within it.

Abruptly, Mason raised the spotlight so that the rays shone through the windshield. Helen Kendal only half checked the exclamation of startled horror which came to her lips.

The body was slumped awkwardly against the steering wheel. The right arm was half circled around the wheel. The head was tilted to one side and rested against the shoulder. A sinister red stream had flowed down from the left temple, had divided at the line of the cheekbone, contrasting in color with the hue of the dead flesh.

Mason stood still, holding the spotlight focused on the inert body. He said over his shoulder to Gerald Shore, "I don't suppose you could identify this man Leech."

"No. I've never met him."

"This isn't your brother?" Mason asked, moving a little to one side so that the spotlight would illuminate the features to better advantage.

"No."

"You're certain?"

"Yes."

Mason deliberated a moment, then said, "Lieutenant Tragg of Homicide is always claiming that I violate the law by moving bodies and destroying clues before the police get on the job. This time I'm going to be above suspicion. If Miss Kendal isn't afraid to stay here, I'm going to leave you two to watch the body while Miss Street and I rush down to the nearest telephone and notify the Homicide Squad."

Shore hesitated for a moment, said at length, "It will only take one to do the telephoning. I'd like more than one witness here."

"Willing to stay?" Mason asked Della Street.

She met his eyes. "Of course."

"Okay. . . . Miss Kendal, what's your aunt's telephone number?"

"Roxwood 3-3987. Why? Are you going to notify her?"

"No," Mason said, "but I thought I might call the house. I may want to ask the houseboy a question."

Mason jumped in his car, hurriedly slammed the door shut, stepped on the throttle, and went snarling in second gear down the winding grade. He stopped at the first house where he saw a light, ran up the steps, and rang the doorbell.

It was a somewhat pretentious mansion, typical of California sidehill construction, one floor on the street side; then descending in a series of floors and balconies on the downhill side away from the road.

Mason saw the figure of a man moving leisurely across a corridor. A porch light clicked, etching him into sharp brilliance. A small window in the door slid back. A pair of keen, gray eyes surveyed the lawyer. "What is it?" a man's voice asked.

Mason said, "My name is Perry Mason. I want to use your telephone to notify the Homicide Squad that a man's body has been found in an automobile up by the reservoir at the top of the hill."

"Perry Mason, the lawyer?" the man asked.

"Yes."

"I've heard of you. Come in."

The door opened. The man, wearing a smoking jacket and slippers, peered curiously at Mason, and said, "I've read a lot about you in the newspapers. Never thought I'd meet you this way. The phone's there on that little stand."

Mason thanked him, picked up the phone, dialed Homicide,

and asked for Lieutenant Tragg. A few moments later, he heard Lieutenant Tragg's crisp, incisive voice on the line.

"Perry Mason," the lawyer said. "I have something to report."

Tragg said, "You aren't going to tell me you've found another body?"

"Certainly not," Mason replied promptly.

"Well, that's better. What's the trouble?"

Mason said, "*I've* quit discovering bodies, but one of the persons who was with me discovered a body in an automobile up near a reservoir above Hollywood. If you want to start now, I'll meet you at the corner of Hollywood and Ivar and show you the way up."

"Oh," Lieutenant Tragg said with elaborate politeness, "someone who was *with* you discovered the body."

"That's right."

"Since you've used up your quota," Tragg said sarcastically, "I presume you've let your very estimable secretary claim the credit for this one?"

Mason said, "It's all right with me if you want to sit at the phone making wisecracks instead of investigating a murder, but it'll sound like hell in the newspapers."

Tragg said, "Okay, you win. I'll be right out."

Mason hung up the telephone and dialed Roxwood 3-3987.

After several seconds during which Mason could hear the sound of the ringing bell at the other end of the line, a woman's voice answered the telephone. "Yes. What is it?" she asked in sharp, high-pitched accents.

"You have a Japanese houseboy," Mason said. "I'd like to talk . . ."

"He isn't Japanese. He's Korean!"

"All right, whatever nationality he is, I want to talk with him."

"He isn't here."

"Oh, he isn't?"

"No."

"When did he leave?" Mason asked.

"About an hour or so ago."

"Who are you?"

"I'm the cook and housekeeper. It's supposed to be my night off, but I came in just as they left and they told me to stay here and answer the telephone in case anyone called."

"Could you tell me if this *Korean* servant had been in the house all the evening?"

"Well—I couldn't exactly—I think he was out for a while."

"And where is he now?"

"Out."

"Can't you give me any more information than that?"

"No."

"I'm Mr. Mason. I'm calling on behalf of Gerald Shore and I want to know where this houseboy is now."

"You're calling for Mr. Shore?"

"That's right."

"If I tell you where Komo is now, you'll see that—there won't be any trouble?"

"No. I'll take care of that."

"He's taken Mrs. Shore to the Exeter Hospital."

"To the Exeter Hospital?" Mason repeated in surprise.

"Yes. She was taken very sick, all of a sudden like, looked as though she'd been . . ."

"As though she'd been what?" Mason asked.

"Nothing."

"When did this happen?"

"About a quarter of nine, I think."

"Looked as though she'd been what?" Mason insisted.

The woman at the other end of the line hesitated a moment, then said sharply, "Poisoned. But don't tell anyone I said so," and hung up the telephone.

7

THE HOMICIDE Squad car, screaming along Hollywood Boulevard, swerved and swayed through frozen traffic. Pedestrians stood staring at the speeding car, watching it swerve and twist until the red tail-light disappeared and the normal traffic once more came to life and motion.

Mason stepped out from in front of his parked car to stand in the beam of the headlights of the oncoming police machine. As the big car slid to a stop, a door swung open, and Lieutenant Tragg said tersely, "Get in."

Mason climbed in, noticing that the rear seat beside Lieutenant Tragg had apparently been reserved for him.

"Where to?" Tragg asked.

Mason took the folded map from his pocket. "There's the map which gave me my directions."

"Where'd you get it?"

"It came in a letter."

"Where's the letter?"

Mason passed it over. Tragg took it, but held it, making no attempt as yet to read it.

The officer who was driving the car looked back at Tragg for instructions.

Tragg said, "Take it easy a minute, Floyd. The man up there in the automobile is dead. *He* isn't going to make any moves that will confuse us. Mr. Mason is very much alive."

"Meaning that *I'm* apt to make confusing moves?" Mason asked with a smile.

Tragg said, "Well, I always like to interview you as soon as possible after one of your nocturnal adventures makes my presence necessary. I find that sometimes simplifies matters."

"I didn't discover this body."

"No? Who did?"

"A lawyer named Gerald Shore."

"Never heard of him."

"He doesn't do much courtroom work and no criminal work. I think you'll find he's a very respectable member of the profession."

There was a certain grudging admiration in Lieutenant Tragg's eyes as he looked Mason over. Tragg was utterly unlike the popular conception of a police detective. Not quite as tall as Mason, he was slender, suave, sophisticated, and thoroughly imbued with a knowledge of his profession. When Lieutenant Tragg started following a trail, he was not easily detoured. He had imagination and daring.

"Now this letter," Tragg said, balancing it in his hand as though trying physically to weigh the evidentiary importance of the document. "Where did you get this?"

"From the clerk of the Castle Gate Hotel."

"Oh, yes. The Castle Gate Hotel, rather a second-rate, shoddy affair; and in case you're interested, Mason, it's down on our list as being somewhat friendly to persons who don't have exactly the best reputations—or perhaps you hadn't heard about that."

"I hadn't heard about it."

"In any event, it's hardly a hotel which *you'd* have picked as a stopping place."

"That's right," Mason admitted. "I wasn't registered there."

"Therefore, it's logical to ask you what you *were* doing there? . . . Drive ahead slowly, Floyd. We're getting too much of an audience around here."

One of the officers in the front seat said, "I can start 'em moving and keep 'em moving."

"No, no," Tragg ordered impatiently without taking his eyes from Mason. "Drive on. Dispersing crowds takes time. Mr. Mason wants to tell us his story while it's still fresh in his mind, don't you, Mason?"

The lawyer laughed.

Tragg pushed the map across to the front seat. "Here, Floyd. Take this map. Follow the road. Don't give her the gun until I tell you to. Now, Mason, you were about to tell me why you went to the Castle Gate Hotel."

"I went there to see a man. If you'd read that letter, you'd understand."

"The man's name?" Tragg asked, still holding the letter in his hand, but keeping his eyes on the lawyer.

"Henry Leech."

"And what did you want to see him about?"

Mason made a little gesture with his hands as though tossing something away. "Now there, Lieutenant," he said, "you have me. I went to see Mr. Leech at the suggestion of Mr. Leech. He wanted to tell me something."

"The invitation came directly from Leech?"

"Indirectly."

"Through a client?"

"Yes."

"The client's name?"

"Helen Kendal, and I presume she came to me through this attorney, Gerald Shore."

"They knew what Leech wanted to see you about?"

"Mr. Leech was to take me to see someone else, as I understood it."

"Oh, a case of a mysterious witness taking you to a mysterious witness?"

"Not exactly. The person I was to see was a man who had disappeared some time ago and . . ."

Tragg held up his hand, half closed his eyes, snapped his fingers twice, said, "Wait a minute—wait a minute! I'm getting it now. What was his name?"

"Franklin Shore," Mason said.

"That's right. The most baffling disappearance of 1932. I've placed your lawyer, Gerald Shore, now. Leech knew something about this disappearance?"

"Of course," Mason said, "I'm only giving you hearsay. You can perhaps do better by communicating with the parties who really know the background."

"Rather subtle that," Tragg conceded. "But I think I'd prefer to have *your* story first, Mason."

Mason said, "Leech was, I understand, going to take Miss Kendal to see Franklin Shore. Really, Lieutenant, I think you'd be wise to try and get up there as soon as possible. What happened there may well be a clue to something more important."

"Yes, yes, I know," Tragg said. "You always have some very acceptable red herring which gets dragged tantalizingly across the trail just when I'm getting somewhere; but there's a little more I want to find out first, Mason. . . . Just keep driving slowly, Floyd. . . . Now, Mason, how did it happen that Leech promised to take you to see Franklin Shore?"

Mason's voice rasped with sudden impatience. "I don't know, and I think you're wasting valuable time. The message came to me through Miss Kendal."

"But he did promise to take you?"

"Who?"

"Leech, of course," Tragg said. "Quit sparring for time."

"No," Mason replied. "So far as I know, Leech didn't talk with Miss Kendal. It was a telephone communication with another party that sent her to Leech."

"Oh, I see," Tragg said. "Someone else did the talking, and I take it you're going to say you don't know who this party was?"

"No," Mason said. "I don't *know* who he was."

"I see. One of those anonymous conversations?"

"Not at all, Lieutenant. The man gave his name, and furthermore gave some rather interesting information to establish his identity."

"And the name?" Tragg asked.

It was Mason's turn to smile. "Franklin B. Shore."

For as long as a second, Tragg's face was changing expression as his mind digested the import of that information; then he snapped a command to the driver. "Step on it, Floyd. Give it everything it's got. Get up there—fast!"

Mason settled back in the seat, took a cigarette case from his pocket, and offered one to Tragg. "I thought you'd like to get up there, Lieutenant. Have a smoke."

Tragg said, "Put that damn thing back in your pocket and hang on. You don't know Floyd."

Mason reached for a cigarette, was all but thrown from his seat as the car lurched around a turn and dodged another automobile coming through an intersection.

"Get that siren going," Tragg ordered. "And get some speed."

The siren started its eerie screaming. The big, powerful car kept picking up momentum as it climbed. Mason, bracing himself, managed to get a cigarette from his case and up to his lips. He returned the case to his pocket, then was forced to hang on with both hands, having no opportunity to strike a match.

The car climbed rapidly, the screaming siren alternately roaring back in echoes from precipitous banks, then being swallowed up in the vastness of deep mountain canyons to return in muffled echoes from distant hillsides. The driver skillfully set the two red-beamed spotlights at such angles that no matter which way the winding road twisted up the mountain, a spot of illumination was thrown on the road.

At length the headlights on the police car illuminated the two parked automobiles, showed Della Street, Helen Kendal, and Gerald Shore standing closely together, their faces white ovals as they watched the approaching car.

Mason said, "Swing your headlights so they illuminate that first car, Lieutenant."

"That the one that has Leech's body?" Tragg asked.

"I don't know," Mason said. "I don't know Leech when I see him."

Tragg looked at him sharply. "You mean this body isn't that of Leech?"

"I don't know."

"Who does?"

Mason said, "I'm sure I couldn't tell you. I don't know whether anyone in my party can make an identification."

The police car lurched to a full stop.

Tragg said, "All right, let's look around, boys. Mason, go over and see if anyone in your party can identify the body."

If Lieutenant Tragg's request had been intended to keep Mason from observing the police inspection of the car, it failed, for Mason merely raised his voice and called, "Come on over here—the three of you."

"I didn't say that," Tragg said irritably.

Mason said, "I thought you wanted to know whether they could identify the body."

"I do, but they don't need to come over here and get in the way."

"They won't get in the way. How are they going to identify a body if they don't see it?"

"They've taken a good look at him by this time," Tragg said. "Trust you for that."

"On the contrary," Mason assured him, "two of these people haven't been near the car."

"How do you know they haven't?"

"Because I left instructions for them not to do so."

"How do you know they followed instructions?"

"Because Della Street was here."

Tragg frowned at him and said, "The elaborate precautions you're taking in this case make it look as though you had already stuck your toe in the water and found it mighty hot."

Mason looked hurt. "You've got a nasty, suspicious mind, Tragg." Then he grinned. "I'll admit, though, that I try to remember the story of the guy who wanted to go swimming at night and dove into the pool without checking on whether it was filled."

By that time, spotlights were blazing on the interior of the car. A photographer had set up his camera on a tripod and was inserting a bulb in the synchronized flash gun.

"Move over to this side," Tragg said. "You can see his face from there. Any of you know him?"

Solemnly they moved around to the side of the car to examine the features.

"I have never seen this man before," Shore said solemnly.

"Nor I," Helen Kendal supplemented.

"You?" Tragg asked Della Street.

She shook her head.

Tragg said, "None of you know Leech?"

There were two "No's" and a shake of the head.

The photographer said, "Okay, Lieutenant, get 'em out of the way."

An officer pushed the group back, and the instantaneous brilliance of the flashlight bulb cut the night apart with a quick stab of light.

"Hold it," the photographer said. "I'll get another shot from this angle, then one from the other side. Then you can have him."

As the little group moved away from the car, Mason managed to get Della Street and Helen Kendal off to one side. "When Lieutenant Tragg questions you," he said, "answer his questions frankly; but it might be a good plan not to *volunteer* any information . . . particularly unimportant information."

"Such as what?" Della Street asked.

"Oh," Mason said, with an elaborately casual manner, "any of the family gossip or anything of that sort. Tragg will ask you what he wants to know. Don't take up his time with a lot of unimportant incidentals, such as the fact that Gerald Shore didn't come into the hotel when we went in to call on Leech—things like that. Of course, if he asks you specifically, that's different, but there's no necessity to waste time telling him things in which he isn't interested. He'll ask you about everything he wants to know."

Helen Kendal nodded innocently enough, but Della Street maneuvered Mason off toward the rear of the car. "Why the secrecy about Gerald Shore not going into the hotel?" she asked. "And what's significant about it?"

Mason's manner was deeply thoughtful. "Hanged if I know, Della. For some reason, I don't think he wanted to go into the hotel."

"You think he really knows Henry Leech?"

"He may—or he *might* have been in there earlier tonight and didn't want the clerk to recognize him."

Della Street puckered her lips to give a low whistle.

"Mind you, that's just a guess," Mason warned. "There's probably nothing to it, but I . . ."

"What are *you* two talking about?" Tragg demanded, coming around from the other side of the car.

Mason said, "Wondering whether he was shot from the left side by someone hidden by the side of the road or from the right side by someone sitting in the car."

Tragg snorted, "Pardon me! From the secret huddle you're in, I thought you might be discussing something confidential—like who won the last World's Series. Just to satisfy your curiosity, he was shot from the left side by someone who was outside the car. The bullet entered the left side of the head, and the murderer stood far enough away so the weapon left no powder burns. Probably it was a .38 revolver, and it *may* have been an automatic. We're going to look for the empty cartridge case. Is there anything else you want to know?"

"Quite a lot," Mason said. "In fact, virtually all of the details."

"Got a nickel?" Tragg asked casually.

Mason pushed his hand down in his pocket. "Yes. Why? Did you want to telephone?"

"No," Tragg said, grinning. "Keep your nickel. You can buy a newspaper with it tomorrow and get *all* the details. Right now, I'm only going to tell you what I want you to know."

Tragg walked past them to the side of the car. By this time, the deputy coroner had completed his examination and the men began searching the body.

A few moments later, Tragg walked over to the police car and said, "I'd like to have you four come over here. Mason, I'm going to ask you to let me do the talking for a moment, and not say anything unless I ask you some specific question."

Mason nodded.

"Now then," Tragg said, turning to the others, "what was it Mason told you *not* to tell me about?"

Mason said, "What makes you think . . ."

Tragg silenced him by holding up his hand. He kept his eyes on Helen Kendal. "All right, Miss Kendal, I'll ask you. What was it?"

In a loud, droning voice Della Street started in reciting: "'*Will you come into my Parlor,' said the Spider to the Fly—*"

"Stop that!" Tragg looked angry. "I'm asking Miss Kendal. Come on, Miss Kendal. What was it?"

Helen Kendal seemed embarrassed for a moment, then, looking straight at Lieutenant Tragg, said, "He told us to answer all your questions fairly and frankly."

"That all?"

"He said not to waste your time by interpolating a lot of trivial little things."

"Such as what?" Tragg asked, pouncing upon her answer with the alacrity of a cross-examiner who has found a weak point in the story of a witness.

Helen Kendal's big, violet eyes were wide. "Such as the things you didn't want to ask us about," she said. "Mr. Mason said that you were very skillful and that you'd ask questions which would cover every single angle of the case about which you wanted information from us."

Tragg's face showed angry determination.

"And don't think I won't," he promised grimly.

8

Iᴛ ᴡᴀs a good half hour before Lieutenant Tragg completed his searching questions. By that time, the men had finished their examination of the body and the car.

Tragg said wearily, "All right, you four stay right here in this automobile. I want to go back to that other car and check up on some things."

Gerald Shore said, as Tragg moved away, "Rather a searching interrogation, it seemed to me. There was an element of cross-examination in it. He would almost seem to suspect our motives."

Mason was soberly thoughtful as he said, "Tragg senses that there's something else behind this. Naturally, he wants to know what that something else is."

Shore said, very casually, "You didn't suggest to *me* that I should withhold any information which might seem trivial from Lieutenant Tragg."

"That's right," Mason conceded.

"What specifically did you have in mind, counselor?"

"Oh, minor matters—things which enter into the general background, but don't seem particularly pertinent to the case."

Shore asked, "Did you have some *particular* thing in mind?"

"Lots of little things," Mason replied. "The poisoned cat, for instance."

Helen Kendal's quick inhalation betrayed her surprise. "Surely, Mr. Mason, you don't think the poisoning of the cat has anything to do with *this?*" and she motioned toward the parked sedan in which the body had been discovered.

Mason said suavely, "I was merely mentioning it to illustrate the trivia in which I felt Lieutenant Tragg *wouldn't* be interested."

"But I thought you said the thing you didn't want us to tell him was . . ." She caught herself abruptly.

"Was what?" Gerald Shore asked.

"Oh, nothing."

Shore looked at Mason suspiciously.

"I think the only thing I specifically mentioned," Mason went on suavely, "was something that I suggested by way of illustration—just as I mentioned the poisoned cat just now."

"What was the illustration that you used?" Shore asked.

Helen Kendal blurted out, "About you not going into the Castle Gate Hotel when we drove up there tonight."

Gerald Shore's body seemed wrapped in that rigid immobility which is the result of a conscious effort not to betray emotion. "What in the world would *that* have to do with it?"

Mason said, "That is just it, counselor. I mentioned it as one of those trivial details which might clutter up the case and unnecessarily prolong the examination of the witnesses. It's in exactly the same category as the poisoning of the kitten."

Shore cleared his throat, started to say something, then thought better of it, and lapsed into silence.

Lieutenant Tragg returned to the automobile, carrying a white cloth bundle.

"Open the car door," he said to Mason. "Move over so I'll have a place to put these things. Now, I don't want anyone to touch any article here. I do want you to look at them carefully—but just look at them."

He spread out the bundle, which proved to be a handkerchief upon which rested a gold watch, a penknife, a leather billfold and card case, a gold pencil, and a fountain pen encrusted with gold and on which initials had been engraved.

"I have some theories about these things," Tragg said.

"But I'm not going to tell you what they are. I want you to tell me if you've ever seen any of these before, if any of them look at all familiar."

They leaned forward to stare down at the articles, Shore peering over Mason's shoulder from the front seat of the automobile, Della Street and Helen Kendal leaning over the back of the front seat.

"They mean nothing to me," Mason announced promptly.

"How about you, Shore?" Lieutenant Tragg asked.

Shore craned his neck, frowning thoughtfully.

Mason said, "He can't see very well from that position, Lieutenant. Suppose I get out, so he can look at them more closely."

"All right," Tragg said, "but don't touch any of the articles."

"Is it in order to ask where you got them?" Mason inquired.

"They were done up in this handkerchief in a little bundle such as you see here, and were on the seat of the automobile beside the body."

"Indeed," Mason said, squirming around so that he could get out of the front door without brushing against any of the articles. "It's all right to touch the handkerchief, isn't it, Lieutenant?"

"Yes. We won't get any fingerprints from the cloth."

Mason fingered the handkerchief. "Good grade of linen," he said. "A man's handkerchief. Touch of rather a peculiar color, isn't there, Lieutenant?"

"There may be."

As Mason slid out of the door, Gerald Shore, leaning over, exclaimed, "Why, that's my brother's watch!"

"You mean Franklin Shore?" Lieutenant Tragg's manner was tense.

"Yes," Gerald said, his voice showing his excitement. "That's his watch all right, and I believe . . . yes, that's his fountain pen!"

"The initials 'FBS' are engraved on it," Tragg said dryly. "It made me think perhaps it *might* have been your brother's."

"It is. It's his."

"How about the pencil?"

"I'm not certain about the pencil."

"Or the billfold and card case?"

"I can't help you there."

"The knife?"

Gerald shook his head. "But that's his watch all right."

"Is the watch running?" Mason asked.

"Yes."

Mason said, "Perhaps we could manipulate the handkerchief so we could look at the face of the watch."

"It's a plain, open-faced watch," Tragg said. "But you'll notice there's a scroll on the back of the watch, a scroll made by the initials 'FBS.'"

"Highly interesting," Mason said. "We might look at the face of the watch to see whether it has any added significance."

The lawyer picked up the handkerchief, moved it around so that the watch slowly turned over.

Mason glanced significantly at Della Street, closed one eye in a quick wink. Della Street promptly lowered her hands to the catch of her purse.

Mason said, "That's interesting. A Waltham watch. There's something written on the dial. What is it? . . ." He bent over the handkerchief. "Hold that spotlight there just a moment if you will, Lieutenant."

"It's a trade name and description of the watch," Tragg said.

Mason bent over it. "That's right. The printing is rather fine. The word '*Waltham*' is printed in a straight line, and down below it in a curve is '*Vanguard 23 Jewels*.' Notice this, Lieutenant. There's a winding indicator on the top, right by the figure twelve. It indicates when the watch has been wound up and when it's run down. There are twenty-four hours on the dial and you can tell roughly from the position of the hand how long since it's been wound—about six hours in this case. Rather interesting—don't you think?"

Tragg said, "Yes. It indicates that the watch was fully wound up about six hours ago—although I can't see that the point has any particular significance."

Mason consulted his own watch. "It's about ten-thirty," he remarked, thoughtfully. "That would indicate the watch was wound up around four-thirty or five o'clock this afternoon."

"Exactly," Tragg said. "But you'll pardon me, Mason, if I don't get very excited over it. Somehow or other, I've always noticed that when you start pointing out clues, it isn't because you're so anxious to have me become interested in the things you're mentioning as to keep me from becoming interested about some other thing which you carefully avoid mentioning."

Helen Kendal grimaced over her shoulder at Della Street and in a loud stage whisper observed, "I'm glad *I'm* not Lieutenant Tragg's wife!"

Mason looked at Helen appreciatively. She was coming on fast. "The lieutenant isn't married," he told her.

"Mr. Mason, I'm not at all surprised. Are you?"

"No, Miss Kendal, I'm not," Mason replied gravely. "They tell me that once . . . All right, Tragg, all right. Carry on."

"That's his fountain pen all right," Gerald Shore said. "I remember now that he was very fond of it."

"Carried it in his pocket all the time?" Lieutenant Tragg asked.

"Yes."

Mason slid out of the car, peered over the back of the seat to make certain that Della Street had interpreted his signal correctly.

She had her shorthand notebook on her knees and was taking down the conversation.

Mason took a pencil and notebook from his pocket and scribbled a series of figures.

Lieutenant Tragg said, "Quite obviously, that is the body of Henry Leech. There's a driving license in his pocket. It shows that it was issued to Henry Leech who resides at the Castle Gate Hotel. Evidently, he must have been a permanent tenant there. There are also some other cards in the wallet. It's Leech all right."

Gerald Shore said excitedly, "Look here, Lieutenant, this man was going to take us to my brother. I think you can appreciate the extreme importance of clearing up that old mystery."

Lieutenant Tragg nodded.

"If my brother is alive and well, that is a matter of the greatest importance. It might even overshadow the murder of this man. I feel that you should lose no time in running down every available clue."

Tragg's eyes narrowed. "Now, why should that overshadow a murder?"

Shore said, "I'm speaking as a lawyer."

Tragg retorted, "Exactly. And I'm speaking as a detective."

Shore glanced at Mason; then turned hastily away. "My brother was a man of some importance. I take it this man Leech who lived at a questionable, second-rate hotel was not."

"Keep talking," Tragg said. "You haven't said anything—yet."

Shore went on rapidly, "Well, there might be a lot of difference in the legal situation. You see—well, I think you'll understand what I mean."

Tragg thought for a moment, then snapped a question. "A will?"

"I wasn't referring to that."

"You had it in mind?"

"Not particularly."

"But it's an angle?"

"Yes," Shore admitted reluctantly. "It's an angle."

Mason intervened with a suggestion. "Look here, Lieutenant, don't you think under the circumstances, we're entitled to see everything that was in the pockets of the dead man?"

Tragg shook his head emphatically. "I'm handling *this* investigation on my own, Mason. You're entitled to see nothing."

"At least," Mason said, "we should be permitted to go with you to Henry Leech's room in the Castle Gate Hotel and see what you uncover there in a search. After all, this is Gerald Shore's brother we're looking for, and Shore should have some rights in the matter."

Gerald Shore said hastily, "As far as I'm concerned, I have unlimited confidence in Lieutenant Tragg's ability. I don't want to do anything which would interfere. However, if there's anything I can do to help, I want to place myself and every bit of my time and ability at the lieutenant's disposal."

Tragg nodded absently. "I'll call on you when I need anything."

Mason said, "Tragg, I want to go to the Castle Gate Hotel with you. I want to see what's in this man's room."

Lieutenant Tragg shook his head in a gesture of finality. "No, Mason, I'm going to run this investigation in my own way without any suggestions or interference."

"But you're going there now," Mason insisted. "At least, we can follow along and . . ."

"Nope," Tragg said. "You're all done. Your car's parked down by Hollywood Boulevard, Mason. Go on down and get in it and go about your business. I'll let you know in case I want anything. I'll leave a man here with this body. I want a fingerprint man to go over every inch of the car. Okay, Floyd, let's get started. And remember, Mason, I don't want you to try following me. You stay away from the Castle Gate Hotel until I've completed my investigation. Good night."

Lieutenant Tragg gathered up the handkerchief and once more tied the corners together, making a compact bundle of it.

Mason slid back into the front seat. "Well, counselor," he remarked to Shore, "I guess Tragg doesn't want any of our assistance. You might drive me back to where I've left my car parked. And," he added in a lower voice, "get started before the lieutenant changes his mind."

"Why, what do you mean?" Shore asked, stepping on the starter.

Mason said, in a low voice, "If I hadn't apparently been so eager to have him let us accompany him to the Castle Gate Hotel, he might have insisted on it."

Shore turned to Mason defiantly. "Well," he asked, "what's wrong with that?"

"Something else has happened that I thought we might want to investigate before the police stepped in. Matilda Shore is in the Exeter Hospital. She's been poisoned."

"Good God!" Shore exclaimed, swinging the car into a quick turn. "Helen, did you hear that?"

"I heard it," Helen said calmly.

"Easy, easy," Mason warned Shore. "Don't make it seem that you're too anxious to get away. Drive along rather slowly until after the police car passes you. And that won't be long. That fellow Floyd drives like the devil."

They had gone about three hundred yards when they saw the

red spotlights on the police car blossom into ruddy brilliance, heard the sound of gears meshing, and then the big car came roaring up behind them.

"Pull over," Mason said, "and let's hope he doesn't think things over and change his mind."

The police car didn't even hesitate, but went screaming on by, swaying into the first down turn of the long, winding grade.

Mason settled back in the seat. "All right," he said to Gerald Shore, "put her in second gear and turn her loose."

9

Matilda Shore, propped up in the hospital bed, surveyed her visitors, her eyes showing her anger.

"What is the meaning of this?" she demanded.

"Why," Gerald Shore explained, "we heard you were ill, and naturally wanted to see if there was anything we could do."

"Who told you?"

"Mr. Mason learned about it."

She turned to Mason. "How?" she demanded.

Mason bowed. "Just casually."

Gerald Shore put in hastily, "We *had* to see you, Matilda. Some things have happened which you should know about."

"I've been sick. I don't want visitors. How did you know where I was? Why did you bring these people?"

Gerald Shore said, "Perry Mason, the lawyer, and Della Street, his secretary, are interested in certain matters which are important to you."

Matilda Shore swung her big head on its thick neck, surveyed Perry Mason, and said, "Humph!"

"How did you know where I was?" she asked after a moment.

Helen Kendal said, "Komo was very much alarmed about you.

He said you'd been poisoned, that you acted just like the kitten. You told him to drive you to a hospital."

"Why, the little slant-eyed hypocrite," Matilda Shore said. "I told him to keep his mouth shut."

"He did," Mason said, "until after he learned that we knew all about it. *I* am the one who found out about what had happened. I didn't talk with Komo. Your niece talked with him *after* I had told her where you were."

"How did *you* find out?"

Mason merely smiled. "I must protect my sources of information."

Heaving herself up to a more erect sitting position, Matilda Shore said, "And will you kindly tell me why my whereabouts and my physical condition should be any of your business?"

"But, Matilda," Gerald interrupted to explain. "There's something about which you have to know. We simply had to reach you."

"Well, what is it? Stop beating around the bush."

Gerald said, "Franklin is alive."

"That's no news to me, Gerald Shore. Of course, he's alive! I've always known he was alive. Ran off with a trollop and left me to twiddle my thumbs. I suppose this means you've heard from him."

"You shouldn't condemn him too hastily, Aunt Matilda," Helen Kendal said in a voice which failed to carry the least conviction.

"No fool like an old fool," Matilda grumbled. "Man who was almost sixty running off with a woman half his age."

Mason turned to Gerald Shore. "Perhaps you'd better tell her how it happens you know he's alive."

"He telephoned us this afternoon—rather, he telephoned Helen."

The bedsprings heaved as Matilda twisted her big body around. She opened a drawer in the table near the bed, took out a pair of steel-rimmed spectacles, adjusted them to her nose, and looked at her niece as though she were examining a bug through a microscope.

"So—he telephoned—*you*. Afraid of me, I suppose."

The door opened. A nurse glided into the room, her starched uniform giving forth a businesslike rustle. "You mustn't excite the patient," she warned. "She really isn't supposed to have visitors. You can only stay a few minutes."

Matilda glared at her. "I'm all right. Please leave us alone."

"But the doctor . . ."

Matilda Shore motioned imperiously toward the door.

The nurse hesitated a moment. "I'll have to notify the doctor," she murmured, then withdrew.

Matilda swung back to Helen Kendal. "So he telephoned you, and you didn't say a word about it. *That's* gratitude. For ten years I devote myself to your—"

Gerald Shore spoke hastily, "You see, Matilda, she thought she might be dealing with an impostor, and she didn't want to disturb you with the news until she had made certain."

"Why did he telephone *her?*" Matilda demanded.

"That's just it," Gerald said placatingly. "Everything indicated that we were dealing, not with Franklin, but with some impostor who wanted to impose upon the family. We thought it would be better to establish a preliminary contact before telling you anything about it."

"I'm not a child."

"I understand, Matilda, but we thought it was better this way."

"Humph!"

Helen Kendal said, "He told me particularly that I couldn't see him unless I followed his instructions to the letter."

"Did you see him?" Matilda asked, peering through her spectacles at her niece.

"No, we didn't. A man by the name of Leech was to lead us to him—and something happened so that Leech couldn't do it."

Matilda Shore said, "It was Franklin all right. Sounds just like him—trying to sneak in the back way—wants to get hold of Helen, play up to her, get her sympathies aroused, and get her to intercede with me. Tell him to stop hiding behind a woman's skirts and come out in the open and meet me. I'll tell him a thing or two. I'll file suit for divorce the minute he shows his face. I've been waiting ten years for this."

Mason said, "I trust your poisoning wasn't serious, Mrs. Shore."

She rolled her eyes toward him, said, "Poisoning is always serious."

"How did it happen?" Gerald asked.

"Got hold of the wrong bottle, that's all. Had some heart medicine and some sleeping tablets in the medicine cupboard. Had a bottle of stout before I went to bed. Then went to get some sleeping tablets. Got the wrong bottle."

"When did you suspect it was the wrong bottle?" Mason asked.

"Had a little spasm," she replied. "Rang for Komo, told him to get out the car, to notify my doctor, and get me up to the hospital. Had enough presence of mind to drink a lot of mustard water and to get rid of as much of the stuff as I could. Told the doctor about how I'd gone to the medicine cabinet in the dark to take some sleeping medicine after I'd had my stout, told him I'd got the wrong bottle by mistake. Not certain he believes me. Anyhow, he got busy and fixed me up. I'm all right now. Want you to keep your mouth shut about that poisoning. I don't want to have the police interfering in my business. Now then, I want to find Franklin. Let's get him out into the open."

Mason said, "Has it ever occurred to you, Mrs. Shore, that there might be some connection between the return of your husband and the two instances of poisoning which have occurred in your household?"

"Two?" she asked.

"The kitten and you."

Matilda Shore studied him for the space of several seconds, then said, "Fiddle-sticks! I got the wrong bottle, that's all."

"I'm asking you if the idea has occurred to you that the drink was poisoned."

"Bosh! I tell you I got the wrong bottle."

"Don't you think you owe it to yourself to do something about it?"

"What should I do?"

Mason said, "At least, you should take steps to prevent a recurrence. If someone has made an attempt on your life, you certainly should do something about it."

"You mean the police?"

"Why not?"

"The police!" she exclaimed scornfully. "I'm not going to have them messing in my life and giving out a lot more stuff to the newspapers. That's what always happens. You call in the police to protect you, and some idiot who wants to see his picture in the paper rushes out to the reporters and tells them the whole story. I won't have it. Besides, I just made a mistake."

Mason said, "Unfortunately, Mrs. Shore, after what's happened tonight, there is going to be a lot of publicity."

"What do you mean, after what happened tonight?"

"This man Leech who was to lead us to your husband failed to do so."

"Why?"

Mason said, "Because someone stopped him."

"How?"

"By a .38 caliber bullet in the left side of his head, fired while he was sitting in an automobile waiting to keep an appointment with us."

"You mean he's dead?"

"Yes."

"Murdered?"

"Apparently."

"When did it happen?"

"We don't know exactly."

"Where?"

"By a reservoir up back of Hollywood in the mountains."

"Who was Leech? I mean how does he fit in?"

"Apparently, he was a friend of your husband."

"What makes you think so? I never heard of him."

Gerald Shore said, "When Franklin telephoned Helen, he told her to get in touch with Mr. Leech, that Leech would take him to Franklin."

Matilda motioned to Helen. "Get these men out of here. Get my clothes out of that closet. I'm going to dress and go home. If Franklin's around, he'll be pussyfooting out to the house, trying to wheedle me. I've been waiting ten years for this, and I'm not going to be shut up in any hospital when it happens. I'll show him he can't walk out on *me!*"

Mason made no move to leave. "I'm afraid you'll have to get your doctor's permission. I think the nurse has gone to telephone him."

"I don't need anybody's permission to get up and go out," Matilda said. "Thanks to that emetic I took, I got off with a very light dose of poison. I have the constitution of an ox. I shook it off. I'm all right now. I'm going out under my own power."

Mason said, "I wouldn't advise you to get up and put any strain

ERLE STANLEY GARDNER

on your heart. We wanted to let you know about your husband, and we wanted to find out what had happened, and what you intended to do about this poisoning."

"I tell you it was an accident, and I don't want the police . . ."

A knock sounded on the door.

Gerald Shore said, "That's probably the doctor or a couple of husky attendants called on by the hospital to eject us forcibly."

Matilda Shore called out, "Well, come on in. Let's get it over with. Let them eject me."

The door pushed open. Lieutenant Tragg and a detective entered the room.

Mason greeted them with a bow. "Mrs. Shore, may I have the honor of presenting Lieutenant Tragg of the Homicide Squad. I think he wants to ask you a few questions."

Tragg bowed to Mrs. Shore, turned, and bowed again to Mason. "Rather cleverly done, counselor. The more I see of you, the more I am forced to respect your very deft touch."

"Referring to what this time?" Mason asked.

"The manner in which you threw me off the trail, temporarily, by insisting that you and your friends should be permitted to accompany me to the Castle Gate Hotel. It wasn't until after I'd left you that it began to occur to me you'd tossed me a bait and that I'd very credulously grabbed at it."

Mason said, "Putting it that way makes it sound very much like a conspiracy."

Tragg said, "Draw your own conclusions. I started checking all angles of the case just as soon as I realized that your insistence on accompanying me had led me to let you go. Now, Mrs. Shore, if you don't mind, I'll hear about the poisoning."

"Well, I *do* mind," Mrs. Shore snapped. "I mind very much."

"That is unfortunate," Tragg announced.

"I ate something that disagreed with me, that's all."

"The hospital records indicate that you took some medicine by mistake," Tragg pointed out.

"All right, I went to the medicine cabinet and took some medicine by mistake."

Tragg was suavely solicitous. "That's unfortunate. May I ask what time this was, Mrs. Shore?"

"Oh, about nine o'clock, I guess. I didn't notice the exact time."

"And, as I understand it, you had prepared for bed, had your regular nightly glass of stout, turned out the light, and went to the medicine cabinet in the dark?"

"Yes. I thought I was taking sleeping tablets. I got the wrong bottle."

Tragg seemed particularly sympathetic. "You didn't notice any difference in the taste?"

"No."

"Your sleeping medicine is in the form of tablets?"

"Yes."

"Kept in the medicine cabinet?"

"Yes."

"And you didn't notice any difference in the taste of the tablets you took?"

"No. I washed them down with water. Had a glass of water in one hand, tossed the tablets into my mouth with the other, and washed them right down."

"I see. Then you were holding the glass of water in your right hand as you tossed the tablets into your mouth with your left hand?"

"That's right."

"And you put the cap back on the bottle and returned it to the medicine cabinet?"

"Yes."

"That took both hands?"

"What difference does it make?"

"I'm simply trying to find out. That's all. If it was an accident, there's nothing to investigate."

"Well, it was an accident."

"Of course," Tragg said soothingly. "I'm simply trying to get the facts so I can make a report that it was an accident."

Mollified, Mrs. Shore explained, "Well, that's what happened. I screwed the top back on this bottle."

"And put it back in the medicine cabinet?" Tragg asked.

"Yes."

"And then picked up your glass of water, holding the tablets in your left hand?"

"Yes."

"Tossed them into your mouth and drank the water immediately?"

"Yes."

"You didn't notice a bitter taste?"

"No."

"I believe it was strychnine poisoning, wasn't it, Mrs. Shore?"

"I don't know."

Tragg's voice showed his sympathy. "Most unfortunate," he said, and then asked casually, "And what were the strychnine tablets doing in your medicine cabinet, Mrs. Shore? You were using them for some particular purpose, I suppose?"

Her eyes studied the detective's countenance. "They're a heart stimulant. I kept them there in case I needed them."

"On a doctor's prescription?" Tragg asked.

"Yes, of course."

"What doctor prescribed them?"

She said, "I don't think that has anything to do with you, young man."

"How many tablets did you take?"

"Oh, I don't know. Two or three."

"And you put the bottle back in the medicine cabinet?"

"Yes. I've told you that before."

"Right next to the bottle of sleeping tablets?"

"I guess so. I tell you it was in the dark. I reached up in that general vicinity and got down the bottle which I thought contained the sleeping tablets."

Tragg said, "It's most unfortunate."

"What is?"

"The fact that a search of your medicine cabinet reveals that there are neither sleeping tablets nor strychnine tablets in it."

Mrs. Shore straightened up still further. "You mean that you've been to my house and searched my medicine cabinet?"

"Yes."

"What authority did you have to do that?" she demanded.

Tragg said, without raising his voice, "Perhaps, Mrs. Shore, I'd better ask you a question instead. What do you mean by lying to the police about an attempt which was made to poison you?"

"There wasn't any attempt to poison me."

"I believe that a kitten was poisoned at your house this afternoon and taken to Dr. Blakely's small animal hospital?"

"I don't know anything about a kitten."

Tragg smiled. "Come, Mrs. Shore, you'll have to do better than that. Falsifying evidence, you know, constitutes a crime. There are two attorneys in the room who will bear me out in that. If there was poison in that bottle of stout, the police want to know about it, and it would be exceedingly unwise for you to hamper their investigation."

The door of the hospital pushed open. A man, entering hastily, said, "What's going on here? I'm the doctor in charge of this case. This patient isn't to be disturbed. She's had a severe shock. I'm going to ask you all to leave—immediately."

Matilda Shore looked at him and said, "I guess you mean well, Doctor, but you got here just five minutes too late."

10

GERALD SHORE, strangely thoughtful and silent, drove his car up to the big, old-fashioned house which had remained virtually unchanged since the night the president of the Shore National Bank had vanished into thin air.

"Better get out here, Helen," he said, "and keep an eye on the house. I'll run Mr. Mason and his secretary out to Hollywood where he left his car."

"I can go and keep you company on the way back," Helen Kendal offered.

"I think you'd better be at the house. Someone should be here to take charge of things."

"When will Aunt Matilda be home?" she asked.

Gerald Shore turned to Mason, silently passing the question on to him.

Mason grinned. "Not until she's answered every question Lieutenant Tragg wants to ask."

"But the doctor insisted that the questioning was to be limited to five minutes. He said that Aunt Matilda's condition wouldn't stand for more than that."

"Exactly," Mason said. "And the doctor is in charge while she's in the hospital. But Tragg will put a couple of men on guard. He'll see that she doesn't leave the hospital until the doctor says she's entirely cured. When the doctor says she's completely recovered, Tragg will get the answer to his questions—either there at the hospital or down at headquarters."

"Lieutenant Tragg seems to be a very clever and a very determined young man," Gerald Shore said.

"He is," Mason agreed, "and don't ever underestimate him. He's a dangerous antagonist."

Gerald Shore was looking searchingly at Mason, but there was nothing in Mason's face which indicated his remark about Tragg had held any hidden significance.

Helen slipped out of the automobile and said, "Well, I'll stay here, then, and hold the fort."

"We won't be long," her uncle promised.

She shuddered a little. "I wonder what's going to happen next. I wish I knew where I could get hold of Jerry Templar."

"Wouldn't you like me to stay with you?" Della said impulsively.

"I'd love it," Helen confessed.

"Sorry," Mason said flatly. "I need Della."

Helen's face fell. "Never mind. I'll be all right—I guess."

Driving out toward Hollywood, Gerald Shore returned to something that seemed to be worrying him. "You've mentioned two or three times, Mason, that Lieutenant Tragg was a dangerous antagonist."

"Yes."

"Am I to assume that perhaps there was some particular significance which was attached to your remarks?"

Mason said, "That all depends."

"Upon what does it depend?" Gerald Shore asked, his manner that of a courteous but insistent cross-examiner.

"Upon what you have to conceal."

"But suppose I have nothing to conceal?"

"In that case, Lieutenant Tragg would not be a dangerous antagonist because he would not be an antagonist. But Lieutenant Tragg would always be dangerous."

Shore studied Mason's profile for a minute, then turned back to keep his eyes on the road.

Mason went on smoothly, "There are several things about this case which are rather significant. In the first place, if you and your brother had parted on the best of terms, there is no good reason why he wouldn't have called you, rather than have subjected his niece to the shock of hearing his voice and learning that he was alive.

"That, however, is a minor matter. The point is, he particularly and specifically suggested that Helen should consult me and take me with her to call on Mr. Leech, that no other member of the family should be present."

Gerald Shore said, "You've either said too much, Mason—or too little."

"Yet," Mason went on calmly, "*you* insisted upon coming along."

"I don't see what you're getting at, Mr. Mason. It was only natural that I should want to see my brother."

"Quite right. But it seemed that you deemed it necessary to see him *before* anyone else talked with him."

"Can you explain just what you mean by that?"

Mason smiled. "Of course I can. I'm looking at it now from the angle a person of Lieutenant Tragg's mentality and temperament would take in approaching the problem."

"Go right ahead."

"Tragg will eventually find out that while you left the house with us, that while you were with us when we drove up to that reservoir to keep that appointment with Leech, you *weren't* with us when we went into Leech's hotel."

"My interest was in my brother, not in Leech," Shore said.

"Exactly. Even Lieutenant Tragg would be willing to concede that, although inasmuch as Leech was the only link with your brother, it would seem that your interest should have been transferred to him. However, Tragg would be quite willing to accept that—*if* there were no other complicating factors."

"Such as?" Shore prompted.

"Oh," Mason said, "let's suppose that, just to be on the safe side, Tragg would get one of your photographs and take it to the clerk on duty in the Castle Gate Hotel, ask him if you'd been making inquiries about Henry Leech, ask if perhaps you'd ever called to see him—or if they remembered having seen you around the hotel at any time."

Gerald Shore was silent for a matter of seconds; then he inquired, "What would be the object in that?"

Mason said, "I am hardly in a position to know all of the facts, but—still looking at it from Tragg's viewpoint—there are things which are most significant. Your brother disappeared abruptly. His disappearance must have been brought about by some rather unusual factors. Immediately prior to his disappearance, he had had an interview with someone who had been either asking for or demanding money. There was some evidence indicating this person was you. There seems to have been some conflict in this evidence. I presume, however, that you were questioned about it, and I presume that the records will show you denied that you had seen your brother the night in question. Now Tragg might reason that it would be rather embarrassing to you if your brother should now appear on the scene and not only tell a story in direct conflict to that, but indicate that what you had been talking about had had something to do with his disappearance.

"Having reasoned that far, Lieutenant Tragg would then doubtless say to himself, Franklin Shore is in existence. For some reason, he doesn't want to make himself known. He doesn't care to go directly to his house. He wants to communicate with some of his relatives. He avoids his own brother and communicates instead with his niece, a very attractive young woman to be certain, but a young woman who must have been only thirteen or fourteen years of age when he disappeared. Gerald Shore, whom the brother has ignored upon his return, immediately steps into the picture and insists that he is going to go along with the niece. Henry Leech is the connecting link between Franklin, who is either unable or unwilling to come directly to the house and his relatives. Henry Leech goes to a lonely spot and is killed. There is a typewritten letter indicating that Leech has gone to this place of his own volition, but there is nothing to indicate that Leech himself wrote that letter. In fact, there is every reason to believe that he didn't write it. Of course, a great deal will depend upon what Lieutenant Tragg finds as to the time of death from a post-mortem examination. However, from certain bits of evidence which I saw when I was at the scene of the crime, I'm inclined to believe the time of death will be fixed perhaps about four hours prior to the time we arrived on the scene.

"Having reasoned that far, if Lieutenant Tragg finds any evidence indicating that you tried to get in touch with Leech earlier in the evening or actually *did* get in touch with him, it would be only natural for him to consider you as a very logical suspect."

Mason ceased talking, took a cigarette from his cigarette case, lit it, and settled back in the seat.

Gerald Shore drove silently for some ten blocks, then said, "I guess it's about time I retained you to act as my attorney."

Mason took the cigarette from his mouth long enough to observe, quite casually, "Perhaps it is."

"How about your secretary?" Gerald Shore asked, indicating Della Street who was sitting silently in the back seat.

"The soul of discretion," Mason assured him. "You may speak freely—and it may be the last opportunity you'll have to speak freely."

"You'll represent me?"

"That will depend," Mason said.

"Upon what?"

"Upon the circumstances, and upon whether I think you're innocent."

"I am innocent," Shore said with feeling, "entirely innocent. I'm either the victim of the damnedest set of circumstances fortune could conjure up, or of a deliberate conspiracy."

Mason continued smoking in silence.

Shore slowed the car so driving it would not require quite so much attention on his part, and said, "I was the one who called on my brother the night he disappeared."

"You denied it afterwards?" Mason inquired.

"Yes."

"Why?"

"For various reasons. One of them was that too much of my conversation had been overheard, and made public. You'll remember that the person who was with Franklin immediately prior to his disappearance had been heard to ask for money and had intimated that his own financial affairs were in desperate straits."

Mason nodded.

"I was engaged in carrying out some promotional transactions at the time. These could have shown a very considerable profit if I carried them through to completion, and could have shown a staggering, ruinous loss if I failed. The only thing which was enabling me to keep my head above water was the fact that the other parties in the transaction never for a moment suspected the possibility that I didn't have ample capital back of me."

"Your brother?" Mason asked.

"Well, my brother's connections perhaps had something to do with it. They didn't think he was directly interested.

They *did* think that I had plenty of capital, and that if anything happened and I found myself in need of more than I had available, my brother was always ready to stand back of me."

"So," Mason said, "you didn't dare to admit that you had been the one who had been with your brother because so much of that conversation had been published in the newspapers."

"That's exactly it."

"Didn't your brother's disappearance have a bad effect upon the transaction?"

"I'll say it did," Shore said with feeling, "but I was able to find and interest a man who furnished me the necessary capital—taking, as it happened, the lion's share of the profits. The fact that the affairs of the Shore National were so promptly investigated, the fact that my brother left so large a cash balance—those all helped."

"You didn't confide to Mrs. Shore perhaps that you were the one who had been with Franklin?"

"I didn't confide in anyone. I didn't dare to at the time."

"And after the necessity for the secrecy was removed?" Mason prompted.

"I stuck with my story. Put yourself in my position, and you'll realize I had to."

"Go ahead."

"Tonight when Helen told me that Franklin had telephoned her, I was sick with apprehension. I felt that I *had* to see Franklin before anyone else did."

"So while Helen returned to the hospital to see how Amber Eyes was getting along, you were out trying to get in touch with your brother. Is that right?"

"Yes. Helen went to the hospital directly after dinner to pick up the kitten. She then took the kitten down to the place where our gardener maintains a little bachelor shack, and then went up to keep her appointment with you."

"And during that interval of time, you went to the Castle Gate Hotel?"

"Yes. That was why I didn't come up with Helen to see you."

"You were trying to see Leech?"

"Yes."

"Any success?"

"No. I inquired first over the telephone, and was told that Leech had gone out with a man, but would be back soon. That left me in something of a spot. I thought the man might well have been my brother, Franklin. So I went to the hotel and waited. I didn't know Leech, but I felt certain he was with Franklin and that he'd be back within an hour."

"You waited?" Mason asked.

"Yes. I sat there waiting until it came time to go and meet you."

"He didn't come in?"

"No. At any rate, I don't think so. I do know Franklin didn't come in."

"And the clerk noticed you?"

"Yes. He spotted me as not being one of the regulars. I sat there by the door, and he kept looking at me. He may have thought I was a detective. As I gather from what Lieutenant Tragg said, the hotel apparently caters to men who have somewhat shady backgrounds, and that must make them suspicious of strangers. At first I intended to park my car near the door and wait in the car; but I couldn't find a parking place within half a block, so I decided I'd go inside and wait."

"And the fact that you were afraid the clerk might identify you as being the man who had been waiting around earlier in the evening made it absolutely essential that you shouldn't be seen in the hotel."

"Yes—that, of course, is in the strictect professional confidence."

Mason said, "I think you can rest assured Tragg will reason all this out for himself."

There was a vacant space at the curb. Shore swung his car to the side of the road, parked it, and shut off the motor. "I can't keep on driving," he said. "Give me a cigarette, will you?"

Mason handed him a cigarette. Shore's hands were shaking so that he could hardly hold the flame from the match to the end of the cigarette.

"Go on," Mason said.

"That's all there is to tell you."

Mason glanced back at Della Street, then said to Gerald Shore, "It's all right, except the motivation."

"What is wrong with the motivation?" Shore asked.

"You wouldn't have done what you did and as you did unless the necessity for seeing your brother before anyone else did had been much greater than would have been the case if you were merely trying to protect yourself against an original discrepancy in your statements."

Shore turned to Mason. "I see that I've got to be frank with you."

"It's always an advantage," Mason observed dryly. "As a practicing attorney, you should realize that."

Shore said, "I think you'll realize that no one ever knows exactly how honest he is. He goes through life *thinking* he's honest, because he's never been confronted with a sufficient temptation; then suddenly he's confronted with some crucial situation where he finds himself facing ruination on the one hand and with a chance to turn defeat into victory by doing something which seems very simple but which is—well, not dishonest, but not strictly legal."

"Never mind the excuses," Mason said somewhat sharply.

"Don't underestimate Tragg. When he works on a case, he works fast. I want facts. You can fill in reasons and excuses later. And get this straight. All that you've told me before this is what I had already deduced. All you've done so far has been to cross the t's and dot the i's. The thing you're coming to now—if you tell me the truth—is going to be the determining factor in whether I represent you."

Shore nervously took the cigarette from his mouth, dashed it out of the window to the sidewalk. He took off his hat and ran his hands through the wavy splendor of his gray hair. "This is something which must never, never come out," he said.

"Go ahead," Mason said.

Gerald Shore said, "I begged and pleaded with my brother. I had to have ten thousand dollars. He read me a lecture on my general business methods—a lecture which I wasn't in a position to appreciate because, if I didn't get that ten thousand dollars, I was completely ruined. If I did, I felt I'd clean up enough money on that one deal so I could quit taking long chances and become more conservative. My brother finally promised that he would help me. He said that he had some other matters to attend to that night, but that before he went to bed, he would make a check for ten thousand dollars and put it in the mail."

"A check payable to you?" Mason asked.

"No. A check payable directly to the party to whom the money was due. Time was too short to have a check go through my account."

"Your brother did that?" Mason asked.

"My brother didn't. He disappeared without doing that."

"Then we can take it for granted that after your visit, he was confronted with a certain urgency which made his disappearance so imperative that he forgot his promise to you."

"I suppose so."

"When did you learn of the disappearance?"

"Not until the next morning."

"And that day was the last day you had in which to take some action?"

Shore nodded.

"You had, perhaps, already assured your associates that the matter had been taken care of?" Mason inquired.

"At nine-thirty that morning," Shore said with feeling, "I rang up the party to whom the payment was due and told him that he would have his check before the banks closed that afternoon, that the check would be made payable to him and would be signed by Franklin B. Shore. About ten minutes after I'd hung up the telephone, Matilda got in touch with me and asked me to come over at once. She told me about what had happened."

"Now, as I remember it," Mason said, "the fact of the disappearance was kept from the public for a day or two."

Shore nodded.

Mason looked at him shrewdly. "During that time, several large checks were cashed," he said.

Shore nodded.

"Well?" Mason prompted.

"Among them," Shore said, "was a check to Rodney French for ten thousand dollars."

"Rodney French was the man to whom you owed the money?"

"Yes."

"And to whom you had promised the payment?"

"Yes."

"And that check?" Mason asked.

Gerald Shore said, "That check was made out and signed by me. I forged my brother's signature. My brother had promised me that I could count on that check. I felt that—that I was entitled to do what I did in all honesty."

11

L had taken off her coat, hat, and gloves and was
when she heard a car in the driveway.
at her wrist watch. Surely no one could be coming
unmistakably, the car was turning into the private
as the driver kicked out the clutch and she heard
of knocks and bangs which came from under the
caught, skipped a beat, then started pounding. She
e was only one motor in the world which was in
te of disrepair, yet still running.
ickly to the door.
r was getting out of the car, moving with that slow
seemed almost to border on awkwardness, yet
managed to accomplish so much. He looked slim
is uniform, and Helen realized the Army training
certain determination, an assurance of his ability to
gs which had not been there a few months earlier.
some ways a stranger to her, a familiar friend who
sted with a new, breath-taking power to affect her
heart skip beats, then pound wildly.
nt would she mention the murder or anything of

"And Matilda Shore never knew that the check was forged?"

"No one ever knew it was forged. I—I made a good job of it. As it happened, my brother had called up his bookkeeper late that night in connection with some other matters, and had mentioned that he was making out this check to Rodney French for ten thousand dollars.

"I don't suppose, Mr. Mason," Shore went on, emotion choking his voice, "I could ever explain to you what all this meant to me. It was the turning point in my career. Prior to that time, I'd been mixed up in a lot of get-rich-quick schemes—legitimate all right, but, nevertheless, promotional gambles. I'd been intent on making money. I guess my brother's influence furnished the spur which goaded me on. I wanted to be like him. I wanted to show that I, too, had the ability to make money. I wanted the things which went with financial security.

"After the devastating experience which I had that time, I took stock of myself. I wasn't particularly impressed by what I found.— That's been ten years ago, Mr. Mason. I think I can truthfully say that I've changed since then—changed in a great many respects."

"Go on," Mason said. "I'm interested."

"For one thing, I've realized that there's something more to life than making money."

"You mean acquiring wisdom, or a philosophy of life?" Mason asked.

"No, I don't," Gerald Shore said. "I mean in the duties and responsibilities a man has toward others."

"In what way?"

"I used to think a man's life was his own to live as he wanted to live it. I realize now that isn't true. A man isn't entirely a free agent. He's constantly influencing others by his character, by what he says, by the way he lives, by . . ." Shore's voice choked, and he became silent.

Mason waited, smoking quietly.

Shore went on after a few seconds, "Take Helen, for instance. She was a girl of fourteen, standing, to use a trite expression, on the threshold of life. She had always looked up to me and respected me. She was approaching a time in life when moral values were about to become more significant to her. If something happened, if she had discovered that—well, Mr. Mason, from that time on, I changed my entire goal in life. I got a completely different set of objectives. I began to try and pattern my life so that those who looked up to me wouldn't— Oh, what's the use?"

"There's a great deal of use," Mason said, his voice kindly.

"That's all there is to it," Shore said shortly. "I quit trying to make money. I began to take more of an interest in people, not for what they could do for me, but for what I could do for them. I realized that, to younger persons at least, I was a trustee for certain standards. And I," he continued bitterly, "a confessed forger, am ranting all this stuff, I who have committed a crime and who thought that crime would go undiscovered, had the temerity to think that I could avoid paying for what I had done."

Mason waited until his emotion had subsided, then inquired, "How about Rodney French? Did he ask any questions?"

"No. He did go so far as to telephone Franklin's bookkeeper and ask him if Franklin had said anything about making out that check. That was when the check wasn't in the morning mail. Upon being assured that Franklin had so advised his bookkeeping department, French took the money and kept quiet."

"Otherwise, French might have resorted to a little blackmail after he learned of Franklin's disappearance?" Mason asked.

"I don't know. I suppose that after he heard of the disappearance and heard my denial that I had been with my brother, French became rather suspicious."

"And just why," Mason a
brother would have become

"Don't you see?" Shore s
"The newspapers dug up a
my brother's financial tran
amount of his bank balanc
the last few days—and ther
fact that the last check whi
of Rodney French to an am

Mason gave the matte
think your brother forgave

"I had hoped that he
said, "but when he saw fi
Helen instead of me, I—W

Mason pinched out t
Tragg ever gets hold of all
first-degree murder."

"Don't I know it!" Ge
ing I can do. I feel like a
current against which he
whirlpool."

Mason said, "There's
"What?"

"Keep your mouth
talking—and that means

HELEN KENDA
reading a book
She glanced
at this hour, bu
driveway. Then
the succession
hood, her heart
felt certain ther
quite such a sta
She went qu
Jerry Templ
efficiency which
which somehow
and straight in
had given him a
accomplish thin
This man was in
had become inv
life, to make her
On no accou

the family complications, Helen decided. He had come tonight, unannounced, to see her. With Jerry, there were more important things to talk about. Perhaps tonight—

"Oh, Jerry!" she exclaimed. "I'm so glad to see you!"

"Hello, darling. I saw lights and thought perhaps you hadn't gone to bed. Can I come in for a few minutes?"

She took his hand, drew him into the hallway, and closed the door. "Yes," she said, rather unnecessarily.

Helen led the way into the big living room and dropped down on the davenport. She watched Jerry curiously to see where he would sit. Was he going to the chair on the other side of the fireplace, or was he coming over to her on the davenport? Shamelessly she willed him to come over beside her, but he just stood there in the middle of the room.

"You look tired, Jerry."

He seemed surprised. "Tired? I'm not."

"Oh! My mistake! Cigarette?" She held a box toward him.

That did it. He crossed the room slowly, took a cigarette and settled down beside her.

"Where have you been all evening?" he demanded.

Helen's eyes dropped. "Out," she said.

"I know that. I've called you four times."

"Twenty cents! You shouldn't throw money around like that, Jerry."

"Where were you?" It was almost an accusation.

"Oh, here and there," she replied evasively. "No place special."

"Alone?"

Helen looked up at him, and her eyes were mocking. "You're mighty curious, soldier," she drawled. "Do all your women sit home every night on the chance you may call?"

"I haven't got any—women," he said roughly. "You know I—"

"Go on."

Instead of going on, however, Jerry jumped up and began pacing the floor.

"Where's your aunt?" he demanded suddenly. "In bed?"

"She was, the last time I saw her." Then, very casually, "So are Komo and the housekeeper."

"Your aunt doesn't like me!"

"Such perception, Jerry! I'm amazed."

"What's she got against me?"

There was a silence.

"I guess I won't answer that one," Helen finally decided.

There was another silence.

"Were you out with George Alber tonight?"

"It's none of your business, of course, but as it happened I was with Uncle Gerald all evening."

"Oh!"

Jerry looked relieved and settled down on the davenport again.

"When are you going to your officers' training camp, Jerry?"

"As soon as I get back to the outfit next week, I guess."

"Monday—six days more," Helen murmured. "You're not thinking about anything much or anybody these days except the war, are you?"

"Well, there *is* a job to be done."

"Yes, but we've still got to live," Helen said softly. If she could only get him to break through that self-imposed wall of silence. If he would only stop being so ridiculously noble, so self-disciplined, and let himself go for once. She turned toward him, chin up, lips half parted. They were all alone in the big house. The ticking of the grandfather's clock in the hall was loud.

Jerry seemed to steel himself against her. He started speaking, and there was no verbal fumbling. His words were swift, close-clipped. His gray eyes looked into hers with tenderness, but with that determination she had seen so much of the last few days. "I don't know what's ahead of me," he said. "You don't know what's ahead of me. There's a nasty job of mopping up. After that, there's got to be some face-lifting in the world. Don't you see that at a time like this a man has to abandon and try to forget some things that mean more to him, personally, selfishly, than anything else in the world? If a man's in love with a woman, for instance—"

His voice trailed off, as suddenly, from Matilda Shore's bedroom, they heard the sound of some article of furniture crashing to the floor. Then, a moment later, came the unmistakable *thump . . . thump . . . thump* of a cane, and the shuffle of heavy steps crossing the floor. The caged lovebirds started throaty, shrill chirpings as they chattered excitedly.

"Your Aunt Matilda," said Jerry in a hollow voice.

Helen tried to speak, but for a moment her throat was constricted so that the words wouldn't come.

Jerry looked at her curiously. "What's the matter, darling, you look scared."

"That's—that's not Aunt Matilda."

"Nonsense. You can't mistake those steps. The shuffle-and-thump; and shuffle-and-thump. You can even hear the peculiar dragging sound of her foot when she . . ."

Helen's fingers clutched his arm. "Jerry, it isn't she! She isn't home. She's at a hospital."

There was a moment while her words and her fear penetrated into Jerry's consciousness; then he was on his feet, brushing her to one side despite her efforts to cling to his arm.

"All right, let's see who it is."

"No, no, Jerry! Don't go alone. There's danger! Something horrible happened tonight. I didn't want to tell you, but . . ."

He might or might not have heard her. She only knew her words had no effect. With his jaw set, he moved swiftly toward the closed door into the corridor leading to Matilda's bedroom.

"Where's the light switch?" he asked.

Helen raced to his side, suddenly aware that Jerry, a stranger to the house, was groping his way through half darkness.

She clicked on the light switch. "Jerry, be careful. Oh, my dear, please . . ."

From behind Aunt Matilda's bedroom door, there was a silence as though the intruder might be standing still—or might be moving with catlike stealth to surprise Jerry when he opened the door. Only the high-pitched chatter of the lovebirds grew to a hysterical crescendo of bird talk.

"Please, Jerry," she whispered. "Don't open it. If someone should be in there and . . ."

He said, "Let go of my arm."

She still clung to him.

"Let go of my arm," he repeated, shaking her off. "I may need that arm. Let's see what this is all about."

He turned the knob of the door, raised his foot, and kicked it open.

A gust of cold air billowing in from an open window came sweeping through the doorway into the corridor. The room was dark save for the illumination which flowed in from the lighted hallway, an illumination which threw a grotesque, distorted shadow of Jerry Templar along the floor of the bedroom. The birds became suddenly silent.

"The lights," Helen said, and darted past Jerry's side to reach for the light switch.

He grabbed her shoulder. "Don't be a fool. Keep out of this. Tell me . . ."

A stabbing spurt of flame came from the dark corner near the head of Matilda's bed. A bluish red spurt of flame that was ringed with orange. The report of the gun boomed through the confines of the room. She heard the bullet smack against the door jamb, even as a swift whisper of air brushed her face. She saw the drab darkness of the wood burst into lighter colored splinters as the wood beneath the aged exterior was ripped into view by the bullet. She felt the blast of fine particles of wood and plaster stinging her skin.

Jerry had her shoulder then, was jerking her back, shielding her body with his own.

The gun roared again.

That second bullet hit with a meaty *"smok"* against something at her side. She felt Jerry's body, close to hers, spin around in a quick half circle. His hand was reaching out, clutching. Then she was frantically trying to support a dead weight. His legs buckled and he went crashing to the floor, taking her with him.

12

MASON, GETTING into his own car, waved good night to Gerald Shore, watched the tail-light on his client's car disappear, then started his own motor.

"Whew!" Della Street exclaimed. "You certainly pick cases! If Lieutenant Tragg ever uncovers those facts . . . Good night!"

Mason grinned. "There's only one way to keep him from uncovering those facts."

"What's that?"

"Give him so many other facts to uncover he won't have time to bother with these."

"That will only hold him back for a while," she pointed out.

"It's the best we can do—now."

Mason swung his car into Hollywood Boulevard, drove halfway to Los Angeles. "I guess the time has come to call in Paul Drake," he decided.

Della sighed. "More overhead! What do you need a private detective for? Couldn't I do it?"

"No, you could not."

"Well, Paul's out anyway. He's taking this week off and he swore that he wouldn't go to the office or take on any job for love or money."

"The devil! I'd forgotten."

"You'll have to get one of his operatives. That sweet little guy who looks like a Bedlington terrier is good. What's his name?"

"He won't do," Mason said decidedly. "I need Paul."

"He'll just hang up on you if you call him. You know Paul."

"Yeah, I know Paul. I guess you're right. He'd just dust me off."

They cruised on down the Boulevard.

"Is it really important, Perry?"

"What?"

"Getting Drake."

"Yes."

Della Street sighed resignedly. "All right, pull up by that all-night lunch counter ahead, and if they've got a telephone booth, I'll see what I can do for you."

"You? What makes you think you can get Paul out of bed in the middle of the night if I can't?"

Della's eyes dropped demurely. "You just don't know how to appeal to Paul's higher instincts," she murmured. "I don't say I can make him *work*, but if I can get him down to the office you ought to be able to handle him from then on."

Perry Mason stopped in front of the lunch counter, and followed Della in. She looked around, frowning.

"Go ahead and do your stuff," Mason said. "I'll order us something to eat."

Della shook her head. "This joint won't do."

"What's the matter? It looks clean enough."

"There's no telephone booth."

"There's a phone on the wall over there, stupid."

"What I've got to say to Paul calls for a *booth*," Della drawled. "A wall telephone won't do. Come on, we'll have to try somewhere else."

A few blocks further on Mason stopped the car again in front of a brilliantly lighted diner. He looked in through plate windows at the interior, shining with chromium and glass, and locked the car.

"We're eating here whether there's a telephone booth or not. I'm hungry."

Inside the door, Mason pointed to the telephone booth and headed for the counter.

"Ham and eggs and coffee for me," she called after him.

Mason said to the man behind the counter, "Two orders of ham and eggs. Keep the eggs straight up and fry them easy. Plenty of French-fried potatoes. Lots of hot coffee, and you might make up two cheeseburger sandwiches on the side."

Five minutes later Della Street joined Mason at the counter.

"Get him?" Perry demanded.

"Yes, I got him."

"Is he coming down to the office?"

"He's coming down to the office—in thirty minutes."

"Swell. Say, what's the matter with your face? You haven't got a fever, have you?"

"I'm blushing, you lug! I'll never do that again, even for you. I want my coffee now."

"Well, I'll be damned," Perry Mason said softly.

The man drew two steaming cups of fragrant, golden-brown coffee, and slid them across the counter. "You'll like that," he said. "Best grade I can buy. I make it in small quantities and keep it fresh."

They perched themselves on stools, placed elbows on the counter, sipped coffee, and watched the food cooking on the gas plate, the appetizing odor of frying ham swirling past their nostrils.

"Now tell me why you need Paul Drake," Della said.

Mason said, "I need a lot of facts dug out before Tragg closes the case with a lot of half truths."

"Do you think Shore was telling you only half truths?"

Mason thoughtfully regarded the steaming surface of the coffee in his cup. "He was telling us the truth as he sees it. But he was seeing only a part of the picture. There's nothing so deadly as a case built on circumstantial evidence composed of half truths."

The cook slid hot, thick platters across the counter. Generous slices of ham, the golden yellow of fried eggs, and the rich brown of French-fried potatoes furnished a tempting visual background for the odors which came drifting up. "We eat," Mason said, "and do our thinking afterwards."

"Your cheeseburgers are coming right along," the man promised, picking up the toasted buns, putting the fillings in them, spreading them thickly with white, chopped onions. "Do you want mustard?"

"Lots of it," Mason said.

They ate silently, concentrating on their food.

Della Street pushed her coffee cup across the counter for a refill.

"Why did Matilda Shore try to keep Lieutenant Tragg from knowing someone had poisoned her?"

"Quite evidently because there's some connection between that and the poisoned kitten."

"Was it an attempt on her life?"

"Looks that way."

"Any ideas?" Della asked.

"It depends on the time element. Apparently the stout was kept in an icebox."

"What makes you think it was?"

"Wouldn't go flat so quickly after it was opened and poisoned. Probably she keeps several bottles in an icebox."

"How did the poisoner make certain she was going to take the poisoned drink if she keeps several bottles on hand?"

"Probably by poisoning the nearest one—or perhaps by poisoning several."

Mason shoved a five-dollar bill across the counter and looked at his wrist watch.

The attendant at the lunch counter made change. "More coffee, yes?"

"About half a cup," Mason said. "That's all I have time for." He pushed back twenty-five cents out of the change, scooped the rest into his pocket, said, "Mighty good grub. We'll be back again sometime."

"In a hurry?" the attendant asked.

"Uh huh."

He peered at them shrewdly through the upper part of his spectacles. "If anybody'd ask me," he said, "looks as though you two was headed for Yuma on a marryin' party."

"Nobody asked you!" Della Street said, smiling.

Mason took another twenty-five-cent piece from his pocket, slipped it under his plate.

"What's that for?" the man asked.

"The idea," Mason said, grinning. "Come on, Della. Let's go."

They raced through the streets to the building where Mason had his office. Paul Drake's detective agency was on the same floor as the lawyer's office but nearer the elevator. Mason opened the lighted door, looked in on the man who ran the office at night. "The boss in yet?"

"Hello, Mr. Mason—no, he is taking this week off. I thought you knew."

"If he should drop in, don't mention me," Mason grinned. "Just forget you saw me."

They walked down the long, vacant corridor, their steps echoing hollowly against the walls. Dark doors on each side lettered with the names of business firms seemed like silent sentinels of dead business. The air in the hallway was musty and stale. Mason opened the door of his private office, switched on the lights. Della

Street paused as he held the door open. "That's the elevator coming up again," she said. "I'll bet this is Paul Drake."

Mason disappeared into the law library and closed the door. He could hear the steady rhythm of the approaching steps.

"It's Paul, all right," Della Street whispered from the other side of the door. "Nothing ever seems to change the tempo of that walk. He's not stopping at his office."

There was a soft knock on the door into the corridor. Della Street opened it a crack. Drake pushed it open the rest of the way, stalked in, slammed the door behind him. He looked at Della with slightly protruding eyes which held no hint of expression. Then he smiled sardonically. Tall, somewhat stooped, he had the manner of a professional undertaker making a midnight round of the mortuary.

"Hello, kid," he said.

"Hello, Paul." Della's voice was uncertain.

"That was a good act. I didn't know you had it in you." He crossed swiftly to the door concealing Perry Mason and flung it open. "Come out of there, you cheap shyster! I'll teach you to try the badger game on me."

Mason came out, grinning. "I had a hunch you didn't fall for it, but I didn't say anything."

There was a wail from Della Street. "You played up and led me on and pretended you thought I was serious, and all the time you were laughing at me!"

"Shucks, Della, I was admiring you. I wasn't laughing at you." His slow drawl was expressive, pungent. "I just know you too well."

"Why did you come, then?" she demanded, pointing at him.

Paul Drake's head drew in like a turtle's, then lunged forward and snapped at the tinted red fingernail a few inches away from his face. "I figured Perry needed me, and I guess I've had enough vacation. I was bored stiff," he confessed, with his peculiar husky chuckle.

"Get this woman off my neck, Perry, and let's get to work." He squirmed his way into his favorite, crossways position in the big, overstuffed leather chair. "What's the excitement?"

For ten minutes Mason talked rapidly. Drake listened with his eyes closed.

"That's the picture," Mason wound up.

"Okay. What do I do?"

"Find out everything you can about Leech. Find out anything you can about all the members of the family, particularly what they've done since the hue and cry over Franklin's disappearance died down."

"Anything else?"

"Yes. This man who telephoned Helen Kendal seems to have identified himself unmistakably as Franklin Shore, but in a case of this sort, you can't overlook the possibility of an impostor. Now, this man Leech has either been in contact with Franklin Shore or else trying to slip over a fast one. Here's a number," Mason went on, opening up his notebook and tearing out a sheet of paper.

"Car license?" Drake asked.

"No. Laundry mark. Laundry mark on a handkerchief that was tied around some personal stuff that seems to have belonged to Shore. It was on the seat of the car beside Leech. Leech evidently brought them along to show that he actually was acting as intermediary for Shore."

"Why the intermediary?"

"You've got me. Maybe Shore didn't want to come back until he'd tossed his hat in the door first."

"Would it have been kicked out?"

"Hard."

Drake gave a low whistle. "Like that, eh?"

Mason nodded.

"Tragg know you've got this laundry mark?" Drake asked.

"I don't think so. I fumbled around and pretended to be interested in the watch. That laundry mark struck me as being peculiar, Paul. I haven't seen laundry marks inked on the hems of handkerchiefs for some time. Most laundries don't do it any more. We should be able to trace Franklin Shore from that laundry mark."

"Anything else?"

"That Castle Gate Hotel seems to be . . ."

"I know the dump," Drake interrupted. "Bunch of promoters hang out there. Slick stock men. Phoney mining-company stuff. Get-rich-quick oil businesses and that sort of thing. They don't promote their rackets from the hotel, but use the Castle Gate as a place to hibernate when things go sour. If they start hitting the jack pot, they move into swanky hotels and apartments and put on the dog. If the police don't get anything on them and the racket pays off, they move into the big-time. If the police do get something on them, they go to San Quentin. But when a racket doesn't pay off, and the police haven't anything on them, they sneak back to the Castle Gate to make contacts with each other and lie low until the beef has passed."

"Okay," Mason said. "Now, here's another angle. Look back in the newspapers in 1932 and you'll find they published a list of checks which had cleared through Franklin Shore's account within a few days of his disappearance. You can be sure the police have dug up everything they could find out about those checks as of 1932. I want you to make a fresh investigation as of 1942."

"Anything else?" Drake asked, jotting down notes in a leather-backed, loose-leaf notebook.

"As an incidental development," Mason said, "a kitten was poisoned out at Matilda Shore's house. I think Tragg will be covering all the drugstores looking for poison purchases, and it won't do any good for us to trail along behind the police. They have the organization and the authority. They'd be bound to get the facts before we could. But you might bear in mind the poison angle."

"What's the kitten got to do with it?" Drake asked.

"I don't know, but Matilda Shore was fed poison from some source—apparently the same sort of poison that was used on the kitten. There's a chap by the name of Komo who works as houseboy. There's some question whether he's Japanese or Korean. Tragg has a letter and map which was mailed, special delivery, around six-thirty from a Hollywood branch post office. It sounds very Japanesy—almost too Japanesy. However, you can't tell a thing by that. Komo might have written it, or it may have been someone who thought Komo, because of his nationality, would make a good bait for the police to snap at. You can probably get a photostatic copy of that letter. Tragg will be searching for typewriters which could have written it, and will have had an expert check it over. You can probably find out from one of the newspaper boys what has been reported by this expert—the make and model of typewriter it was written on. It looked to me like a portable owned by someone who didn't do any serious typewriting, quite probably a man who's owned the machine for some time."

"What gave you that impression?" Drake asked.

"Letters badly out of line, a faint ribbon which looked as though it had dried out from lack of use, dirt in the loops of the e's and the a's, a few strike-overs and cross-outs, poor spacing of the letter on the sheet of paper, and irregularities in the letters which indicated a ragged touch. However, Tragg will have seen all that almost at a glance, so don't waste too much time on the letter. There's no use duplicating the police effort, and we can't expect to engage in competition with them on the things they'll be covering."

"Okay," Drake said, "I'll . . ."

Della Street said, "The phone keeps ringing in the outer office. Hear that peculiar buzzing sound? That's the way the switchboard sounds when the lines are out and someone's ringing on the main line. It's been doing that at intervals for the past five minutes."

Mason glanced at his watch, said, "On a hunch, Della, see who it is."

She got up and went through to the outer office and in a few minutes came running back.

"What is it?" Mason asked.

"Helen Kendal. Someone broke into the house and shot her boy friend—the one who's on leave from the Army. She notified the police and called for a taxicab. She's at the hospital now. They're operating, on a desperate chance. They don't expect him to live through the operation. She's been calling for the last five minutes."

Mason nodded to Paul Drake. "Let's go, Paul."

Drake shook his head. "*You* go. By the time you get there, Lieutenant Tragg will have things sewed up so tight you'll have to pay admission to get within a block of the place. I'll put in the time working these other angles while Tragg's busy out there."

Mason said, "There may be something to that."

"This new development will keep him occupied," Drake said, "and leave my hands free."

Mason was struggling into his overcoat. "Want to come, Della?"

"Try holding me back."

Drake looked at Mason, with his peculiar, lopsided smile twisting his features. "Where was *your* client when this last bit of shooting took place?" he asked.

Mason looked at his wrist watch, narrowed his eyes thoughtfully as he made a rapid mental calculation, and said, "That's one of the first things Lieutenant Tragg is going to ask. For all I know, he's asking it right now—and getting an answer. And, as I figure out the time element, my client could have made it back to the house in time to do the shooting."

13

THE BIG, old-fashioned house in which Franklin B. Shore had reigned as a financial power was lighted from cellar to garret. Two police cars were parked in the driveway. Under the contagion of excitement, adjoining houses showed lighted windows, mostly in the upper stories, and these oblongs of light, in a neighborhood which was otherwise wrapped in slumber and darkness, held in themselves a certain portent of tragedy.

Mason drove past the house twice, then parked his car on the opposite side of the street and said to Della Street, "I'll make a preliminary survey. Do you want to sit here in the car?"

"Okay."

"Keep your eyes open. If you see anything suspicious, strike a match and light a cigarette. Otherwise, don't smoke. When you strike the match, hold it for a second close to the windshield, then cup your hands and bring it up to the cigarette. It won't do any harm to let the first match go out and strike a second, just in case I'm where I don't get your first signal."

"Are you going up to the house?"

"Eventually. I want to snoop around the yard first."

"Want me to go in with you when you do make the house?"

"I'll let you know. I want to check up here first. Notice that window over on the north side of the house, the one on the ground floor. It's wide open and the curtains aren't drawn. I saw the light from a flash bulb on the inside of that room just now. It looks as though they were photographing the window. That's significant."

Della Street settled down in the car. "I suppose Tragg's already on the job in person."

"Oh, sure."

"And your client, Gerald Shore?"

"May have walked right into the middle of things," Mason said. "I hope he has sense enough not to give them his alibi."

"What *is* his alibi?" Della Street asked.

"He was with us—I hope, I hope."

She said, "I don't think we've ever furnished an alibi for a client, have we?"

"No. That's why I hope he keeps his mouth shut."

"Wouldn't Tragg accept your word?"

"Tragg might, but put yourself in the position of someone in a jury box. A lawyer comes into court defending a man charged with one murder. Another murder gets linked up with him. He says, 'At that time I was with my lawyer,' and the lawyer who is defending him, and his secretary, get on the stand and glibly try to prove the alibi. Doesn't look very well, does it?"

She shook her head. "Not to a jury it wouldn't."

"That is why the better lawyers withdraw from a case when they have to be witnesses," Mason said.

"You mean you'd withdraw if you had to make an alibi for Shore?"

"I wouldn't want to be both a witness and an attorney in a case."

"*I* could be a witness."

"We'll talk it over later," Mason said, and buttoning his overcoat against the chill of the night wind which was sweeping down from the northeast, walked diagonally across the street toward the lighted house.

Della Street watched him through the windshield of the car, her eyes darting about, searching the shadows. As Mason neared the yard and started to cut across the strip of lawn, Della saw the motion of a shadow near the hedge.

Mason had turned so that he was facing the window on the north. The shadow was moving toward him.

Della Street hurriedly lit a match. Mason, with his back to her, didn't notice the signal. Della reached to the dashboard and switched the headlights on and off, twice.

Mason turned, then—too late.

Della Street, rolling down the window of the car, could hear the conversation.

"Mr. Mason?"

Only one who had been intimately associated with Perry Mason for years would have noticed anything unusual in his voice as he said, "Yes. This is Mr. Mason. Why?"

The man moved forward.

"Lieutenant Tragg wants to see you. He said you'd probably be along and for me to keep an eye out for you."

Mason's laugh was hearty. "My compliments to Lieutenant Tragg. When do we see him?"

"Now."

"Where?"

"Inside."

Mason linked his arm through that of the officer. "It's a little chilly outside, anyway. Care for a cigar?"

"Don't mind it I do."

They marched up the steps and into the house.

Della Street settled back against the cushions of the automobile. Lights in the hallway beat into the lawyer's eyes, so that he squinted against the sudden glare. A plain-clothes officer, seated by the door, got to his feet.

"Tell Tragg Mr. Mason's here."

The guard looked curiously at Mason and said, "Okay," and vanished.

Mason's escort held a match to the cigar, tilted his hat back on his head. "We stay here," he said. "I don't think the lieutenant would like to have you rubbering around the house until he's ready to talk with you."

Mason heard the sound of quick steps. Tragg came through the door which opened from the living room. "Well, well, Mason," he said, "nice of you to call! I wanted to talk with you. Called your office but you weren't there."

"I endeavor to anticipate your every wish," said Mason with mock formality.

"That's very thoughtful of you."

Lieutenant Tragg turned, pushed his head through the door, called out to someone, "Close that bedroom door."

He waited until the sound of a door slamming shut indicated that his order had been obeyed.

"Come on in, Mason."

Tragg led the way into the living room. Mason's eyes, by this time thoroughly adjusted to the light, took in the significant details with photographic clarity.

Gerald Shore, apparently perfectly calm and composed, was sitting in an easy chair, his knees crossed, puffing placidly at his pipe. A plain-clothes officer stood unobtrusively in the shadows, his hat brim pulled down so that his face was completely in the shadow. The ruddy tip of a lighted cigarette glowed and paled alternately as he smoked. A man whom Mason took to be Komo, with a distinctly Oriental cast of countenance, was seated within a few feet of the officer.

That end of the long room was shadowed by a relatively dim illumination, but the end over toward the hallway leading to Matilda's bedroom and the hallway itself blazed with the brilliant light thrown by powerful floodlights in reflectors which were supported on metal stands. These lamps quite evidently had been used to give illumination for photographic purposes. The wires which led to them from outlets in various parts of the living room and hall criss-crossed over the floor.

The closed door and the end of the hall concealed the interior of the room beyond. The blazing floodlights standing just outside the door, showed quite plainly that Lieutenant Tragg had wanted photographs of the bedroom, and the sinister red stain on the hardwood floor by the door showed why.

"Sit down, Mason," Tragg said. "I don't want to take any unfair advantage of you. I have asked you for cooperation in times past. I'm not doing that now, because I'm in a definitely hostile position."

"How so?" Mason asked.

"Mr. Shore says you're his attorney. He isn't doing any talking. I don't like that."

"I don't blame you," Mason said.

"And," Tragg went on, "I don't propose to stand for it. When a man tries to conceal something from me in a murder case, I consider it an admission of guilt."

Mason's nod was sympathetic.

"I'm hoping," Tragg said to Mason, "that *you'll* talk. It's going to be unfortunate for your client if you don't."

Mason nodded to Gerald Shore, sat down in a chair by the table, and said, "Of course I'll talk, Tragg. I'm always willing to talk."

Tragg drew up a chair.

Shore removed the pipe from his mouth. "Lieutenant Tragg has been asking me questions. I told him you were my lawyer."

Tragg said, "That doesn't prevent you from answering questions about an entirely different matter."

"How do you know it's an entirely different matter?" Mason asked.

"Because it must have occurred *after* he'd employed you."

"I see."

Shore tamped the tobacco down into the bowl of the pipe with his finger and said, "It's an axiom of the profession, Lieutenant, that a lawyer who seeks to advise himself has a fool for a client."

Tragg said, "The point is, Shore refuses to tell me where he was when this crime occurred."

Mason said, "Suppose you tell me what crime we're talking about, Tragg."

Tragg said, "All right—I'll tell you that. Helen Kendal was sitting on that davenport talking with Jerry Templar, her—well, if she's not engaged to him, she ought to be. They heard a noise in Mrs. Shore's bedroom."

"What sort of a noise?" Mason asked, his eyes showing keen interest.

"As though a bedside stand or something of the kind had been knocked over."

"By an intruder climbing in through that window on the north side?" Mason asked.

Tragg hesitated for a moment, then said, "Well, yes."

"Go on."

"Naturally, Helen Kendal was startled," Tragg said, "as she knew that her aunt was not in her bedroom. After that they both heard sounds that *should* have been Matilda Shore walking across the room, the thump-thump of a cane and the slightly dragging steps. It's significant that if Miss Kendal hadn't known that Mrs. Shore was in the hospital, she would not have paid any attention to the sounds, thinking that her aunt had accidentally overturned some object in getting out of bed to go to the bathroom. But since she knew Mrs. Shore was not in the house, they started to investigate."

"Mrs. Shore *was* in the hospital?" Mason asked.

Tragg said, "She was. I can vouch for that. Templar opened the door. While he was fumbling for the light switch, someone who was in the room shot him with a revolver. Two shots were fired. The first missed. The second struck him in the left side."

"Killed?" demanded Mason quickly.

"No. I understand his chances of recovery are about fifty-fifty. The doctors are performing an emergency operation."

"This seems to be one of your more lurid nights, Tragg," Mason broke in dryly.

Tragg ignored him. "They ought to have that bullet shortly, if they have not already recovered it. I've got here, though, the bullet which missed him and which hit the woodwork just to the side of the door. It missed Helen Kendal's head by a scant inch or two. It's a .38 caliber slug, apparently fired from a conventional doubleaction, self-cocking revolver. I haven't as yet matched it up with the bullet which killed Henry Leech, but I won't be at all surprised if all three shots were fired from the same gun. That means, of course, they were fired by the same person."

Mason drummed softly with the tips of his fingers on the arm of the chair. "Interesting," he observed.

"Isn't it?" Tragg said acidly.

Mason nodded. "If we concede in advance that all three shots were fired from the same gun and that, therefore, they must have been fired by the same person, we can exclude Leech because he is dead, Matilda Shore because she was in a hospital at the time the last crime was committed, Gerald Shore because he has a perfect alibi for that same period, also Helen Kendal and Jerry Templar. Moreover . . ."

"I'm quite capable of working out the theory of elimination," Tragg interrupted. "What I am interested in is your statement that Gerald Shore has an alibi."

Mason said, "He has."

"Well, what is it?"

Mason smiled. "You haven't told me the time the crime was committed."

"Then how do you know he has an alibi?" Tragg countered quickly.

"That's right," Mason said, smiling, "I don't, do I? Now let's see. The person who entered that room knew that Mrs. Shore wasn't in the room, but *didn't know that Helen Kendal knew it.*"

"How do you make that deduction?" Tragg asked, interested.

Mason said, "Because he tried to deceive Helen by impersonating Mrs. Shore, and walking across the room just as Mrs. Shore would have done. That proves Gerald Shore couldn't have done it. Gerald knew that Helen knew her aunt wasn't in the house."

Tragg frowned. It was plain that Mason's reasoning impressed him, and also upset some theory he had formed.

Suddenly the guard at the other end of the room said, "This Jap's doing a lot of listening, Lieutenant. His ears are sticking out a foot."

Tragg turned, his face showing annoyance. "Get him out of here."

Komo bowed. "Excussse please," he said with dignity. "I am not Japanese. I am Korean. My sentiments for Japanese are not friendly."

"Get him out!" Tragg repeated.

The guard clapped a hand on Komo's shoulder. "Come on, Skibby," he said. "Out!"

Tragg waited until Komo had been escorted from the room to the kitchen. Then he turned to Mason. "Mason," he said, "I don't like your attitude, nor that of your client."

Mason grinned. "If we're going to play a game of Truth, Lieutenant, it's my turn. I don't like the way you dragged me in here as though I were a second-story man."

Tragg said, "And perhaps you won't like what I'm going to do now any better. When my men checked on the Castle Gate Hotel, the clerk said there were *three* of you in there when the letter was received. Four of you went up to the mountain. Now, why didn't one of your party want to go in the hotel? Just hold everything a moment."

Tragg got up, walked out to the telephone in the hallway, leaving the door open behind him. He dialed a number, and after a moment said, "The Castle Gate Hotel? The night clerk? . . . This is Lieutenant Tragg, Homicide. . . . That's right. . . . What time did you come on duty last night? . . . Six o'clock. All right, do you know a man named Gerald Shore? . . . Let me describe him. About sixty-two years, rather distinguished looking, a high forehead, clean-cut profile, five-feet-eight or eight and a half, weight a hundred and sixty-five pounds, flowing gray hear which sweeps back from a high forehead, wearing a gray checked suit, a light blue shirt, and a blue-and-red necktie with a black pearl scarf pin. . . . He was! When? . . . I see. . . . For how long? . . . I'll be up and see you within the next half hour. In the meantime, don't talk with anyone about this."

Tragg slammed up the telephone receiver and came back to stand where he could look from Gerald Shore to Perry Mason. "I think I begin to see a very great light," he said. "Perhaps, Mr. Shore, you will tell me why you went to the Castle Gate Hotel early this evening and waited—and waited—and waited."

Gerald Shore calmly removed the pipe from his mouth and pointed the stem toward Perry Mason. "He's my lawyer."

Tragg nodded. His smile was triumphant. "Okay, Jerry," he called to the guard in the hall, "Mr. Mason has got to go. If you see him hanging around remind him that he has an engagement elsewhere—until we meet again, counselor!" Then he held up his hand for attention. "And I'm telling everyone here that as soon as Franklin Shore is found I want him as a witness to testify before the grand jury—and you'll all kindly remember that."

Mason turned without a word and started for the front door and opened it. Tragg said to Gerald Shore, "This is going to be about your last chance to say something."

Mason hesitated, listening for Shore's reply.

"Have you got a match, Lieutenant?" Shore asked calmly.

The guard bustled Mason out to the front porch. The door slammed shut.

Another officer, evidently waiting to see that he left the grounds promptly, stepped up beside him. "I'll walk you to your car."

"No need to."

"Oh, I'd better. No telling what might happen around here to-night. Wouldn't want anything to happen to *you,* Mr. Mason."

Perry walked down the driveway, the officer marching at his side. Peering across the street, he saw only the vacant curb. There was no sign of his automobile nor of Della Street. For a moment only, the lawyer was puzzled. He hesitated just enough to throw the officer out of step with him.

"What is it?" the officer asked.

"Little kink in my leg," Mason said, walking toward the corner.

"Say, Mr. Mason! Your car's on the other side. You'd better . . . Where the hell *is* your car?"

Mason said, "My chauffeur took it back to the office. I had an errand I wanted done."

The officer looked at him suspiciously. "Where you goin' now?"

"I'm going to take a walk—a long walk—to get some air. Would you like to come along?"

Said the officer, with feeling, "Hell, no!"

14

MASON'S UNLISTED telephone was ringing as he opened the door of his apartment. He switched on the lights, crossed over, picked up the receiver and said, "Let's have it."

It was Della Street. As soon as she started talking Perry realized that she was in a nervous funk and trying to cover up. "Gosh, Chief, is that you?" She was off at the tempo of a pneumatic riveter exploding into action. "I think I may be violating the form, force and effect of the statutes in such cases made and provided, and my actions are probably against the peace and dignity of the People of the State of California. I guess I've graduated into a full-fledged criminal."

"They tell me prison is a great experience," Mason assured her. "You'll learn a lot."

Her laugh was high-pitched, and there was a catch in the middle of it. "Paul Drake warned me that I'd wind up in jail if I went on working for you, but I was too stubborn to listen to him."

"Well, you haven't been sentenced yet. What have you done?"

"I've k-k-k-kidnaped a witness," she wailed.

"Done what?"

"Snaked him right out from under Lieutenant Tragg's nose, and am holding him incommunicado."

"Where?"

"In my automobile—or rather, your automobile."

"Where are you?"

"At a service station about four blocks from your apartment."

"Who's the witness?"

"He's sitting out in the car now. His name's Lunk, and he . . ."

"Wait a minute," Mason interrupted, "what was the name?"

"Lunk. He's the gardener out at the Shore place. And he's the temporary custodian of the poisoned kitten."

"How does he spell his name?"

"L-u-n-k. Thomas B. Lunk. That part's on the up and up. I've already managed to get a look at his driver's license."

"What does he know?"

"I don't know exactly, but I think it's awfully important."

"Why?"

"He got off a street car about two blocks from the house. It was just after that guard collared you and took you inside. I saw the street car come to a stop and this man get off. He's an old, weather-beaten, outdoor type of man. He came hurrying toward the house. Occasionally he'd break into a run for a few steps. You could see he was in a great rush."

"What did you do?"

"Followed a hunch," she said, "started the car, and drove down a block to meet him, got out of the car and asked him if he was looking for the Shore residence."

"Then what?" Mason asked, as she hesitated.

"I'd rather not tell you all this over the phone."

"You've got to. At least the part that you don't want him to hear."

"Well, he was so excited he was stammering. He just kept nodding his head and couldn't talk at first. Then he said he had to see Mrs. Shore right away. I turned on my best manner and asked him if he knew Mrs. Shore when he saw her—just sort of sparring for time and trying to find out what it was all about. He said then that he'd worked for her. That he's the gardener who's been with the place for twelve or thirteen years."

"But doesn't live there?" Mason asked.

"No. The address on his driving license is 642 South Bilvedere. He says he lives in a little bachelor shack in back of a house. He used to live in a room over the garage up at the Shore place. Then he went down to live in this little shack."

"What's he know?"

"I don't know. He was so excited he could hardly talk. He said he had to see her at once, that something had happened, and I told him that Mrs. Shore wasn't at home, that I happened to know where she was and I could take him to see her. I got him in the car, drove away from the place, and then started stalling, pretending that I needed oil and gas, and then let the attendant at the service station here talk me into changing spark plugs. I told him that Mrs. Shore was where she couldn't be disturbed right away, but that we could see her in fifteen or twenty minutes and I'd take him to her. All the time, of course, I kept calling up, hoping that you'd get a taxi and come in. When I didn't hear anything from you, I bribed the service station attendant to let the air out of one of my tires and tell me that I had a puncture that had better be fixed right away. He got the tire off and kept fooling around with it. Now my boy friend's getting nervous and a little suspicious. I've got to let the attendant here put that tire back on, and you'll have to get here in a rush."

"What's the address of the service station?"

"On the corner, four blocks down the boulevard from your apartment."

"I'm coming right down. Wait there," Mason said.

"What'll I do when you get here?"

"Just follow my lead," Mason said. "I'll size him up. Tell me about him."

"He has steady, blue eyes, with a far-away squint, a weather-beaten face with high cheekbones, a drooping mustache, about fifty-five or maybe sixty, gnarled hands, stoop shoulders, long arms, slow-moving, and has a single track mind. Sort of simple, but obstinate and sullen when he gets suspicious. I think he'll believe anything you tell him, if you can make it sound plausible. But I was so excited and—well, he's getting terribly suspicious. You'll have to get down here right away or he'll walk out on me."

"On my way," Mason promised, and hung up.

He switched out the lights, went down in the elevator, crossed the street and waited in the shadows to make certain he wasn't being followed. Having convinced himself on that point, he walked rapidly for three blocks, and paused long enough to once more be certain no one was on his trail. Then he walked to the all-night service station where an attendant in white uniform was just finishing tightening the bolts on the left hind wheel of Mason's car.

Mason walking up to Della Street, apparently without noticing the man in his late fifties who sat at her side, raised his hat, said, "Good evening, Miss Street. I hope I didn't keep you waiting."

Della searched his eyes for a signal, hesitated a moment, then said, with some show of feeling, "Well, you certainly *were* late! If it hadn't been for finding a nail in this tire I couldn't have waited."

"Too bad," Mason said. "I was unavoidably detained. You know, I told you I could get you an audience with Mrs. Shore. But, you see, she's . . ."

He broke off, apparently seeing, for the first time, the man beside Della.

Della said, "It's all right, this is Mr. Lunk. He's working out at the Shore place as a gardener. He wants to see Mrs. Shore, too."

Mason said, "Mrs. Shore is at a hospital. She was poisoned. She *says* she took poison by mistake, but that isn't what the police think, and they're making it a matter for police investigation."

"Poison!" Lunk ejaculated.

Della Street registered dismay. "Can't we see her? Mr. Lunk says his business is terribly important."

Mason said, "We can try at least. I thought everything was arranged, but the way things have turned out . . ." He shifted his position so he could watch Lunk from the corner of his eye. "You see," he went on, "with a police guard on the premises, the minute we tried to see her, they'd begin asking *us* questions."

"I don't want no police," Lunk burst out. "I've got to see Mrs. Shore personally and private."

Mason raised his eyebrows. "You say you work there?"

"I'm the gardener."

"Live there?"

"Nope. I come to work on the street car and go home on the street car. I lived there for a while. That was years ago. She wanted me to stay on, but I can't stand having a darned Oriental snooping around. I want to be by myself and be private-like."

"Oriental?" Mason asked.

"Yeah. That houseboy she's got. I don't know why she hasn't fired him long ago. To tell you the truth, I've been looking for the FBI to come around and . . . Well, I guess I ain't goin' to say nothin' more."

Mason didn't press him, but nodded sympathetically. "Well, as I understand it, if we can fix things so we can see Mrs. Shore without the police grabbing us, you want to see her. Otherwise, it can wait. Is that it?"

Lunk said, "It *can't* wait."

"That important?"

"Yes."

Mason gave the matter thoughtful consideration. "Well, let's go down and see if the coast is clear."

"Where is she?"

Mason said, "She's in a hospital."

"Yeah, I know. But what hospital?"

"I'll drive you there."

Mason eased the car past the street intersections. "At this hour of the night, you don't ordinarily meet anyone on these intersections, but if you do meet someone, he's driving like the devil. You can get smacked at an intersection as easy as not."

"Uh huh."

"So you've been working for Mrs. Shore for some twelve years?"

"Yes, goin' onto thirteen."

"You knew her husband then?"

Lunk glanced at Mason sharply, saw nothing except an expressionless profile as Mason's eyes held steady on the road ahead.

"Yes. One of the finest men that ever set foot in a garden."

"So I've heard. Peculiar about his disappearance, wasn't it?"

"Uh huh."

"What do *you* think about it?"

"Who? Me?"

"Yes."

"Why should I think anything about it?"

Mason laughed. "You do think, don't you?"

"I'm paid for gardening."

Mason said, "It's an interesting family."

"You know 'em?" Lunk asked. "All of 'em?"

"I've met some of them. I'm doing some work for Gerald Shore. How do you like him?"

"He's all right, I reckon. He ain't like his brother Franklin, though, about the lawn and flowers. He don't seem to care much about 'em, so I don't see much of *him*. Mrs. Shore gives the orders—except when that damned Jap tries to horn in. Know what that heathen devil was trying to do just a little while ago?"

"No."

"Get her to go take a trip for her health. Wanted the whole family to get out and let him give the house a thorough cleaning inside and out. Guess he wanted to take three or four months doing it. Wanted her to go to Florida and take the niece with her. And I happen to know he'd been talking with George Alber about it. May have been Alber's idea. You know him?"

"No."

"He's the fair-haired boy child right now. Seems like the old lady liked his daddy—or he liked her—ain't sure which. I do my work and want to be left alone. That's *all* I ask."

"How is Komo? A pretty good worker?"

"Oh, he *works* all right, but you always have the feeling that his eyes are staring through your back."

"You said you lived at the Shore place for a while. Have any trouble with Komo while you were living there?"

"No fights—nothing open. My brother was the one that had the trouble with him."

"Your brother?" Mason asked, taking his eyes from the road long enough to flash a quick glance at Della Street. "You had a brother living there with you?"

"Uh huh. For about six, seven months."

"What happened to him?"

"Died."

"While you were living there?"

"Nope."

"After you moved, eh? How long after?"

"Week or two."

"Sick long?"

"No."

"Heart trouble, I suppose?"

"No. He was younger than me."

Della Street said soothingly, "I know just how he feels about it. He doesn't want to talk about it, do you, Mr. Lunk?"

"No."

Della Street went on rapidly, "It's that way when someone near to you passes away. It's a shock. Your brother must have been smart, Mr. Lunk."

"What makes you say that?"

"Oh, just little things in the way you describe him. He seems to have been a man who wasn't taken in by anybody. That is, the Japanese houseboy didn't fool *him* any."

"I'll say he didn't!"

"It must have been rather hard to start doing the work by yourself after having had your brother help you in the garden."

"He didn't help me. He was there visiting. He hadn't been well for quite a while—not able to do any work."

"People of that sort sometimes live a lot longer than the husky, strong people who don't know what an ache or a pain is."

"That's right."

Della said, "Mr. Shore must have been a very fine man."

"Yes, ma'am. He sure was. He was certainly nice to me."

"Letting your brother stay in the house that way. I don't suppose they charged him board."

"Nope. They didn't," Lunk said. "And I'll never forget how Shore acted when my brother passed away. I'd been spending my money on doctors and things, and—well, Shore just called me in and told me how he understood the way I felt, and—know what he did?"

"No. What did he do?"

"Gave me three hundred and fifty dollars so I could ship him back East, and gave me time off from work so I could go along with him on the train. My mother was alive then, and it meant a lot to her having me bring Phil home that way and having the funeral right there."

"She's passed away since?" Della asked.

"Uh huh. Five years ago. Never had anything hit me quite as hard as the way Mr. Shore acted about that. I thanked him at the time. I wanted to thank him some more, but he was gone when I got back from burying Phil."

Mason nudged Della Street with his knee so that she wouldn't pounce on that opening and alarm the gardener. Then, after a moment or two, Mason asked casually, "That was right about the time he disappeared?"

"Just that time."

Mason said, "Those Japs certainly are clever. The Orientals know a lot about drugs that we don't know."

Lunk leaned forward so he could look searchingly into the lawyer's face.

"What made you say that?"

"Oh, I don't know," Mason said. "I was just thinking out loud. I sometimes get funny ideas."

"Well, what was funny about that idea?"

"It wasn't even an idea," Mason said. "I was just thinking."

Lunk said, significantly, "Well, *I've* been doing a lot of thinking too."

Mason waited a few seconds, then observed, casually, "If I had a Jap around and I didn't like him—I'd sure hate to be living in the house with him. . . . Have him fixing or serving food for me. I don't trust 'em."

"That's the same way I feel," Lunk said. "I'm going to tell you something, Mr.—what'd you say your name was?"

"Mason."

"Well, I'll tell you something, Mr. Mason. There was a while after I heard about Mr. Shore disappearing that I'd have bet dollars to doughnuts the Jap had something to do with it. And then, later on, I began to wonder if maybe the Jap hadn't had something to do with the way Phil died. It could have been something, you know."

"Poison?" Mason asked.

"Well, I ain't saying anything. Personally, I ain't got any use for the sneaking, treacherous race, but I want to be fair. I've done him one injustice already."

"Oh, is that so?"

Lunk said, "Well, to tell you the truth, I sort of suspected him of having a hand in—well, I'll tell you. I thought for a while that maybe he wanted to get Mr. Shore out of the way, and he sort of practiced first on my brother to see if he had the right dose and— you know, the way Mr. Shore disappeared and all that, and coming right on top of Phil's death. . . . I didn't think so much of it at the time, but I got to thinking more about it later on."

Mason again nudged Della Street with his elbow as he piloted the car around a corner toward the hospital. "Well, I don't see that that's doing the Jap any injustice."

"Nope," Lunk said positively. "He didn't do it. But up to a few hours ago, you couldn't have convinced me of that if you'd argued all night. Just goes to show how we get an idea through our heads and it sticks. To tell you the truth, the reason I didn't want to live on the place any more was on account of the way that Jap was hanging around. Phil was gettin' worse all the time. I got to feeling kind of sick myself and went to a doctor, and the doctor couldn't find nothing wrong with me, so I up and left."

"Did that cure you?" Mason asked.

"Perked right up," Lunk said, warming to his subject. "I got a place of my own, did all my own cooking, and carried my lunches with me. And I'll tell you something else, Mister, I didn't leave my lunches hanging around where anybody could open up a box and sprinkle something on my sandwich, either. No siree!"

"And you were cured immediately?"

"Within a week or two. But Phil was sick anyway. He didn't make it. He was all shot."

"What did Komo say when you moved out?"

"The damn Jap didn't say nothin'. He just looked at me, but I knew he knew what I was thinkin', and I didn't care."

"What made you change your mind? Why don't you think he poisoned Mr. Shore?"

"Nope," Lunk said, shaking his head positively. "He didn't poison the boss. I do think he poisoned Phil though, and I think he tried poisoning me; what's more, he poisoned that kitten, and if Matilda Shore got a dose of poison, you'll never convince me that Komo didn't do it. He ain't foolin' me none. You mark my words, he wanted to poison someone, but he wanted to see how the poison worked first. Ten years ago he used Phil to try things out on. Last night he used this here kitten. Thought for a while ten years ago he was practicin' up on Phil to have a go at the boss. Now I know it was me he was after."

"But if you thought your brother was poisoned, why didn't you go to the police, and . . ."

"Didn't have a thing to go on. When Phil died, I asked the doc about poison. He laughed at me. Said Phil had been living on borrowed time for five years."

Mason said, "Well, here's the hospital. You want to go in with me and see if the officers are still on duty?"

"I don't want to see no officers."

"Of course," Mason said. "But there's just a chance we can get through to see Mrs. Shore."

Della Street looked at Mason apprehensively. "I can run up, Chief," she said, "and see if they're on duty, and . . ."

"No," Mason said significantly. "I want to take Mr. Lunk up

with me. You see," he explained to Lunk, "I was in to see her once this evening."

"Oh," Lunk said. "Didn't you say you were working for Gerald Shore?"

"Yes. He's a client of mine. I'm a lawyer."

Mason opened the car door. "Come on, Lunk. We'll run up. Della, you won't mind staying here?"

She shook her head, but there were little creases of worry down the center of her forehead.

Mason took Lunk's arm, and the two climbed up the stone steps to the hospital.

As they walked down the long corridor past the receiving and admittance desk, Mason said to Lunk, "Probably just as well to let me do the talking. But you listen carefully, and if I'm not doing all right, give me a nudge."

"All right," Lunk said.

Mason rang for the elevator, went up to the floor on which Matilda Shore's room was located. A nurse, working on some records at a desk, looked up from her work. Two men got up out of chairs at the far end of the corridor and came marching toward the visitors.

Mason had his hand on the door of Mrs. Shore's room when one of the men said, truculently, "Hold it, buddy."

The other man said, "That's Mason, the lawyer. He was here before. Lieutenant Tragg had a talk with him."

"What you want?" the man who seemed to be in charge asked.

"I want to talk with Mrs. Shore."

The man shook his head and grinned. "Nix on it. Nix on it," he said.

Mason said, "This man with me wants to talk with her."

"Well now, does he?" The officer grinned, surveying Lunk as

though enjoying a huge joke. "So you *both* want to talk with her, eh?"

"That's right."

The man jerked his thumb down the corridor, and said, "Back down the elevator, boys. I'm sorry, but it's no go."

Mason, raising his voice, said, "Perhaps this man could do you some good if he could talk with Mrs. Shore. He's her gardener. I think Lieutenant Tragg would like to see him, too."

The officer nodded to his companion as his hand clapped down on Mason's shoulder. The other officer hooked his fingers in the back of Lunk's collar. "Come on now, boys. On your way, and don't act rough about it."

Mason said, "I think we're really entitled to see her."

"Got a pass?" the officer asked.

The nurse came efficiently forward on rubber heels. "There are other patients on this floor, and I'm responsible for them. I want no noise, no argument, and no disturbance."

One of the officers rang for the elevator. "There won't be any disturbance, Miss," he said. "These men are going *out*. That's all."

The elevator came to a stop. The door slid open. Propelled by insistent pressure from behind. Mason and Lunk entered the elevator.

"And don't try comin' back without a pass," the officer called as the elevator doors clanged shut.

Lunk started to say something as they walked down the corridor, after the elevator had left them at the street level, but Mason motioned him to silence. Nor did the lawyer speak until they were out on the sidewalk.

Della Street, sitting in the parked car, opened the door. "Things as you expected to find them?" she asked Mason anxiously.

Mason was smiling. "Just exactly. Now then, we'll go some place where we can talk."

Lunk said doggedly, "I've got to reach Mrs. Shore. I don't want to talk to nobody else."

"I know," Mason said. "We'll see if we can't work out some plan of action."

Lunk said, "Listen, I ain't got all night to work on this thing. It's hot. It's got to be handled right now. I've simply *got* to see her."

Mason turned the car into a broad street which, at this hour of the night, showed no traffic. Abruptly, he swung into the curb, parked the car, switched off the headlights, and the ignition, turned to Lunk, and said sharply, "How do you *know* Franklin Shore is alive?"

Lunk started as though Mason had jabbed him with a pin.

"Come on," Mason said. "Speak up."

"What makes you think I know any such thing?"

"Because you gave yourself away. Remember you said that up until a short time ago, all the talking in the world wouldn't have convinced you that Komo hadn't been mixed up in Franklin Shore's disappearance. You've held that belief for several years. You've held it so deeply and sincerely that it's become a fixed obsession with you. Now then, there's only one thing that could have changed your mind so suddenly. *You've seen or heard from Franklin Shore.*"

Lunk stiffened for a moment as though preparing to deny the statement; then settled back in the seat as the resistance oozed out of him.

"All right," he admitted, "I've seen him."

"Where is he?" Mason asked.

"He's at my place."

"He came there shortly before you took the street car to go to see Mrs. Shore?"

"That's right."

"And what did he want?"

"He wanted me to do something for him. I can't tell you what it was."

Mason said, "Wanted you to go to Mrs. Shore and find out if she'd take him back, or something of that sort."

Lunk hesitated a moment, then said, "I ain't goin' to tell you what he told me. I promised him I wouldn't ever tell that to any living man."

Mason asked, "How long was it after Franklin Shore came to your house that you went out to take the street car?"

"Quite a little while."

"Why the delay?"

Lunk hesitated, then said, "There wasn't any delay."

Mason glanced at Della Street, then asked Lunk, "Had you gone to bed when Franklin Shore called on you?"

"Nope. I was listening to a news broadcast when he knocked at the door. I like to fell over dead when I seen who it was."

"You recognized him without any difficulty?"

"Yeah. Sure. He hadn't changed so much—not near as much as she has. Looks about like he did the day he left."

Mason glanced significantly at Della Street and said, "There's no reason why you should stay up any longer, Della. I'll take you down the street a few blocks to a taxi stand. You can take a taxi home."

She said, "You're not keeping me up. I wouldn't miss this for worlds. I . . ."

"You need *some* sleep, my dear," Mason interrupted solicitously. "Remember, you have to be at the office promptly at nine, and it will take you a *long* time to get home."

"Oh! I see—I guess so."

Mason switched on the ignition, drove rapidly to a nearby hotel where a taxi was parked at the curb. Della Street jumped out with a quick "Good night. See you in the morning, Chief," and walked across to the taxicab.

Mason drove down the street for a couple of blocks, then

parked the car again. "We'd better get this thing straight, Lunk," he said. "You say Franklin Shore *knocked* at your door?"

The gardener was sullen and suspicious. "*I've* got it all straight. Sure he knocked. The doorbell wasn't working."

Mason shook his head. "I'm not certain that you did right. It might make trouble for you with Mrs. Shore—trying to intercede on behalf of her husband."

Lunk said, "I know what I'm doin'."

"You owe Franklin Shore a debt of gratitude," Mason went on. "You want to do everything you can to help him, don't you?"

"Yes."

"And you know Mrs. Shore hates him, don't you?"

"No."

Mason said, "You must have talked with Franklin Shore for a couple of hours before you started out to see Mrs. Shore."

"Not that long."

"An hour, perhaps?"

"Perhaps."

"How did he seem mentally?" Mason asked abruptly.

"How do you mean?"

"Was his mind keen?"

"Oh, sure. He's smart as a steel trap—remembers things I've even forgotten. Asked about some poinsettia plants I'd put out just before he left. Damned if I hadn't clean forgotten about 'em until he asked. They didn't do so good and the old lady had 'em pulled up. We got some rose bushes in there now."

"Then he doesn't seem to have aged much?"

"No. He's older; but he's pretty much the same."

Mason said, "Why don't you tell me the truth, Lunk?"

"What are you getting at?"

Mason said, "Franklin B. Shore was a banker, a keen-minded businessman. From all I can learn, he was clearheaded and quick thinking. A man of that type wouldn't have come to you to ask you to intercede with Mrs. Shore on his behalf."

Lunk remained sullenly silent.

Mason said, "It's a lot more likely that he'd have gone to your place knowing that you were under a debt of gratitude to him, looking for a place to spend the night where no one would be apt to look for him. You pretended you were going to give him a place to hide out, and then, after he'd gone to bed and to sleep, sneaked quietly out in an attempt to go and tell Mrs. Shore where he was."

Lunk clamped his lips together in stolid, defiant silence.

"You may as well tell the truth," Mason said.

Lunk shook his head doggedly.

"The Homicide Squad wants to question Franklin Shore. They want to examine him about what happened after he communicated with a man named Henry Leech."

"What's that got to do with it?"

"Leech was murdered."

"When?"

"Some time early last night."

"Well?"

"Don't you see," Mason said, "if you conceal a witness, knowing he's a witness and wanted as such, you're guilty of a crime."

"How do *I* know he's a witness?"

"I'm telling you so. Now then, you'd better tell me everything that happened."

Lunk thought things over for a few minutes, then said, "Well, I guess I might's well. Franklin Shore came to my place. He was excited and scared. He said somebody was trying to kill him. That he had to have a place to hide. He told me about what he'd done for me in giving me a home for my brother and all that and said it was up to me to help him out."

"And you asked him why he didn't go home?"

Lunk said, "I asked him some questions, but he wouldn't talk much. He acted like he was still the boss and I was just a hired man. He said he didn't want Mrs. Shore to know anything about his bein' here until after he'd found out what had been done with certain property. He said his wife was going to try to strip him of every penny and he didn't propose to stand for it."

"Then what?"

"So then I told him he could stay with me. It was just the way you doped it out. I got a spare bedroom in the back, and I put him to bed. After he got to sleep I sneaked out and went to tell Mrs. Shore."

"You hadn't gone to bed at all?"

"No."

"And you didn't go to bed?"

"Nope. Told him I had some letters to write."

"And Franklin Shore didn't know you had sneaked out?"

"Nope. He was lyin' on his back with his mouth open, snoring, when I left."

"To betray the man who had once been so kind to you," Perry added.

Lunk's eyes shifted uneasily. "I wasn't going to tell her *where* Mr. Shore was—just that I'd heard from him."

"Did you know Henry Leech?" Mason asked suddenly.

"Yes, I knew him—a long time ago."

"Who was he? What did he do?"

"He was a plumber—used to come to the house and do some work once in a while. Franklin Shore liked him. Mrs. Shore never did go much for him. He and my brother Phil used to get along pretty well, but I never cared too much for him. Thought he was full of hot air—always tellin' about how he was goin' to get rich in some mining deal. Told Phil a while before Phil died that Franklin Shore was goin' to finance him on a mining proposition—said he was goin' to be living on Easy Street in a couple of months. I've been wondering if maybe Franklin hadn't gone in partners with him, and when Franklin left he went out to work on that mine."

"Where was it?'"

"In Nevada somewhere."

"Did Leech continue working after Franklin Shore disappeared?"

"No, he didn't. Mrs. Shore never liked him. Soon as she got in the saddle she canned him. He was puttin' in a lot of new plumbing up in the north end of the house, and every time he'd get a chance, he'd talk over this mining deal with Mr. Shore and with my brother. For some reason or other, Shore liked him, and would take time out to kid with him about his mine, an' when he was goin' to strike it rich."

Mason said, "When Franklin Shore showed up at your house, you asked him *some* questions about where he'd been, and whether he'd put any money in this mining deal. Now go ahead and tell me the truth."

Lunk blurted out, "The boss ran away with this woman. He went to Florida, but he had an interest in some mine out in Nevada. I don't know whether it was Leech's mine or not. They struck it kinda rich, and Shore's partner froze him out for a few thousand, when he could have made a lot more money if he'd held on."

"And that partner was Leech?" Mason asked.

Lunk faced Mason then with steady-eyed candor. "I'm goin' to tell you the truth, Mr. Mason. I don't know who that partner was. Shore wouldn't say. He dried up when I tried to pump him. It might have been Leech, and it might not."

"Didn't you ask him?"

"Well, I didn't come right out and ask him in so many words. When I was talkin' with him, I'd forgotten what Leech's name was. I did ask the boss what'd ever become of that plumber that was trying to interest him in a mining proposition, and the boss dried up like a clam."

"And you didn't press the inquiry?"

Lunk said, "I guess you don't know Franklin Shore very well, do you?"

"I don't know him at all."

"Well," Lunk said, "when Franklin Shore don't want to tell you a thing, he don't tell you. And that's all there is to it. I don't s'pose he's got any dough at all now, but you'd think he was still a high-and-mighty millionaire, the way he acts when you try to get any information out of him.

"Now, I can't stay away no longer. I've got him out there at the house and I've got to get back before he wakes up. If he wakes up and finds me gone, there's goin' to be hell to pay. Now you drive me back home and I'll find some way of gettin' in touch with Mrs. Shore. Ain't she got a telephone in that hospital?"

Mason said, "I was in the room for a few minutes. I saw that she had a telephone by the bed, but I don't think I'd try to telephone her except as a last resort. Even then, I wouldn't dare to tell her anything important over the telephone."

"Why?"

"Because Lieutenant Tragg will either have taken the telephone out, or have left instructions at the switchboard not to put through incoming calls."

"But she could call out all right?" Lunk asked.

"She *might* be able to."

Lunk creased his forehead in thought. "I got a phone," he said, "and if we could think up some way of gettin' her to call my number, I could give her the message."

Mason said, "I'll drive you home and after we get there, we may be able to think up some way of getting her to put through a call. You might send her some flowers with your card on them and your telephone number on the card. The flowers would be delivered. The officers wouldn't stop them. When she saw your name and telephone number on the card, she'd know that you wanted her to call you on the phone. That might be a good way to work things."

Lunk said, "Now you're really talkin' sense. That'd work all right. The first thing she'd think of when she saw my card on the flowers would be what the hell I was sending her flowers for. But you understand they'd have to be bought flowers. If I sent her flowers out of the garden, it would be a natural thing to do. But bought flowers would tip her off right away that there was some reason for sending 'em."

Mason said, "I know a flower shop that's open all night. We can get an immediate delivery to the hospital. Have you got any money?"

"Only about a dollar and a half."

Mason said, "It should be a good big bouquet of expensive flowers. I'll drive up to the florist's with you, and then take you back home. I'll pay for the flowers."

"That's mighty white of you."

"Not at all. I'm glad to do it. Now there's one question I want to ask you, and I want you to think carefully before you answer it."

"What is it?"

"Henry Leech was interested in mines. Now, do you know whether he ever hired Gerald Shore as a lawyer to do anything in connection with his mining company?"

Lunk thought that question over for almost a minute, then said, "I can't tell you for sure, but I *think* he did. I'll let you in on something, Mr. Mason. I think Franklin Shore was double-crossed somehow—after he'd left."

"How do you mean?"

Lunk fidgeted uneasily, said, "Last time the boss was down in Florida he ran on a guy who looked just like him. They had their pictures taken together, an' this guy certainly was a ringer for the boss.

"Well, the boss kept kidding about it after he got back, said he was going to use this guy as a double when his wife had some of her social doings that he wanted to get out of. Mrs. Shore would get hopping mad every time he'd mention it.

"Now, I got an idea that the boss went down to Florida with this woman of his, and intended to educate this here double to go back and pretend *he* was Franklin Shore. This guy could live a swell life and send Franklin Shore money, and the boss could be happy with this woman he'd gone away with. Well, I think that after he'd sort of educated the guy, the bird got cold feet, or he may have died or somethin'.

"Get me? I think the boss was plannin' to have this other bird show up, claimin' it had been a loss of memory that was responsible for everything. People would have believed that, because the boss didn't take any money with him when he left. Well, somehow or other, it didn't pan out. Maybe he couldn't get this other guy educated right, or something. That left the boss with his bridges burnt."

Mason held his eyes steadily on those of the gardener. "Might it not have been the other way around?"

"What do you mean? What you gettin' at?"

"This double might have got the idea and then made way with Franklin Shore, and returned to take his place."

"Nope. This man who came to my place is Franklin B. Shore. An' I knew from what he told me . . . say, wait a minute. I'm talkin' too damn much. You an' me will start gettin' along a hell of a lot better, Mr. Mason, if you quit askin' questions—beginnin' right now. Come on, let's go where we're goin' . . . or you can let me out right here an' I'll handle things myself."

Mason's laugh was good natured. "Oh, come on, Lunk. I didn't mean to be nosey."

15

Houses in the neighborhood were dark and silent as Mason stopped his car at 642½ South Bilvedere. The chill which comes an hour or so before dawn was in the air.

Mason switched off the headlights and ignition and eased the automobile door shut after he and Lunk had alighted at the curb.

"You live in back?" Mason asked.

"Uh huh. That little house around in back. You walk in along the driveway. My place is built onto the garage."

"You have a car?" Mason asked.

Lunk said, grinning, "Well, it ain't a car like yours, but it gets me there all right."

"Keep it here in the garage?"

"Uh huh. I'd've taken it to go up to Shore's place tonight, only I was afraid opening the garage door and starting the car would wake Franklin Shore up. So I sneaked out and took the street car."

Mason nodded, started walking quietly up the driveway.

"Look here," Lunk protested, "you ain't comin' in."

"Just far enough to make sure Franklin Shore is still there."

"You don't want to wake him up."

Mason said, "Certainly not. Those flowers will be delivered at almost any time now, and Mrs. Shore may call you up. When she does, you'll have to talk with her in such a way she'll know you have a message for her without telling her what it is."

"Why can't I tell her over the phone?"

"Because Franklin Shore will wake up when he hears the phone ring and listen to the conversation."

"Maybe he won't," Lunk said. "The phone is right by my bed. I can sort of muffle what I'm saying with a pillow."

"You might do that," Mason conceded, all the time walking toward the little bungalow on the back of the lot. "Or, you could just tell her that you'd seen me and that she could get in touch with me, and give her my number."

"Yes. That might work. What's your number?"

"I'll come in and write it out for you," Mason said.

"You can't make no noise," Lunk warned.

"I won't."

"Can't you write it down out here?"

"Not very well."

"Well, come on in. But don't make no noise."

Lunk tiptoed up the two stairs which led to the wooden porch, inserted a key in the lock, and noiselessly opened the door. He switched on a light which illuminated a small room cheaply furnished and bearing unmistakable evidences of masculine occupancy. It seemed even colder inside than it had been out in the air. The house was a flimsy structure, and the chill had penetrated through the walls. The air was impregnated with the odor of stale cigar smoke, and a cigar butt, soggy and cold, was lying on an ash tray.

Mason bent over to look at it. "His?" he asked.

"Yep. Expensive, too, I guess. Smelled good when he was smokin' it. Pipe and cigarettes are what I smoke."

Mason continued to lean over the little table on which the ash tray reposed. Directly beside it was a card bearing the printed words, "George Alber," and, in a man's handwriting, "Called to see about the kitten. Rang the bell, got no answer. Guess everything's O.K. Knew Helen was worrying."

Lunk lit a gas heater.

"Nice little place," Mason said in a low voice.

"Uh huh. Over here's my bedroom; other bedroom's in back of that, with a bath between."

Mason said, "Better close the doors between the bedrooms so Franklin won't hear the phone ring."

"That's a good idea," Lunk said. "I think the door from the bathroom to the boss's room was left open. I closed the one from my room."

He tiptoed into the bedroom, and Mason followed along close behind.

The bedroom was a small, square room, furnished with a cheap bureau, a table, a straight-backed chair, and a single iron bed with a thin mattress and sagging wire springs.

In the light which filtered through from the living room, Mason saw that the door to the bathroom was open, that the bed had not been made, and in the low spot in the center of that bed, lying in the middle of a soiled and crumpled sheet, curled up in a furry ball, was a sleeping kitten.

The drawers of the bureau had been pulled out, the contents dumped on the floor. A clothes closet had been opened and garments pulled out and dropped into a careless pile near the closet door.

Lunk, standing halfway between the door and the bed, looked around him in dazed surprise, and said, "Well, I'll be a son of a gun!"

Mason walked past Lunk through the open door into the bathroom and looked into the adjoining bedroom.

It was empty.

This bedroom was even smaller than the other. A window in the far side of the bedroom and which looked out on the alley, was standing wide open. A night breeze blew somewhat grimy lace curtains in bellying folds. Covers had been turned back on the spring cot. Clean sheets were slightly rumpled. A pillow case had a depression in it where a man's head would have rested.

Lunk came to stand beside Mason, looking with open-mouthed dismay at the bed and the window.

"He's skipped out," he said ruefully. "If I could've got to Matilda Shore while he was still here, she'd have . . ."

He stopped talking suddenly as though afraid he had said too much.

Mason made a cursory examination of the room. "These bathroom doors open when you left?" he inquired.

"I think this one was, but the one into my room wasn't. I was very careful to close it when I sneaked out."

Mason indicated a second door. "Where does this go?"

"Kitchen. And then from the kitchen you can get to the living room."

"You have to go through one of the bedrooms to get to the bathroom?"

"That's right. This house is just a square box. The front room an' kitchen on one side, an' the two bedrooms on the other, with the bathroom in between the bedrooms."

Mason said, "I notice this door to the kitchen is open a crack—just an inch or two."

"Uh huh."

Mason said, "You can see the kitten walked through that door. There are the tracks of a kitten outlined in something white."

"That's right."

Mason bent over and touched his finger to the floor, rubbing it across one of the white tracks. "Feels something like flour. You can see where the kitten came through the door, walked over toward the bed. Yes, there are four tracks right together where the kitten must have stood to jump up on the bed. Then the kitten came down on the other side. You can see just a trace of the white powder here."

"That's right. But I don't think that powder is flour."

"Why not?"

"Because I keep my flour in a big tin, and I keep the lid on the tin. And I know the pantry door was closed."

"Let's take a look," Mason said, going into the kitchen.

Lunk opened the door of a little pantry, said, "Of course, I don't waste a lot of time keeping house. I cook my own grub and my cooking suits me all right. It might not suit some finicky housekeeper, but it suits me. Yep, there's the cover on the can all right. Of course, I spill a little occasionally when I'm gettin' it out for cooking. There's a little on the floor around the can, and it looks like the cat was chasing a mouse or somethin' an' jumped right into that pile of stuff. That's the most careless damn kitten I ever saw in my life. He ain't got sense enough to be afraid of anything. He'll run and butt his head up against a wall if he happens to be chasing something, or get on the back of a chair and fall down on his head. He's just awful careless. Either ain't got good sense, or don't know enough to be afraid."

Mason stood staring down at the flour. "If this pantry door was closed, how did the kitten get in here?"

Lunk thought that over. "Only one answer to that. Franklin was lookin' for somethin', an' he came snooping around in here, an' the cat followed him."

Mason said, "How about that stuff in the front bedroom where the drawers have been pulled out and the clothes dumped on the floor?"

Lunk said, somewhat ruefully, "I guess I slipped up. Shore must have got up right after I went out. When he found I was gone, he realized I'd gone out to tell Matilda Shore that he was here. Gosh, why did I let him catch me at that?"

"And then you think he searched the place?" Mason asked.

"He must have, what with him opening the pantry door and all that."

"What was he looking for?"

"I wouldn't know."

"You must have had *something* that Franklin Shore wanted."

Lunk thought for a moment or two, then said, "I'm not certain but what Shore was down on his luck. He may have been looking for money."

"Did you have any?"

Lunk hesitated. then said, "Yes, I had a little salted away"

"Where?"

Lunk was silent for eight or ten seconds, and Mason said, "Come on. Come on. *I'm* not going to hold you up."

"I kept it in the hip pocket of my best suit, hanging in the closet," Lunk said.

"Well, let's look and see if it's there now."

Lunk returned to the front room. The kitten opened its sleepy eyes, yawned, got up to its four feet, arched its back as high as it could possibly stretch, then reached out with its forepaws, elevated its hind legs, flexed its back in the other direction, and said, *"Mi-aow."*

Mason laughed. "I think your kitten's hungry. Have you got any milk in the house?"

Lunk said, "No fresh milk. I got some canned milk. Helen Kendal brought the kitten here so it wouldn't get no more poison." He walked across to the pile of clothes, picked them up, and started going through the pockets. An expression of dismay came over his face. "Cleaned out!" he muttered. "Damn him, he took every cent I had saved up."

"Tell me exactly how much it was," Mason said.

"Pretty close to three hundred dollars. He could get a long ways on that."

"You think he wants to get away?" Mason asked.

Once more, Lunk's mouth firmed into a position of sullen silence.

"Think he'll be back?" Mason asked.

"I don't know."

"Have you got any money at all?"

"Some in the bank. I ain't got no cash."

"Matilda Shore will be ringing up any minute now," Mason reminded him. "Are you going to tell her Franklin Shore was here and you let him get away?"

"Good gosh, no!"

"What *are* you going to tell her?"

"I don't know."

"What about the flowers? How are you going to explain sending her a bunch of hothouse roses with instructions to deliver them immediately—at around three o'clock in the morning?"

Lunk made a frowning effort at thought, then surrendered to say doggedly, "I don't know *what* I'm going to tell her—not now."

"Why tell her anything? Why not simply skip out?"

Lunk said, with feeling, "Gee, I'd like to do that, if I could get away with it?"

"Well, why not? I could take you to a hotel, let you register under an assumed name, and then you could get in touch with Mrs. Shore whenever you wanted to, and make whatever explanations you wanted. In that way, you wouldn't have to tell anyone anything. You could keep in touch with me."

Lunk was nodding slowly. "I *could* stick some stuff in a bag," he said, "and maybe get a check cashed . . ."

Mason peeled off a couple of ten-dollar bills from a thick roll.

"You don't need to cash a check," he said. "I'll give you some money, and when you need more, you can telephone me. I've given you a number where you can always reach me."

Lunk suddenly gripped strong fingers around the lawyer's hand. "You're acting mighty square," he said, and, after a moment, added, "You stick by me in this, and I'll stick by you. And maybe later on, I'll tell you just what Franklin Shore *really* wanted. You let me think it over, and I'll give you a ring later on."

"Why can't you tell me now?"

The old sullen look came over Lunk's face. "Not now," he said. "I gotta be sure of somethin' first, but I *may* tell you later on—maybe around noon. Don't try to get it out of me now. I'm waiting for somethin' before I can tell you."

Mason studied his man. "Is that something," he asked, "the morning newspaper with the account of Leech's death?"

Lunk shook his head.

"Or the police report on Matilda Shore's poisoning?"

"Don't crowd me. I'm tellin' you straight," Lunk warned.

Mason laughed. "All right, come on, I'll put you in a nice, quiet hotel. Suppose you register as Thomas Trimmer? And I'll take the kitten along with me and see it's taken care of."

Lunk regarded the kitten somewhat wistfully. "You take good care of it."

"I will," Mason promised.

16

HELEN KENDAL sat dry-eyed in the waiting room at the hospital. It seemed she had been there for endless hours, so nervous she couldn't sit still, so physically weary that she couldn't summon the energy to get up and pace the floor. A hundred times in the last hour she had looked at her wrist watch. She knew now that it simply *couldn't* be much longer.

She heard the sound of quick, nervous steps in the corridor. Her tortured mind wondered if that might be someone coming to take her to the bedside of a dying man. Her heart choked up her throat with the thought that if it was only to tell her everything was all right, the messenger would be walking more slowly. These staccato footsteps could only indicate one thing, that they were coming for her and that seconds were precious.

White-lipped she came up out of the creaking rattan chair, started running toward the door of the reception room.

The steps turned into the door. A long, overcoated figure smiled reassuringly at her. "Hello, Miss Kendal. I guess you re-member me."

Her eyes widened. "Why, Lieutenant Tragg! Tell me, have you heard . . . anything . . ."

Tragg shook his head. "They're operating on him. They had

some delay getting donors for blood transfusions. They should be finished about now," Tragg said. "I've been talking on the telephone with the nurse."

"Oh, tell me, how's he standing it? How's he coming? Is it going to be . . ."

Tragg placed a hand on her quivering shoulder. "Take it easy," he said. "Take it easy. Things are going to be all right."

"They . . . they aren't sending for you because it's the last chance he'll have to tell . . ."

"Now listen," Tragg said, "take this thing like a soldier. You've been through so much tonight you're all unstrung. They're operating on him, and the last I heard was that he's taking it all right. I'm here right now to get just one thing."

"What?"

"That bullet—and a statement from him if he's able to talk."

"Not what they call a dying declaration?"

Tragg grinned. "You've been here all alone fighting your nerves, and you're jumpy."

She said, "I can take it! I want to know how he is—that's natural. And I'd be lying to you if I tried to tell you I wasn't frightened. But I'm not getting any heebie jeebies over it. I guess we used to think we were entitled to happiness as a matter of right. Now, people are dying all over the world and . . . well, I've got to learn how to take it—and so has everyone else."

Tragg's eyes were sympathetic. "You haven't been crying?"

"No—and don't you make me—either. Don't sympathize with me, and don't look at me like that. But, for heaven's sake, if you can really find out how he's coming and what his chances are, go to it."

"You engaged?" Tragg asked abruptly.

Helen's eyes dropped and she flushed. "I—I—honestly don't know. He never—quite—asked me, but on the way over here in the taxi—Well, I guess I let him see how much I cared. I didn't mean to, but I was so frightened that everything broke down. He was so game—and brave—I shouldn't have, of course."

"Shouldn't have *what*? You love him, don't you?"

Helen raised her head and looked at him defiantly. "Yes, I love him. And I told him so. I belong to him, and always shall, no matter what happens. I told him that, too, Lieutenant Tragg. And I told him I wanted to marry him *now*."

"What did he say to that?"

Helen turned away. "He didn't say anything," she replied dully. "He fainted."

Tragg controlled his twitching mouth. "Jerry lost a lot of blood, you know. I'm not surprised. Tell me, Miss Kendal, how long had you been home last night before Jerry arrived?"

"I don't know. Not very long."

"How did he happen to call—so late?"

Helen laughed nervously. "He said he tried to telephone me earlier, but of course I was out. He was passing and saw the house all lit up, so he just dropped in for a minute. We were talking, and then we heard this sound from Aunt Matilda's bedroom . . ."

"You said the noise sounded as though someone had knocked something over. The room was dark?"

"Yes."

"You're certain about that?"

"Yes. Unless whoever was in there had a flashlight. That may have been it, because the lovebirds started chirping."

"But there was no sign of a flashlight when you opened the door?"

"No."

"And the lights were on in the hall?"

"Yes. I never thought about *not* putting them on. I guess it would have been better if we'd kept the hallway dark and turned on the lights in the bedroom."

"It would," Tragg said, "but that's all done now. No use bothering about it. What I'm getting at is that the lights *were* on in the hall and there were no lights on in your aunt's bedroom."

"That's right."

"And who opened the door? You or Jerry?"

"Jerry."

"And then what?"

"We knew, of course, someone was in there. Jerry was groping for the light switch and didn't know where it was, and I suddenly realized how terribly important it was to get the light on, so I ducked under his arm and reached for the light switch. It was then it happened."

"Two shots?"

"Yes."

"You never did get the lights on?"

"No."

"Was your hand near the light switch when the first shot was fired?"

"I think it was, but I can't be certain. That bullet whizzed right past my head, and smacked into the woodwork around the door. It threw splinters or plaster or something into my face, little stinging particles. I jumped back."

"And the next shot came how soon?"

"Almost at once."

"What happened after that?"

White-faced, she shook her head. "There's just a lot I can't remember. I heard that peculiar sound of the bullet—hitting Jerry."

Tragg said, "You're a brave kid. Don't think about Jerry. Just think of facts. Remember that's all we're interested in. That second shot came right after the first one, with hardly any interval in between, and it hit Jerry."

"Yes."

"Did he fall down immediately?"

"He seemed to spin right around as though something had hit him, you know, a blow."

"Then he fell?"

"I felt his knees buckle; then he was a dead weight against me. I tried to ease him to the floor, but he was too heavy. We both went down in a heap."

"What happened to the person who was in the room?"

"I don't know. All I can remember is seeing that awful pallor on Jerry's face. I put my hand down to his side, and it came away all bloody. He was unconscious. I thought he was dead. Naturally, I didn't think much about anything else. I talked to him—and told him things—and then his eyelids fluttered—after a while, then he smiled up at me and said, 'Let's see if I can get my legs under me, Babe.'"

Tragg frowned. "Has it occurred to you that the person who was standing in that room wasn't shooting at Jerry?"

"What do you mean?"

"I mean," Tragg said, "he was shooting at you. He shot at your head the first time, and almost hit it; then you jerked back, and in jerking back, you swung around so that your body was behind Jerry's; and when he took that second snap shot at you, he hit Jerry. Remember, the person who was there in the room could see *you* very plainly."

Her eyes were wide and startled. "I hadn't thought of that. I just thought that someone was in the room and didn't want to be discovered, and . . ."

"And you haven't any idea who that someone might have been?"

"No."

"Anyone who would find it to his advantage to have you out of the way?"

She shook her head.

"Not even if your aunt should die?"

"What makes you ask that?"

"Someone had made an attempt to poison your aunt earlier in the evening. He perhaps had reason to think he'd been successful, and that she was dying or dead. He might have come to the house to get you out of the way."

"No, I can't imagine anything like that."

"You can't think of anyone who would have stood to gain if . . ."

"No."

The efficient tread of rubber heels sounded just outside the door. The rustle of a stiffly starched uniform brought a nurse to the doorway, smiling. "He's down from the operating room, Miss Kendal. You *are* Miss Kendal, aren't you?"

"Yes, oh, yes! Is he going to live? Is he conscious? Is he . . ."

"Of course he is, and you can go up if you want."

Tragg moved along at Helen Kendal's side. The nurse looked at him inquiringly.

"Lieutenant Tragg. The police," Tragg explained.

"Oh, yes."

"I came to get the bullet."

"You'll have to talk with Dr. Rosllyn. He'll be down from the operating room very shortly."

Tragg said to Helen Kendal, "I hate to butt in on this, but I've got to ask him a question if the doctor thinks he can answer it."

"He's conscious," the nurse said. "They used a spinal anesthetic."

Helen Kendal looked up at him pleadingly as they reached the elevator. "Aren't you more interested in that bullet, Lieutenant? That's awfully important. You know doctors are sometimes careless. He might throw it away or lose it—or something—unless you went right up."

Tragg burst out laughing. "All right, you win. Go in and see him alone. But don't get him tired, because I'm coming down in just a minute to talk to him."

The nurse frowned. "He's full of hypos, you understand, Lieutenant. He's groggy, and you can't rely too much on what he says."

"I know," Tragg said. "I only want to ask him a couple of simple questions. What floor is the operating room?"

"Eleven. Mr. Templar is on the fourth. I'll show Miss Kendal the way."

Tragg gave Helen an imperceptible nudge when the elevator stopped at the fourth floor. Then he turned to the nurse. "Couldn't you let Miss Kendal find Mr. Templar's room by herself, and take me up to the operating room?"

"Why, yes. His room is 481—just down the corridor."

"She can find it."

Helen flashed Tragg a grateful glance. "Thanks," she breathed, and sped down the corridor.

The elevator door slid shut, and the cage started on its upward journey.

"What are his chances?" Tragg asked.

The nurse shook her head. "I wouldn't know."

At the eleventh floor, she led the way to the operating room. Dr. Rosllyn, stripped to the waist, was drying his arms on a towel.

"Lieutenant Tragg," the nurse announced.

"Oh, yes, Lieutenant. Got that slug for you. What the devil did I do with it? Miss Dewar, where's that bullet?"

"You put it in a tray, Doctor, and said you didn't want it touched."

"Damn it," Rosllyn said, "bet I put some bandages in on top of it. Here, wait a minute . . . Here, come this way."

He led the way into a room which opened off the operating room. The peculiar acrid smell of blood assailed Tragg's nostrils. A nurse pulled blood-soaked bits of cloth from an enameled container, handed it, not to Tragg, but to the doctor. The doctor took a pair of forceps, reached in, and pulled out a red-stained chunk of metal. "Here you are, Lieutenant"

"Thanks. You'll have to swear that this is the bullet you took from the body of Jerry Templar, you know."

"Sure, this is the one."

Tragg turned the bullet over. "Make some identifying mark on the base here so you'll know it again."

The doctor took out his pocket knife, scratched three parallel lines on the base of the bullet, then put crosses on each line. Tragg slipped the bullet in his vest pocket. "How are his chances?" he asked.

"Pretty good, so far. I'd have given him fifty-fifty before I started working on him. I'll give him nine out of ten now. Barring complications, he'll be all right. Strong, rugged type. That Army training does wonders for 'em, Lieutenant. That lad has the stamina of a billygoat. Came through the operation in fine shape."

"All right for me to talk with him for just a minute?"

"I think so. He's full of dope, of course. Don't tire him, and don't ask him complicated questions. Simple things that he can hold his mind to. He'll start rambling if you let him keep on talking, but if you hold his mind to it and ask him simple questions, he'll give you the answers. Don't have any stenographer there, though. Some of his talk will be rambling and an isolated answer or two may be incorrect."

"All right," Tragg said. "Now, if there's any change, I want to know about it. And if it looks bad, I'll want to get a death-bed statement."

Dr. Rosllyn laughed. "I don't think you're going to have the chance. That boy *wants* to live. He's nuts over some girl or other, and, until I put him under with a whiff of gas, was rambling on how glad he was he got shot because that way he found out how much she loves him! Can you beat it? The only thing that's bothering him is that the bullet knocked him over and he couldn't get the man who did it. All right, Lieutenant, let me know when you want me to be a witness and identify that bullet."

Lieutenant Tragg made his way down to the fourth floor, tiptoed down the corridor to 481, gently pushed open the door.

A nurse was standing in the far corner of the room. Helen Kendal, self-conscious and embarrassed, was seated on a chair by the foot of the bed. "I'm so glad," she was saying as Lieutenant Tragg opened the door.

Jerry Templar frowned at the new interruption standing in the doorway.

Tragg smiled at him cheerfully. "Hello! You don't feel much like talking now, but I've got a couple of questions to ask you. Lieutenant Tragg of Homicide."

Templar closed his eyes, let the lids flutter open, looked at Tragg for a moment as though having some difficulty getting his eyes in focus, then grinned back and said, "Shoot!"

"Not twice in the same night," Tragg protested. "Now you answer as briefly as you can, because you're not supposed to talk much."

Jerry nodded.

"Who fired the shots?" Tragg asked.

"I don't know."

"Could you see anything at all?"

"Just a little motion—a blurred figure moving."

"Tall or short?"

"Couldn't say . . . a corner of the room moved, then came the shots."

"Could this person have been shooting at Helen instead of you?"

That thought galvanized Templar into hard-eyed attention. "How's that? Shooting at Helen?"

"Could that have been the case?"

"Don't know. Can't think that out. Yes—yes—might have. I never . . ."

"I'm sorry, but the patient mustn't be excited," came a droning voice from the nurse in the corner.

Lieutenant Tragg looked at Helen Kendal's proudly stiff figure, thought of the baffled, thwarted expression on Templar's face as he opened the door. He grinned at the nurse, and said, "Sister, I've been talking with the doctor, and I can tell you right now you're in the right church, but in the wrong pew. This shooting, mysterious as it is, has started to clear up some mighty important things that would get *all* cleared up once and for all if you'd just relax and go and get yourself a cup of coffee. I may not know a darn thing about medicine, but I know something of human nature, and if you'd get out of here for about five minutes and leave these two people alone, it would do your patient more good than anything in the world. He was telling the doctor all about it during the operation. Why not give him a chance to tell her about it now?"

The nurse glanced at Templar, then her garments rustled as she moved quietly around the foot of the bed toward the door.

Lieutenant Tragg said, "Well, I'll be seeing you."

"You only have a minute," the nurse warned Helen Kendal.

Tragg held the door open for the nurse, caught the glint of Helen Kendal's eyes, and pushed the door shut behind him. "Give her as long as you can," he said to the nurse.

She walked with him down toward the elevator. "You certainly spoke *your* piece."

Tragg grinned. "I had to. Pride has busted up more romances than jealousy. Guy didn't want to say anything because he's in the Army. Girl shows how she feels when she's riding up to the hospital with him, and then becomes suddenly self-conscious, thinks she's been forward, and waits for him to make the next move. He's afraid perhaps she's changed her mind. Neither one of them want to say anything, and you standing there . . ."

"I stood back in the corner out of the way."

Tragg grinned and said, "Well, I've started something, anyway."

Whistling a little tune, Tragg pushed the button for the elevator, went down to the street floor, walked through the long lines of hushed corridors out into the cold, stinging tang of the night air.

He got into his police car, and drove rapidly to headquarters. An irritable Scotchman in the laboratory said, "I dinna suppose this could a' waited until nine o'clock."

"It couldn't," Tragg said. "You've got the bullet the autopsy surgeon gave you from the body of Henry Leech?"

"Yes."

Tragg handed him two bullets from his vest pocket. "The one with the three straight lines on it was recovered in an operation performed on Jerry Templar. The other one was dug out of some woodwork beside the door in which Templar and the girl were standing when Templar was shot. Now then, how long will it take you to tell me whether those three are from the same gun?"

"I don't know," the Scotchman said with singular pessimism. "It'll all depend. It may take a long while. It may take a short while."

"Make it take a short while," Tragg said. "I'm going down to my office. Give me a ring. And don't mix those bullets up. Perry Mason's on the other side of this case, and you know what he'll do to you on cross-examination."

"He'll na do a thing to me in cross-examination," the man at the laboratory bench said, adjusting the eyepieces on a comparison microscope. "He'll have no chance. I'll take micro-photographs, and let the camera speak for me. A man's a fool to talk wi' his tongue when he can get a camera lens to do it for him."

Tragg smiled, then pausing in the doorway, announced, "I've

declared open season on Mr. Perry Mason. I'm going to teach that boy not to cut corners."

"You'd better be buyin' yourself an alarm clock," Angus Mac-Intosh grunted as he settled himself to his task. "Ye'll be gettin' up early in the morning, Mister Lieutenant."

Tragg paused in the act of closing the door to say, "I've already got one." Then he gently slipped the door shut and walked down to his office.

Tragg made a little grimace, as the dead odor of stale smoke assailed his nostrils. He went to the windows, opened them, and shivered slightly as the dry cold of the before-dawn air stole into the room. He rubbed exploratory fingers across the angle of his jaw, feeling the stubble, and frowned as he noticed the oil which had been transferred from his skin to his fingertips. He felt sticky, dirty, and tired.

He crossed to the coat closet which contained a wash stand, turned on hot water, washed his hands and face, and was drying himself with a towel when the telephone rang.

Tragg walked over to pick up the receiver.

"Yes?"

The voice of the Scotchman in the laboratory department said, "I havena got 'em in the most advantageous positions yet so that I can make the best possible photograph, but I can tell you one thing. The three bullets came from the same gun. Noo then, how soon will ye be wantin' photographs?"

"Just as soon as I can get 'em," Tragg said.

The Scotchman groaned. "Ye was always an impatient lad," he observed, and hung up the receiver.

Tragg grinned his satisfaction.

Once more the telephone rang. The man on duty at the switchboard said hurriedly, "Here's an anonymous tip for you, Lieutenant. Won't talk with anyone else. Says he's going to hang up in exactly sixty seconds, and there's no use trying to trace the call."

"Got it so you can listen in?" Tragg asked.

"Yes."

"Okay, put him on."

A click came over the line as the operator plugged in a key and said, "Here's Lieutenant Tragg on the line."

"Hello," a peculiarly muffled voice said. The man at the other end of the line might well have been holding his fist cupped between his mouth and the transmitter. "Is this Lieutenant Tragg?"

"This is Tragg. Who is this talking?"

"Never mind. I'm just telling you something about Perry Mason, the lawyer, and the girl who drove him out to the Shore place a while after midnight."

"Go ahead," Tragg invited. "What d'you know about 'em?"

"They picked a man up. He's an important witness, one you want. They spirited him away where they've got him sewed up."

"Go on," Tragg said impatiently. "Who's the man, and where is he?"

"I don't know who he is, but I can tell you where he is."

"Where?"

The voice suddenly speeded up its tempo as though anxious to get the conversation terminated.

"Maple Leaf Hotel under the name Thomas Trimmer. Registered about quarter past four this morning. He's in room 376."

Tragg said quickly, "Now, wait a minute. Let me get one thing straight. Are you absolutely certain that Perry Mason, the lawyer, is the one who put this man in the hotel? Is he back of that?"

"Back of it, hell," the voice said. "Mason was the one who came in with him, carrying a canvas-covered telescope bag. The girl wasn't with him then."

The receiver abruptly slammed up at the other end of the line.

Lieutenant Tragg jiggled the hook. "Able to trace that call?" he asked.

"Pay station, block from the hotel," the exchange operator said. "I got the call traced, and two radio cars rushing out there with instructions to pick up anyone they see within three blocks of the place for questioning. We'll know in fifteen minutes if they get any results."

There was the glint of a triumphant hunter in Tragg's eyes. "I'll wait fifteen minutes just on a chance."

It was twenty minutes before the report came in. Two radio cars had converged on the place. It was an all-night restaurant with a phone booth near the door. There was only one man on duty behind the counter, and he had been busy waiting on some customers. He had vaguely noticed a man enter the phone booth, but he couldn't describe him. The radio cars had picked up two men within a radius of four blocks of the place. It didn't seem probable that either man had put in the call, but the police had secured names and addresses from driving licenses. Then the officers, stopping at the Maple Leaf Hotel, had found that a Thomas Trimmer had been checked in about four o'clock. He was a man in the late fifties with a slight stoop. He weighed a hundred and forty pounds, was about five feet six, wore somewhat shabby, but clean clothes, had high cheekbones, and a gray drooping mustache. His only baggage had been an old-fashioned canvas telescope case, fairly heavy. Trimmer had been brought in by a tall, well-dressed man.

A little pulse in Lieutenant Tragg's forehead began to pound as he listened to the report. "Keep the radio cars on the job," he ordered. "Sew the place up so Trimmer doesn't get out. I'm on my way out there right now."

17

MASON DROVE the car slowly. The long hours of sleepless activity had lowered his resistance to the cold chill of the night air.

The kitten curled up on the seat beside him, snuggling closely for warmth. Occasionally, the lawyer, steadying the wheel with his left hand, placed his right hand down on the kitten's fur, leaving it there for a few seconds until Amber Eyes would start purring in drowsy contentment.

In the east, the stars were shrinking into invisibility. A faint illumination furnished a backdrop against which the roofs of the clustered apartment houses showed in a serrated silhouette. Mason slowed the car as he neared the place where Della Street lived. The entire apartment house was dark, save for that one vaguely lighted orange oblong which would be Della Street's window.

Mason parked his car, picked up the relaxed form of the purring kitten, and slipped it under his overcoat, holding it against the warmth of his body. He paused before the long list of tenants beside the mail boxes, and pressed the bell of Della Street's apartment.

Almost instantly, the electric buzzer which released the catch on the street door brought her answering signal. Mason pushed through the door, and into the stuffy, warm air of the lobby. He crossed to the automatic elevator, pressed the button, and ascended to Della Street's floor. Amber Eyes, nestled under the lawyer's coat, became apprehensive as he felt the upward motion, and squirmed around, digging sharp little claws into Mason's clothing until an inquiring, startled head pushed its furry way out from the overcoat to stare curiously at the walls of the elevator cage.

The elevator came to a stop. Mason opened the door, walked down the corridor and paused before Della Street's door to tap lightly with the tips of his fingers, giving their private code knock.

Della Street opened the door. She was still wearing the clothes in which she had been attired when Mason had deposited her in front of the taxi stand at the hotel.

"Gosh, I'm glad to see you. Tell me, did I get your signals right?" she asked in a half whisper, as Mason eased his way through the door and entered the cozy warmth of her apartment.

"Darned if I know. What did you think I wanted?"

"For me to go out to Lunk's place."

"Right. What did you do with him?"

She said, "He wasn't there. Oh, you've got the kitten!"

Mason took off his hat, placed the kitten in Della Street's outstretched hands, and sat down without taking off his overcoat. He frowned thoughtfully at the carpet. "Got a drink?"

"Been keeping a pot of coffee hot for you. Spiked with brandy, it will fix you up in a jiffy—" She deposited the kitten on the davenport. "You sit there, Amber Eyes, and be a good kitten."

Mason said, "Wait a minute, Della. I want to talk with you about . . ."

"Not until you've had that coffee," she said, and vanished through the door into the kitchenette.

Mason sat motionless, elbows resting on his knees, staring fixedly at the pattern in the carpet.

Amber Eyes investigated the davenport, jumped down to the

floor, allowed his nose to guide the way to the kitchenette, and stood at the door giving a high-pitched "*miaow.*"

Della Street laughed and opened the door, saying, "And I suppose *you* want some warm milk."

Mason was still in the same position when she returned carrying a tray on which were two cups of steaming black coffee. The aroma of fine brandy mingled with that of the beverage to caress the nostrils.

Mason lifted a cup and saucer from the tray, and grinned at Della Street.

"Here's to crime," he said.

She sat down on the davenport, balanced the saucer on her knee and said, "Sometimes that toast of yours scares me."

Mason sipped hot coffee, felt the brandy warming his blood into circulation. "What happened?" he asked.

She said, "I wasn't certain you could keep Lunk occupied much longer. I told the cab driver to hurry."

"Give him the Bilvedere address?" Mason asked.

"Not the address. I told him to stop at the corner of a cross street and wait. Then I walked back a block, turned the corner, checked the numbers until I came to the driveway which led into Lunk's place. It's a little square house tacked onto the garage and . . ."

"I know," Mason interrupted. "I was inside the place. What did *you* do?"

"I saw the house was dark, so I barged up on the steps and rang the doorbell, big as life. No one answered. I kept leaning against the doorbell, and couldn't hear it ring, so I started to knock, and then I noticed that the front door wasn't quite closed. Believe me, Chief, I wished I'd been a mind reader right then and known what you wanted me to do. But, after a while, I pushed the door open and went in."

"Turn on the lights?" he asked.

"Yes."

"What did you find?"

"There was no one in the house. The bed in the front bedroom hadn't been made. In the back bedroom . . ."

"Wait a minute. How did you get into the back bedroom? Through the kitchen or the connecting bathroom?"

"The connecting bathroom."

"Now be sure about this, Della. Were the doors between the two bedrooms open?"

"Yes, about halfway open—that is, the first door was about half open. The door from the bathroom to the back bedroom was *all* the way open. There was a window in the back bedroom that opened on an alley. That window was raised, and the wind was coming through there, gently blowing the curtains."

"How about the door from the bedroom into the kitchen?"

"It was open just an inch or two."

"Did you go through that?"

"No. I went into the kitchen by going back through the front bedroom and the living room. But let me tell you about the front bedroom first. Drawers had been pulled out of the bureau and clothes from the closet were piled on the floor."

Mason said, "I know. Let's get back to the kitchen. Did you look in the pantry?"

"Yes."

"Was the pantry door open or closed?"

"Closed."

"Did you turn on a light in the pantry?"

"No. I opened the door, and enough light came in from the kitchen so I could see there was no one in the pantry. I wanted to make sure—I thought perhaps Franklin Shore had heard the bell ring and decided to hide, just in case it might be someone whom he didn't want to see."

"Did you notice any flour on the floor around the flour can in the pantry?"

"No—but I wouldn't have noticed it unless there'd been quite a bit of flour on the floor, because the light was back of me and I was only searching to make certain someone wasn't hiding in there."

"Feel pretty shaky?"

"I'll say! Chills were chasing one another up and down my spine. If Franklin Shore *had* been standing in that pantry, he'd have scared the boots off me."

Mason finished the coffee, got up to put the cup and saucer over on the table. He slipped out of his overcoat, stretched his long arms, then lowered them to shove his hands down deep in his pockets. From the little kitchen, the kitten *"miaowed"* a peremptory command to be readmitted to the room which contained human companionship. Della Street opened the door, and the kitten, its stomach bulging with warm milk, marched awkwardly into the room, made a little throaty noise of satisfaction, jumped up on the davenport, and settled down, curling its forepaws in under its chest. The alert interest slowly left its eyes, and, after a moment, they closed enough so white membranes could be seen at the corners as the kitten settled down to purring slumber.

Mason, still standing, jerked his head toward the kitten. "Where was Amber Eyes when you came in?"

"Curled up on the sheets right in the middle of the bed in the front bedroom."

"Near the center of the bed?"

"Yes. The bed sags a little, and there was a low place right near the center. The kitten was curled up, fast asleep."

Mason took his hands from his pockets, hooked his thumbs in the armholes of his vest, and started pacing the floor.

"More coffee?" Della asked.

He might not have heard her, but continued pacing the carpet, head pushed slightly forward, eyes lowered.

Abruptly, he turned, "Did you notice any tracks on the floor, such as might have been made if the kitten had walked through some white powder?"

Della Street frowned, said, "Let me think. I wasn't looking for anything smaller than a man, and I was scared stiff, but . . . I *think* there were some cat tracks across the kitchen. I carried away the general impression that it was a place in which a man had been living by himself, and that it needed a darn good cleaning. The sheets on the bed in the front bedroom were pretty soiled, and the pillow case was filthy. The lace curtains needed cleaning. The dish towels were in pretty bad shape. Oh, just a lot of little things like that. And I *think* there was something in the kitchen, some cat tracks or something spilled on the floor."

"But the pantry door was closed? You're certain of that?"

"Yes."

Mason said, "How the devil could the kitten have got into flour in the pantry and left tracks across the floor—if the pantry door had been closed? It didn't go in when *you* opened the door?"

Della Street thought that over for a few seconds, then shook her head. "It's beyond me. The kitten never moved while I was there."

Mason thoughtfully regarded the sleeping kitten, abruptly picked up his overcoat, whipped it on, and reached for his hat.

Della Street came to stand at his side as he reached for the doorknob.

"Please go to bed and get some sleep, Chief. You'll need it."

He looked down at her, and the granite lines of his face softened into a smile. "Get some yourself. *You'll* need it.

"When you were in the house, did you notice a calling card on the ash tray with George Alber's name and some handwriting on it?"

"A card was there. I didn't notice the name on it. Why?"

"Oh, nothing. Forget it."

He circled her waist with his arms, drew her close to him. She raised half-parted lips. His other arm circled her shoulder. For a moment, he held her close, then said, "Keep a stiff upper lip, Kid. I think we've pulled a boner."

Silently opening the door, he slipped out into the hallway.

18

DELLA STREET fought against the clamor of the alarm clock.

Her sleep-drugged struggle against the first spasm of ringing was successful. The bell ceased its clanging summons and Della Street slipped off once more into deep slumber, only to be aroused by the irritating insistence of the second alarm.

She raised herself on one elbow, eyes still closed, groped for the shut-off. The clock eluded her, making it necessary for her to open her eyes.

The clock was not in its accustomed place by the bed, but over on the dresser where she had placed it as a precaution against shutting it off and going to sleep again.

Reluctantly, she threw back the covers, swung her legs out of bed, and started for the clock.

A faint "*miaow*" of protest came from the bed.

It took her a moment to account for that strange sound, then, switching off the alarm, she pulled up the covers which she had thrown back over Amber Eyes.

The kitten curled in a warm little nest on top of the bed, purred its gratitude, got to its feet, arched its back, stretched, yawned, made two awkward zigzag cat jumps which brought it within reaching distance of Della Street's fingers.

The kitten accepted the ministrations of Della's fingertips behind his ears, ventured in purring exploration over the slippery treachery of the rounded bedclothes, seeking to regain the warmth of Della Street's body.

Della laughed and pushed him away. "Not now, Amber Eyes. The strident clang of the alarm calls me to industry."

She knew that she didn't have to get to the office on time, but there were some matters in the mail which needed attention. A new typist was working on an important brief, and Della knew she'd have to check over that brief before letting Mason see it for final reading.

Warm needles of water from the shower, the scented lather of soap, then, at the last, the sting of the cold water, tingled her into life. She vigorously toweled her skin into glowing health, inspected stockings for possible runners, and was standing before the mirror in her underthings, getting her face made up when the buzzer on her inner door exploded into noise.

For a while, Della ignored it, then she opened the door a scant inch, said, "Go away, I'm a working girl. I don't want to buy anything, I can't subscribe to anything, and I'm late for the office now."

Lieutenant Tragg's voice said, "Well, I'll drive you down to the office. That will save time."

Della Street tilted her head, placing her eyes close to the crack in the door so that she could see Lieutenant Tragg's face.

"How'd you get past the street door?"

"It's a secret. You look sleepy."

"You look worse than that."

Tragg grinned. "As far as I can tell, no one west of the Mississippi got any sleep last night."

"I'm dressing."

"How long will it take you to finish?"

"Five or ten minutes."

"Breakfast?"

"Not here. I grab a cup of coffee at the drugstore on the corner."

"Bad for the health to eat that way," he told her.

"Swell for the figure."

"I'll wait outside the door," he said.

"Is it that important?"

"It's that important," Tragg said.

Della closed the door. Her mirror showed her the reflection of a scowling countenance. She moved over to the telephone, picked up the receiver, started to dial Mason's unlisted number, then changed her mind, dropped the receiver back into place, got into her dress, kicked off her bedroom slippers, put on shoes, and then realized the problem presented by the kitten.

She snatched the little fluff of fur up in her arms, said softly, "Now listen, my love, that cop outside *eats* kittens, eats 'em alive. What's more, he'll want your presence explained, and, frankly, you'd be harder to laugh off than a man under the bed. It's the kitchen for you, and I'm praying that lots of warm milk will keep you quiet."

Amber Eyes purred contentedly.

Della Street stepped out into the little kitchenette, poured some top-milk from a bottle, warmed it until it felt just the right temperature, then fed the kitten.

"The doctor says you aren't to have anything solid," she told Amber Eyes, "and unless you want to give the show away you've got to be a good little kitten and keep your mouth shut. A good full stomach should help, so go ahead and fill up."

Purring its pleasure, the kitten lapped up the warm, creamy milk, and Della Street, slipping quietly out of the kitchen, gently closed the door so Tragg wouldn't hear the click of the latch. She hastily threw the covers back into place on the bed, tucked the sheet in, fluffed the pillows, placed them in the clips at the foot of the bed, and pushed the bed back up against the wall, turning the revolving door so the bed was concealed in the closet. She pushed the chairs back into position, working against time.

She put on her street coat, adjusted her hat more by instinct than any desire for facial adornment, opened the door and gave Lieutenant Tragg the benefit of her best smile. "All ready," she said. "Nice of you to offer to drive me to the office. I suppose, however, it's not entirely philanthropic."

"It isn't," Tragg said.

"A Greek, bearing gifts?"

"Exactly. Nice place you have there. Nice southeast exposure."

"Isn't it," Della Street said, tugging at the doorknob.

"You're all alone here?"

"Of course."

Tragg took a step forward so that his shoulder blocked the closing door. "Tell you what, Miss Street, we may as well talk in here for just a minute."

"I haven't time. I've got to be at the office."

"I think this is more important than being at the office," Tragg said.

"Well, we could talk in your car, or . . ."

"It's hard to talk, driving a car," Tragg said, moving on into the apartment and walking apparently in a most casual manner over to the davenport.

Della Street sighed in exasperation, stood in the doorway, fully aware of the fact that his sharp, police-trained eyes, were taking in every detail.

"I'm sorry, Lieutenant, but I simply *have* to get to work. I haven't time either to be interviewed or to argue about being interviewed . . . and I can't leave you here."

Tragg apparently didn't hear her. "Certainly is a nice place. Well, if you insist, I'll come along, although I'd prefer to talk here."

He paused, apparently to adjust his tie in the mirror, but Della realized that from the position in which he was standing he could see a reflection of the bathroom through the open door.

"Will you *please* come, Lieutenant."

"Coming," he said. "Lord, I certainly look as though I'd been up all night. You won't mind driving with such a disreputable specimen?"

"Just so we get started," Della Street said firmly.

"What's this door?" Tragg asked, indicating the kitchen door.

"It's a door," she said angrily. "Surely, you've seen doors before, Lieutenant. They're composed of wood. They're hung on hinges, and they swing back and forth."

"Do they indeed!" Tragg said, his eyes fastened on the door.

Della Street came angrily back into the apartment. "Now you look here," she said sharply. "I don't know what you're after. You're not going to come in and snoop around my apartment any time you want to. If you want to search my place, go get a warrant. If you have anything to say to me, say it on the way to the office. I'm starting now, and you're getting out!"

Tragg looked into the angry defiance of her eyes, said with an ingratiating smile, "Surely, Miss Street, you don't object to my looking around your apartment."

"I most certainly do."

"Why? Are you hiding someone?"

"I give you my word of honor, there's no other human being in this apartment except myself. Now, does that satisfy you?"

He met the steady anger of her eyes and said, "Yes."

She let him start first for the door, followed along close behind, this time ready to slam the door shut and let the spring lock snap into position.

Tragg was just stepping over the threshold, and Della Street's hand was on the doorknob when there came an ear-piercing scream of feline anguish, a scream which changed both its pitch and location with great speed.

"Oh, my heavens!" Della Street exclaimed, suddenly remembering that she habitually left the kitchen window open a few inches for ventilation.

There was no mistaking the sound. This was no mere cry of feline impatience, but a squall of agony.

That cry appealed to the maternal in Della Street. She would no more have abandoned that kitten to its fate in order to save herself from a felony charge than she would have refused to rush to the aid of a child.

Lieutenant Tragg was right behind her as she raced through the apartment's living room into the kitchenette. His head was at her shoulder as she flung open the kitchen window.

What had happened was only too apparent. The pulley which held the manila rope clothesline was fastened directly beside the kitchen window. Amber Eyes, crawling to the sill and peering out, had been intrigued by the rope. He had hooked a paw around it and, in trying to withdraw that paw, his claws had caught and held. As his weight came against the clothesline, it had started to slide through the well-oiled pulley. There was plenty of slack in that line and Amber Eyes had found himself sailing out through space at a dizzy height above the ground. His other paws had locked around the clothesline, leaving him hanging head downward, squalling with pop-eyed terror, his tail switching back and forth, then fluffing out to huge proportions.

"You poor thing!" Della Street exclaimed and, reaching for the upper rope, started pulling Amber Eyes in. "Hang on now, kitty," she exhorted. "Don't let go."

The cat swayed to and fro, eyes shifting from Della Street in the safety of the window to the courtyard far below.

Tragg grinned. The grin became a chuckle, and, as Della

brought the kitten to within reaching distance and clutched it in her hand, the chuckle became a burst of laughter.

Not only did Amber Eyes have no intention of letting go, but terror had locked his claws into the rope so that Della Street had to disengage them as though they had been so many fish hooks. She held the trembling little body close to her, speaking reassuringly to it, quieting its fear.

"Go on and laugh," she blazed at Lieutenant Tragg. "I suppose *you* think it's funny!"

"I do for a fact," Tragg admitted. "The cat makes a playful swipe at the rope, and the next thing he knows, he's flying through the air with the greatest of ease. It must have been a startling sensation for a kitten."

"Startling," Della said indignantly. "I'm glad you think it's funny."

"I didn't know you had a kitten," Tragg said.

"Indeed. I suppose the police department feels aggrieved that I should have adopted a kitten without consulting it. I suppose if I should tell you that my Aunt Rebecca had sprained her ankle ice skating, you'd call me on the carpet because I let her go out without permission from the police. If you'll just let me get to the office, I'll write you a letter 'Dear Lieutenant Tragg: I have a kitten. Does it meet with your approval?'"

Lieutenant Tragg said, "That is a very effective burst of indignation and sarcasm—but it doesn't tell me anything about the cat; and it isn't distracting my attention in the least."

"Oh, is that so!"

"How long have you had the cat?"

"Not very long."

"What do you mean by that?"

"It isn't a very old kitten."

"Have you had it ever since it was born?"

"No."

"About how long then?"

"Not so very long. Long enough to get to feel attached to it. You know how it is, after an animal has been with you a few weeks—or as far as that's concerned, even a few minutes, if you love animals, you get to feeling an attachment that . . ."

"Has the cat been with you a few weeks?" Tragg asked.

"No, I suppose not."

"Even a few days?"

"I fail to see where this concerns you in any way."

Tragg said, "Ordinarily, I would say you were quite right, Miss Street, but there are some circumstances which might alter the case."

"Such as what?" she asked impulsively, and then wished she had kept her mouth shut, realizing that she had given him just the opening he had been angling for.

"Oh," Tragg said casually, "in case the kitten happened to be the one that belonged to Mrs. Matilda Shore, one that had been poisoned last night."

"Even so, what would that have to do with it?"

"The question of how that cat came into your possession," Tragg said, "might be interesting to the police. However, as you suggested, we can talk it over while we're riding to the office."

"Yes, I'm late now."

Tragg's smile was apologetic. "Perhaps," he said, "you are not referring to the same office that I am."

She turned to face him, fighting back a wobbly feeling in her knees.

"You know perfectly well to what office *I* am referring," Della Street said, managing to keep firmness in her voice.

Lieutenant Tragg was not in the least impressed. He announced, "I am referring to the office of the district attorney. And you may as well bring the kitten along. Not only does it seem to be too careless to be left alone, but it may be a bit of very significant evidence."

19

PERRY MASON soaked up slumber. The consciousness of broad daylight knifed its way through to his brain. He sat up in bed long enough to look at his watch, fling the pillows into a new position, and drop back with a sense of languid comfort. He started drifting comfortably down into the welcome warmth of nerve-healing oblivion. . . . The ringing of the buzzer on his doorbell irritated him into consciousness.

Mason decided to ignore the summons. He turned over, frowning in the determination of his concentration . . . damn the doorbell anyway . . . probably someone wanting to sell something. Why hadn't he shut it off. . . . The bell again . . . well, let them ring. He wouldn't pay any attention to it.

Again and again the bell rang. Mason found that his very determination to sleep was marshaling his faculties into wakefulness. He heard quick steps in the corridor, then knuckles banging imperatively on his door.

With an exclamation of irritation, Mason climbed out of bed, unlocked the door and jerked it open.

Paul Drake stood on the threshold, grinning at him. "How do you like it?" he asked.

Mason said, "Damn it. I *don't* like it. Come in."

Drake followed the lawyer into his apartment, selected the most comfortable chair, twisted himself into a pretzel of comfort, and lit a cigarette. "Nice place you have here."

"Isn't it," Mason said sarcastically.

Drake said, "A little chilly. I'll close this window. The breeze is coming in through there. Sunlight's pouring in through the other one. It's eleven-thirty, Perry."

"What the devil do I care what time it is?"

Drake tried to blow a smoke ring, watched the blue clouds of smoke drift out into the shaft of sunlight, and said, "You're always getting me up around the middle of the night, when you and Della have been out making whoopee—and seem to think it's fun. Thought I'd interfere with your sleep just so you can see how it feels."

Mason, pulling the covers over his bare toes, grinned at the poetic justice of Drake's position, said, "It feels like hell," and reached for a cigarette.

"Thought you'd like a report of what's going on."

Mason tapped the end of the cigarette, carefully moistened the end with his tongue, lit a match, and said, "As soon as I finish with this cigarette, I'm going to throw you out and go back to sleep." He placed the match to the end of the cigarette.

"Lots of things have been happening," Drake said. "Those bullets all came from the same gun."

"That's nothing new."

"Tragg's turned the whole police force upside down. He's working on every angle of the case, squeezing out every last bit of information."

"I'm glad he is."

"The doctors give Jerry Templar nine chances out of ten to pull through. He stood the operation in fine shape."

"That's good."

"The kitten that was poisoned was taken down to the gardener's house for safekeeping—chap by the name of Thomas Lunk."

Mason said, "Uh huh."

"Lunk's disappeared. So has the kitten."

Mason said, "Listen, Paul. I can keep abreast of the current developments by reading the newspapers. I wanted you to get some angles everybody didn't know about, not trail along a few steps behind the police."

Drake went on as though he hadn't even heard Mason's remark, "Chap by the name of George Alber seems to stand acehigh with Her Majesty, Matilda Shore. Seems as though Matilda thinks Alber and Helen Kendal should get spliced. Alber thinks so too. Alber's going places. He's going to amount to something in the world. He's attractive and magnetic. Helen is throwing herself away on a man who isn't at all worthy of her. Aunt Matilda may leave her dough to Alber if Helen isn't a good girl."

Mason sucked in a prodigious yawn. "You are very annoying at times, Paul."

Drake looked at him with humorless eyes. "Do you find me that way?"

Mason knocked ashes off the end of his cigarette, snuggled back down under the covers.

"Matilda is out of the hospital and back at the house. Seems as though she's made a will in which she's tried to exert some pressure on Helen Kendal to make her marry young Alber. Alber apparently gets a very, very nice chunk of the Shore fortune one way or another. Either he gets it by marrying Helen, or, if Helen doesn't marry him, he is taken care of very handsomely. . . . Oh, yes, your friend Lieutenant Tragg is having the last few checks that went through Franklin Shore's account carefully experted. A ten-thousand-dollar check to a man by the name of Rodney French seems to be the one he's particularly interested in. Rodney French is being looked for by the police. He seems to have taken a little vacation for himself, commencing yesterday evening. He neglected to tell anyone just where he was going."

Mason said, "Franklin Shore telephoned his bookkeeper he was putting that ten-thousand-dollar check through."

"That's right," Drake said, grinning, "he did."

"Well?" Mason asked.

"Tragg's working on a theory that perhaps Franklin *intended* to put that check through, but pulled his disappearing act before he'd made out the check. . . . That would make an interesting situation, wouldn't it, Perry? Put yourself in the position of a man who is depending on a ten-thousand-dollar check from a chap whose name on the bottom of a check would have made it as good as a certificate of the United States Mint. Then the chap disappears and can't be found, and you've already committed yourself to the things you're going to do, on the assumption that check is going through."

"Anything else?" Mason asked.

"Oh, yes. Tragg's really working on that disappearance. It's a shame he wasn't in on it when it happened, but that was during the regime of our old friend, Sergeant Holcomb. Tragg's going over all the unidentified bodies that were found around that time—getting the records out for an airing. He's found one body. The description doesn't check, however. He's also checking up on all the suicides around Florida in 1932, and he's checking up on some mining property Leech was interested in, also making a very close check on the finances of Gerald' Shore as of January, 1932. A very, very resourceful chap, Tragg."

Mason said, "Phooey! Tragg's just a damned misanthrope."

"Of course, he covers a lot of territory," Drake went on. "Seems to think that kitten is rather an important factor in the entire situation."

"The kitten, eh?" Mason observed.

"Uh huh. Interesting chap, Tragg. When he goes after something, he really gets it."

"The kitten for instance?" Mason asked, very casually.

"Oh, of course, the kitten. He has that kitten up at the district attorney's office."

Mason sat bolt upright in bed. "How's that?" he asked.

"Has the kitten up at the district attorney's office. Don't know just what he's doing with it, but . . ."

"Where did he get it?"

"I don't know. I pick up a lot of stuff from the newspaper boys, things that leak out through the police. He's asking questions of the chap who does the gardening out there, man by the name of Lunk. He . . ."

Mason became a moving mass of arms and legs, pinching out the cigarette, kicking the covers off, grabbing the telephone. The dial whirred through a number. Mason said, "Hello. . . . Hello. That you, Gertie? . . . Where's Della this morning?

"No word from her, eh? . . . Let me talk with Jackson. . . . Hello, Jackson. This is an emergency. Give it a right of way over everything in the office. Make out an application for a writ of *habeas corpus* for Della Street. Make it wide enough, big enough and broad enough to cover everything from rape to arson. She's being detained against her will. She's being examined concerning privileged communications, she's held without any charge being placed against her. She's abundantly able to furnish bail in any reasonable amount. Ask for a writ of *habeas corpus* and ask that she be admitted to bail pending the return and hearing on the writ. I'll sign and verify it. Get going on the thing!"

Mason slammed up the telephone, peeled off his pajamas,

splashed hurriedly into the shower, came out drying his body, jerking clean underwear out of a bureau drawer.

Drake sat curled up in the chair watching with a puzzled expression of growing concern while Mason hurried into his clothes.

"I have a six-volt electric razor in the glove compartment of my car," Drake said. "If you wanted to drive uptown with me, you could shave in the car."

Mason jerked open the door of a coat closet, struggled into his overcoat, grabbed his hat, pulled gloves out of his overcoat pocket, said, "Come on, Paul. What's holding us back?"

"Nothing," Drake said, uncoiling his double-jointed frame in a series of convolutions that would have done credit to a contortionist. "We're on our way. Your office or the D.A.'s?"

"My office first," Mason said. "When I talk with a D.A. I always like to be able to slap him in the face with a writ of *habeas corpus* in case he gets rough."

"This bird getting rough?" Drake asked.

"Uh huh. Where's that razor?"

20

HAMILTON BURGER, the district attorney, was a man with a huge chest, a thick neck and heavy shoulders. There was about him a suggestion of the massive strength of a bear. He was given to making unpredictable moves with the swiftness of a man who concludes his deliberations before taking action. Once he started to act, he threw himself into that action with a concentrated force that eliminated any possibility of re-examining the situation. Lawyers who had come to know him well said that once Hamilton Burger started charging, it took a brick wall to stop him. As one attorney had expressed it, "Once Burger starts moving, he keeps moving until he's stopped, and it takes a hell of a lot to stop him."

Mason knew that a reception had been prepared for him as soon as he entered the outer office of the district attorney. No assistant or trial deputy was assigned to interview him; but with the clocklike precision of a carefully-thought-out bit of campaign strategy, Mason was whisked down the corridor and into the district attorney's office almost as soon as he had announced himself at the reception desk.

Hamilton Burger surveyed Mason with glittering, steady eyes. "Sit down," he said.

Mason took the chair across from Burger's desk.

"Do you want to talk to me or am I going to talk to you?" Mason asked.

"I'm talking to you," Burger said.

"Go ahead," Mason told him, "do your talking first. I'll say what I have to say when you've finished."

Hamilton Burger said, "You're unorthodox. Your methods are spectacular, dramatic, and bizarre."

"You might add one additional word," Mason said.

For a moment, there was a flicker in the district attorney's eyes. "Effective?" he asked.

Mason nodded.

"That is the thing which bothers me," Burger said.

"I'm glad to hear you admit it."

"It doesn't bother me in the way that you think, however," Burger went on. "It simply means that if your spectacular, dramatic, swashbuckling methods *continue* to be effective, we'll have every attorney at the bar trying to cut corners, playing legal sleight of hand to outwit the police. And heaven knows, one of you in this county is *plenty*."

"If I beat the police to the correct solution of a crime, does that constitute outwitting the police?"

"That isn't what I meant," Burger objected. "It's not our policy to prosecute the innocent. And understand this, Mason, I'm talking, not only about what you do, but about how you do it."

"What's wrong with my means?"

"You don't try your cases in a courtroom. You don't sit in your office and interview clients. You go tearing around the country, working by a catch-as-catch-can method of grabbing evidence, refusing to take the police into your confidence, and . . ."

"Wait a minute," Mason said. "Do the police take me into their confidence?"

Burger ignored the question. "There have been times when I've co-operated with you because I thought you were co-operating with me. But it's always been that same spectacular, flamboyant, pulling-the-rabbit-out-of-the-hat business with you."

Mason said, "Well, if the rabbit I'm looking for happens to be in a hat, why not pull him out?"

"Because you usually furnish the hat. You can't justify a legal hocus-pocus simply because you eventually squirm your way out. Now I'll quit talking generalities with you. I'll get down to specific instances."

"That would be fine."

"Specifically," Burger said, "last night you uncovered a valuable, vital witness in a murder case. If the police had had the testimony of that witness, they might have solved the case by this time. As it was, they were given no opportunity. You and your secretary whisked this witness out from under the noses of the police."

"You mean Lunk?" Mason asked.

"I mean Lunk."

"Go ahead."

"You took him to a hotel and secreted him. You did everything in your power to keep the police from finding him. The police have found him."

"What are they going to do with him?" Mason asked. "If he's so valuable, let him go ahead and solve the case."

"I'm afraid it isn't that simple," Burger said.

"Why not?"

"We've uncovered some evidence that up to now has been unnoticed in connection with Franklin Shore's disappearance."

"What?" Mason asked.

"Specifically, that ten-thousand-dollar check which was given to Rodney French may have been a forgery."

Mason settled back in his chair, crossed his long legs. "All right, let's discuss that."

"I'll be glad to hear your ideas on it," Burger said with stiff formality.

"In the first place," Mason replied easily, "Franklin Shore told his bookkeeper he had put through such a check."

"I will correct you there," Burger interrupted, consulting his notes. "The testimony of the bookkeeper as given ten years ago was to the effect that Franklin Shore said he *was putting* through such a check."

Mason waved the point aside. "All right, suppose he said he was putting through that check. That establishes its authenticity. But if the check *was* forged, the statute of limitations has run out. At present, that check business can have no legal significance."

Burger said, "The check could furnish a motivation."

"For what?"

"For murder."

"Go ahead. I'm listening."

"If we had been able to get in touch with Lunk last night, it is quite possible we could have uncovered some very valuable additional evidence."

"Do you want to be more specific?"

"Yes. I think we could have found Franklin Shore."

"And I am accused of keeping you from getting in touch with Lunk?"

"Exactly."

Mason said, "I'll puncture that theory right now. The first thing I did with Lunk was to take him down to the hospital to see Matilda Shore. That was where he wanted to go. But—and get this point straight, Burger, because it's legally important—in place of trying to keep away from the police, I took him to the hospital knowing the police were guarding Matilda Shore. I told the police guards who Lunk was. I told them that he wanted to see Mrs. Shore, that he might have some important evidence, and that Tragg might want to see him. What more can anyone ask?"

Burger nodded. "That's an outstanding example of your cleverness, Mason. As far as Lunk is concerned, that one very clever move virtually gives you immunity from any prosecution. You could make that stand up in front of a jury. And yet you know, and I know, that you deliberately staged that entire visit so that the guards *would* eject you and the man with you. You did it simply to give yourself a legal insurance policy."

Mason grinned. "I can't help it if you fill up your police force with morons. I took Lunk there, and told them who he was. They pushed him back in the elevator, told him to get out and stay out."

"I understand," Burger said patiently. "Now let me call your attention to something. Under our law, any person who willfully prevents or dissuades a person who is, or who may become a witness, from attending upon any inquiry authorized by law is guilty of a misdemeanor."

Mason nodded.

"And, under another law, if any person gives or promises to give such a witness a bribe to keep him away, he's guilty of a felony."

"Go right ahead," Mason said. "I'm interested in your theory."

"Under the decisions," Burger said, "it isn't necessary that this attempt should be successful. Nor does the witness have to be actually kidnaped. It's been held in one of our sister states that it's a crime within the meaning of a similar law to get a witness intoxicated so he couldn't testify."

Mason said, "Well, I didn't bribe anyone, and I didn't get anyone intoxicated. What's all the shooting about?"

Burger said, "Lunk adopts a sullen, defiant attitude toward the police, and won't tell us what he knows. However, he isn't too intelligent. Once you understand his peculiar psychology and take the time to work with him, it's possible to get a story out of him—a bit at a time."

"Well?"

"Lunk has told us enough so that we know Franklin Shore was at his house, that your secretary went out and picked him up. Tragg had told you specifically he wanted Franklin Shore as a witness to appear before the grand jury."

Mason said, "Go ahead and finish what you have to say, and then I'll tell you how I feel about it."

"You want the last word, eh?"

Mason nodded.

Burger said, "Mason, I'm going to hit you where it hurts, and I'm going to hit you hard."

"By picking on my secretary, I suppose?"

Burger said, "You got her into this. I didn't. You kept Lunk tied up while she jumped in a cab and went to Lunk's residence, got Franklin Shore out of bed, told him that he had to get out, and made arrangements to conceal him."

"You can prove all this, I presume?"

"I can prove it by circumstantial evidence. You know very well, Mason, that you wanted to talk with Franklin Shore before the police did. You sent your secretary out there to pick up Franklin Shore and conceal him."

"Does she admit that?"

"No, she doesn't. She doesn't have to admit it. We've got the evidence to prove it."

"When you say prove, what do you mean?"

"I mean to the satisfaction of a jury."

"I don't believe it."

"It's circumstantial evidence," Burger said, "but we have it."

"You've got it like I've got the Hope diamond!" Mason said insultingly.

Hamilton Burger met his eyes unflinchingly. "I've sympathized with some of the things you've done in times past, Mason. I have been so intrigued by your rapid-fire methods and the results you have achieved that I haven't realized that as far as justice was concerned the vicious-ness of those methods more than offsets the benefits achieved. Now then, I'm going to pull your house of cards down."

"How?"

"I'm going to convict your secretary of spiriting off a material witness in a murder case. After that, I'm going to try you as an accessory and I am going to convict you. Then I am going to have you disbarred on the strength of those convictions. Now, you probably have a writ of *habeas corpus* in your pocket that you've been preparing to slap down on my desk as your last word. Go ahead and slap it. I have no desire to be unduly harsh with Miss Street. I am proceeding against her because that's the only way I can get at you. I don't intend to confine Miss Street in jail. I am perfectly willing to let you have a writ of *habeas corpus.* I am perfectly willing to see that she is admitted to bail. I am, however, going to convict her of a crime. If she wants to apply for probation, that's all right. I won't stand in her way. Then I am going to convict you of a crime. I am not going to ask for a jail sentence. I am going to see that a fine is imposed, and then I am going to use that conviction to terminate your activities as a member of the Bar."

Burger pushed back his swivel chair and got to his feet. "Now then, that last word that you were talking about—that business of slapping the writ of *habeas corpus* on my desk, loses some of its dramatic punch, doesn't it, Mason?"

Mason also got to his feet, stared across the desk at the district attorney. "All right, I told you I was going to have the last word. Now I'll have it.

"Burger, the trouble with you is that you've hypnotized yourself by looking at law entirely from the viewpoint of a district attorney. District attorneys have organized themselves and they've organized public sentiment. You have gradually lulled the public into a feeling of confidence that it can trust you to see that no innocent person is ever knowingly prosecuted."

Hamilton Burger said, "I am glad to hear you admit that, Mason."

"You shouldn't be. You should be sorry."

"Why?"

"Because the public has sat idly by and let the organized prosecutors amend the law until the constitutional guarantees of the public were swept away. We're living in a period of changing times. It's quite possible that the definition of crime will be broadened to include things which we might at present list in the category of political crimes. When the ordinary citizen is dragged into court, he'll find that the cards have been stacked against him. Ostensibly, they were stacked against the professional criminal by organized public servants, but actually they've been stacked against Mr. and Mrs. Ordinary Citizen, because the whole legal procedure has been completely undermined.

"It's high time for citizens to wake up to the fact that it isn't a question of whether a man is guilty or innocent, but whether his guilt or innocence can be proved under a procedure which *leaves in the citizen the legal rights to which he is entitled under a constitutional government.*

"You object to spectacular, dramatic methods of defense. You overlook the fact that for the past twenty-five years you have beguiled the public into releasing its constitutional rights so that the only effective methods of defense which are left are the spectacular and the dramatic. Now then, Mr. District Attorney, you go ahead and arrest Della Street, and we'll thrash this thing out in a court-room."

Burger said, "That's right, Mason. We'll thrash it out in a court-room. And, if you ask me, your last word didn't amount to much."

Mason paused in the doorway, his face hard with anger. "I haven't had that last word yet," he said. "I'll have it in court."

And he slammed the door behind him.

21

JUDGE LANKERSHIM came to the bench amidst a swish of whispers from the crowded courtroom, which subsided as a bailiff pounded a gavel.

"The People of the State of California versus Della Street," Judge Lankershim called.

Mason got to his feet. "The defendant is in court and on bail. Let the records show that she has surrendered for the purpose of trial."

"The record will so show," Judge Lankershim said. "She will remain on the same bail during the trial. I understand this action has been brought on for immediate trial pursuant to stipulation of counsel."

"That is right," Hamilton Burger said.

"I would like to hear from the prosecution as to the nature of the case."

Burger said, "Your Honor, I will make a brief preliminary statement. It is the contention of the prosecution that while the police officers were investigating a felony, to wit, an assault with a deadly weapon with intent to commit murder, committed by persons unknown upon one Jerry Templar, the defendant in this case willfully spirited away a certain witness, one Franklin Shore, who had information which, if communicated to the police, would have materially aided the police in the solution of the crime. Specifically, it is charged that the defendant in this case, fully aware of the full significance of the facts which this witness knew, concealed him from the police and continues to so conceal him."

"And the defendant has pleaded not guilty?" Judge Lankershim asked.

"The defendant has pleaded not guilty, and asked for a trial by jury," Mason said. "And to prove our good faith in the matter, we will accept, without examination, the first twelve names which are called to the jury box as jurymen to try this cause."

Judge Lankershim looked over his glasses at Perry Mason. "You are, however, insisting upon a trial by jury?"

"Exactly," Mason said. "Trial by jury is guaranteed by the constitution to the citizens of the state. We have lost too many of our constitutional guarantees by not insisting upon them. Upon behalf of this defendant, I insist upon a jury trial more as a gesture than otherwise. I would be perfectly willing to submit the matter to Your Honor's discretion otherwise."

"Do you wish to accept Mr. Mason's stipulation that the first twelve names called to the jury box may constitute a jury, Mr. District Attorney?"

Hamilton Burger, who had personally embarked upon the trial of the case, relegating his assistants to subordinate positions at the far corners of the counsel table, got to his feet. "No, Your Honor, we will examine the jurors in the regular way."

Mason settled back in his chair. "I have no questions to ask of any juror," he announced with a smile. "I waive my challenges for cause. I waive my peremptory challenges. I am satisfied that any twelve American citizens who file into that jury box will give the defendant the benefit of a square deal when the evidence is in— and that's all the defendant wants."

"The Court will observe," Burger said acidly, "that counsel is using the excuse of waiving his rights as a peg upon which to hang a dramatic statement intended to impress the jurors in advance with . . ."

"The Court understands the situation," Judge Lankershim interrupted promptly. "The jurors will pay no attention to the extraneous comments of either counsel. Let's get on with this case. Under the circumstances, Mr. Burger, it devolves upon you to examine the jurymen on their *voir dire*."

And examine them Burger did, with the painstaking, mathematical, searching questions which a man might have expected a prosecutor to use in a murder case, while Mason tilted back in his chair, an amused smile on his face, his bearing indicating that he was paying no attention either to questions or answers. And, somehow, the more Burger examined the jurymen, the more he made it appear that he was suspicious of their probity, of their impartiality, an attitude which contrasted unfavorably with that of counsel for the defense. Twice his associates tried to warn him of this, but Burger paid no attention to their warnings. He went doggedly ahead with his questions.

When he had finished, Judge Lankershim said, "Under the law, the Court is called upon to examine the jurors for prejudice. It has never been the policy of this Court, however, to restrict the questions of counsel. Therefore, the Court has always permitted counsel to interrogate the jurors in the usual manner. But, under the circumstances of this case, the Court feels that it is incumbent upon it to see that no member of the jury is prejudiced for or against either side." Whereupon, the judge asked a few searching, but impartial questions, and said to Hamilton Burger, "The defendant has waived both challenges for cause and peremptory challenges. Do you have any challenges?"

Burger shook his head.

Mason turned to smile at the jury. Gradually it dawned on the courtroom that the ultimate effect of the entire procedure had been to accomplish what Mason had proposed in the first instance, namely, that the first twelve persons called should sit as jurors.

The jury smiled back at Mason.

Hamilton Burger made a brief statement to the jury, outlining simply what he expected to prove, followed that up by saying, "I will call as my first witness Helen Kendal."

Helen Kendal, obviously conscious of the eyes of the spectators in the crowded courtroom, came forward and was sworn. She gave her name and address to the clerk, looked at Hamilton Burger expectantly for questions.

"You have occasion to remember the thirteenth of this month?"

"I do."

"I will call your attention to the evening of that day and ask if anything unusual happened."

"Yes, sir."

"What?"

"In the first place, my kitten was seized with spasms, and I rushed it to a veterinary, who said it was . . ."

Burger held up his hand. "Never mind what the veterinary said. That's hearsay. Just state what you know of your own knowledge."

"Yes, sir."

"Now, at about the time the kitten became ill, did anything else unusual happen?"

"Yes. I received a telephone call—from my uncle."

"What?"

"I received a telephone call."

"From whom?"

"From my uncle."

"You have two uncles?"

"Yes, sir. This call came from Uncle Franklin."

"And by the words Uncle Franklin, you refer to Franklin B. Shore?"

"Yes, sir."

"When had you last seen Franklin B. Shore?"

"Some ten years ago, shortly prior to his disappearance."

"Your uncle, Franklin Shore, had disappeared mysteriously some ten years earlier?"

"Yes, sir."

Hamilton Burger said to the Court, "I am asking leading questions on some of these points which are not disputed, but which I want to get before the jury."

"No objection," Mason said.

"What did your uncle say to you over the telephone?"

"Objected to," Mason said, "as hearsay. Incompetent, irrelevant, and immaterial."

"If the Court please," Burger announced, "I am not seeking to adduce any facts which will bind the defendant as to this conversation, but only as to show the condition which existed there that night, and as to that only to the extent that it will be considered a part of the *res gestae*, explaining the moves of the various parties on that night."

"I will overrule the objection," Judge Lankershim said, "but will later limit the purposes for which the answer may be considered by the jury."

"What did your uncle say?"

"He asked me if I knew who was speaking. I told him that I didn't. He then told me his name and went on to prove his identity."

"That's a conclusion," Hamilton Burger said hastily. "That may go out. What did he say?"

"Well, he called my attention to certain things that only my uncle would have known about."

"What I am after particularly," Hamilton Burger said, "is what he told you to do."

"He told me to go to Mr. Perry Mason, the attorney, and then to go to the Castle Gate Hotel and ask for a Mr. Henry Leech, who, he said, would take us to him. He told me that I wasn't to take anyone else into my confidence; that, particularly, I wasn't to let my Aunt Matilda know anything about it."

"Your Aunt Matilda is the wife of Franklin Shore?"

"Yes."

"And later on that evening, in company with Mr. Mason, did you make any effort to get in touch with Mr. Leech?"

"Yes."

"What did you do?"

"We went to the Castle Gate Hotel. We were advised that Mr. Leech wasn't there. A note was delivered telling us where we could . . ."

"Just a moment," Hamilton Burger said. "I'll produce that note and ask you if this is the note."

"Yes."

Burger said, "I'll ask that it be received in evidence as People's Exhibit A, and I will then read it to the jury."

The document was duly stamped, and Burger read it to the jury.

"Now," he asked Helen Kendal, "what did you do with reference to that. In other words, what was your next step after you received that document?"

"We went to the place mentioned."

"There was a map with it?"

"Yes."

"I will show you this map and ask if this is the one."

"Yes, sir."

"I ask that this be received in evidence as People's Exhibit B."

"No objection," Mason said.

"So ordered," Judge Lankershim announced.

"And you went to the place indicated on that map?" Burger asked the witness.

"Yes."

"What did you find there?"

"It was up in the hills back of Hollywood. There was a reservoir. A car was parked near the reservoir. A man was sitting in the car, sort of slumped over the wheel. He was dead. He . . . he had been killed."

"That man was a stranger to you?"

"Yes."

"Who was with you at that time?"

"My uncle, Gerald Shore, Mr. Perry Mason and Miss Street."

"By Miss Street you mean Miss Della Street, the defendant in this action?"

"Yes, sir."

"And what happened next? What was done immediately after that?"

"We three remained near our car while Mr. Mason went to telephone the police."

"Then what happened?"

"The police came and asked questions and then my Uncle Gerald drove us home. After that, we went to a hospital to call on Aunt Matilda, and then Uncle Gerald drove me home again."

"By home, you mean to the Shore residence?"

"Yes, sir."

"Then what happened?"

"They let me out at the residence. The others went to . . ."

"Never mind stating where they went, because you don't know—only what they told you. But the others left, did they?"

"Yes."

"Then what happened?"

"A friend came to call on me."

"What was his name?"

"Jerry Templar."

"He was a man with whom you had been quite friendly?"

"In a way, yes."

"And who was in the house at that time?"

"Komo, the servant, was sleeping in the basement. Mrs. Parker, a cook and housekeeper, was in her room over the garage. Mr. Templar and myself were in the living room."

"What happened?"

"We heard a peculiar sound coming from my Aunt Matilda's bedroom, a sound as though something had been tipped over. Then we heard the chatter of her caged lovebirds. Then, after a moment, we heard a peculiar noise which sounded like my aunt walking."

"Is there anything peculiar about her walk?"

"Yes, sir. She drags her right foot when she walks, and uses a cane. The thump of the cane, and the peculiar dragging noise of the right foot are very distinctive."

"And this walk sounded like your aunt's walk?"

"Yes, sir."

"Then what happened?"

"I knew that my aunt wasn't in the house. I told that to Jerry. He immediately walked down the corridor and opened the door of the bedroom. Jerry had always been so big and strong that I guess I considered him invincible. I never realized the danger in which I was placing him. I . . ."

"What happened?" Burger asked.

"Someone in the room shot twice. The first bullet just missed my head. The second one . . . hit Jerry."

"What did you do after that?"

"I don't know. I dragged Jerry away from the door, and then he recovered consciousness. He was unconscious for some little time. I don't know just how long. When he opened his eyes, I told him I must get an ambulance and a doctor. He said we could get a taxicab quicker, and I telephoned for a taxicab. We rushed him to the hospital, and an hour or two later on, Dr. Everett Rosllyn operated on him."

"You remained at the hospital?"

"Yes, sir, until after the operation, and until after—after I'd seen he was going to be all right."

"Cross-examine," Burger snapped.

Mason said, "You don't know how long Jerry Templar was unconscious?"

"No. It was all a nightmare to me."

"You don't know how long it was after the shot was fired before you got to the hospital?"

"No, sir. I can't tell you the time."

"And you don't know exactly how long it was after we left you at the house that last time before the shooting took place?"

"Well . . . it might have been . . . it might have been an hour. It might not have been more than half an hour. It was perhaps somewhere between half an hour and an hour."

"You can't fix it any closer than that?"

"No."

"You were about fourteen years of age when your uncle disappeared?"

"Yes, sir."

"Can you fix exactly the time when the kitten was first taken sick—that is, with reference to the time of that telephone conversation with your Uncle Franklin?"

"It was immediately after I had hung up the telephone that I noticed the kitten was sick."

"Did *you* notice that?"

"My attention was first called to it by my aunt."

"By your aunt you mean Matilda Shore?"

"Yes, sir."

"What did you do with the kitten?"

"I took it to the veterinary."

Burger said, "Just a moment, Your Honor, one important question I forgot to ask. I would like to interrupt to get it in the record."

"No objection," Mason said affably.

"After dinner that night, did you go back to see the veterinary?"

"Yes, sir."

"And what was the condition of the kitten at that time?"

"The kitten seemed to be well, but weak."

"What did you do with him?"

"I took him with me. The veterinary suggested that . . ."

"Never mind what the veterinary suggested."

Mason said affably, "Oh, go ahead, let her tell it. I take it, Miss Kendal, the veterinary suggested that if some person were trying to poison the kitten around the house, that it would be better to take it away from the house, and so you took it down and left it with Thomas Lunk, the gardener, did you not?"

"Yes, sir."

Mason said, "That's all." And Burger nodded.

Hamilton Burger called Lieutenant Tragg to the stand. Tragg testified in the close-clipped, efficient manner of the police officer who has been on the witness stand on numerous occasions. He testified to receiving a telephone call, to going to the hills back of Hollywood, finding the body, identified the articles which were tied up in a handkerchief near the body, and testified as to the identity of the body.

Tragg then stated positively that he had advised Mr. Mason

that night, while the lawyer was at the Shore residence, that he desired the presence of Franklin B. Shore as a witness to appear before the grand jury, and that he stated to Mason the importance to the police of finding and examining Franklin Shore.

Tragg then went on to state his experiences at the Shore home later on that night when he had been summoned to investigate the shooting of Jerry Templar. He testified what he had found, calling particular attention to a writing desk on which a lock had been forced open. He identified photographs showing the condition of the bedroom when he had arrived on the scene. Burger introduced these photographs in evidence.

On cross-examination, Mason adopted a manner of good-natured affability.

"Lieutenant, referring to this handkerchief, I call your attention to a laundry mark. Have you made any effort to trace that laundry mark?"

"Well, yes."

"And you found, did you not, that it was a mark given to Franklin Shore by a laundry in Miami, Florida, and that the laundry had been out of business for some six years?"

"That is right."

"You'll remember that when you first showed me the watch up in the hills back of Hollywood, I pointed out to you that, according to the indicator, the watch must have been wound at approximately four-thirty or five o'clock the day of the murder?"

"Yes."

"Now, have you examined the fountain pen?"

"Yes."

"And what was the condition of that fountain pen?"

Tragg said, "It was dry."

"According to your observations at the scene of the shooting of Jerry Templar, the assailant had entered through a ground-floor window on the north side of the house. Is that right?"

"Yes."

"And, in entering the room, had knocked over a night stand or taboret which was by the side of Mrs. Shore's bed?"

"Yes."

"Then had picked up a cane which apparently was in the room, and had imitated the steps of Mrs. Shore?"

"I think that's a fair deduction from the evidence. Of course, I don't know that of my own knowledge."

"But you did find a cane which was lying on the floor near the corner from which the shots had been fired?"

"Yes."

"By the way, Lieutenant, you stated, I believe, that you took Thomas Lunk into custody at a downtown hotel where he was registered under the name of Thomas Trimmer?"

"Yes."

"How did you happen to go to that hotel to make the arrest?"

Tragg smiled. "I am not going to divulge that."

"It's not proper cross-examination," Hamilton Burger objected. "The witness certainly is entitled to protect the source of his information."

Mason said, "I will withdraw that question and ask this in its place. Isn't it a fact, Lieutenant, that you went to that hotel because you received an anonymous telephone tip from some person who told you where Lunk was, the name under which he was registered, and the number of his room?"

"Same objection," Burger said.

Judge Lankershim deliberated the matter thoughtfully, then asked Mason, "What is the reason for asking this question, Mr. Mason?"

"It simply goes to show the entire *res gestae*," he said. "As a matter of fact, Your Honor, it may be quite material. Suppose, for instance, that *I* had been the one who had given Lieutenant Tragg that telephone tip?"

"You don't claim that you were?" Judge Lankershim asked.

"Not at present, Your Honor. But I think it's only fair to the defendant that the witness should answer that one question."

"I'll overrule the objection," Judge Lankershim said. "I doubt that it's entirely pertinent, but I am going to give the defense the benefit of the widest latitude in cross-examination. The question doesn't call upon the lieutenant to divulge in any way the source of his information. Answer the question."

Tragg picked his words cautiously. "I received an anonymous telephone communication, giving me approximately that information."

Mason smiled. "That's all."

"I call Matilda Shore as my next witness," Burger said.

Matilda Shore, who was sitting next to the aisle, raised herself from the seat by clinging to her cane with one hand, the back of the seat in front of her with the other, and walked to the witness chair, where the clerk administered the oath. While she was walking, the jurors, as well as the spectators, had an opportunity to listen to the peculiarly distinctive sound of her steps.

When she had given her name and address, Burger lost no time in getting to the point.

"You are the wife of Franklin B. Shore?"

"I am."

"And where is Mr. Shore now?"

"I don't know."

"When did you see him last?"

"Approximately ten years ago."

"Can you give us the exact date?"

"January 23, 1932."

"And what happened on that date?"

"He disappeared. Someone was talking with him in his study, someone who wanted money. The voices were raised for a while in angry altercation. Then they quieted down. I went to bed. I never saw my husband after that. He disappeared. I knew, however, that he wasn't dead. I knew that some day he would show up . . ."

"Never mind what you felt or surmised," Burger interrupted hastily. "I just want to establish certain things to prove a possible motivation for the entering of your house by a person who was interrupted before he could achieve the purpose for which he had come. For that purpose only, I'll ask you if there were some checks which were cashed just before and after your husband's disappearance?"

"Yes."

"One of those checks was for ten thousand dollars?"

"Yes, sir."

"To whom was it payable?"

"A man named Rodney French."

"There were several other checks?"

"Yes, sir."

"Now, where were those checks when you saw them last?"

"They were in my bedroom in a pigeonhole in a desk which was pushed back against the wall."

"That was a roll-top desk?"

"Yes, sir."

"An old one?"

"Yes, sir. It had been in my husband's study. It was his desk."

"You mean he had used it continuously up to the time of his disappearance as his desk?"

"Yes, sir."

"And you were using it on the thirteenth of this month?"

"That's right."

"And these checks which I have mentioned were in there?"

"Yes, sir."

"How many of them?"

"There were about a dozen of them in an envelope, checks which had been put through the account within the last few days prior to his disappearance, or checks which had been written immediately before his disappearance and were cashed afterwards."

"Why were those checks segregated in that manner?"

"Because I thought they might prove to be evidence. I put them in an envelope and kept them in this drawer."

"When did you leave your house on the night of the thirteenth?"

"I don't know exactly what time it was. I was getting ready for bed. It was probably around ten o'clock. I followed my usual custom of drinking a bottle of stout and shortly afterwards became violently ill. Remembering that the kitten had been poisoned, I took an emetic and went at once to the hospital."

"Where were the checks which you have mentioned when you went to the hospital?"

"In that pigeonhole in the desk."

"How do you know?"

"I had been looking at them shortly before, and I hadn't left the bedroom except to go to the icebox and get a bottle of stout and a glass."

"When did you next enter your bedroom?"

"The next morning about nine o'clock when I was discharged from the hospital."

"Did anyone accompany you?"

"Yes."

"Who?"

"Lieutenant Tragg."

"At his suggestion, did you search through your room to see if anything was missing?"

"Yes."

"Did you find anything missing?"

"No."

Burger produced the watch and fountain pen which had been identified as having been found near Leech's body. Mrs. Shore stated positively they were the property of her husband, that he had had both of these objects in his possession the night he had disappeared, and that she had never seen them again until the police had shown them to her.

"Cross-examine," Burger said.

"You couldn't find that *anything* was missing from your room when you searched it after your return from the hospital?"

"No."

Mason said, "That's all."

Swiftly Hamilton Burger laid the foundations for a complete case. He called the autopsy surgeon, called Dr. Rosllyn, identified the bullets which had been taken from the wound inflicted on Jerry Templar and from the body of Henry Leech. He then recalled Lieutenant Tragg to get the bullet which had embedded itself in the woodwork of the Shore home; following which he called the expert from the criminal laboratories who introduced photographs showing the distinctive scratches made by the rifling and by pits in the barrel of the gun, showing that these bullets had all been fired from the same gun.

Judge Lankershim glanced at the clock. "You will understand," he said to Burger, "that we are not trying the murder case at this time."

"Yes, Your Honor, but we are showing the circumstances which surrounded the commission of the alleged crime in this case. We are showing the significance of what had happened and the importance of having the police unimpeded in their efforts to solve these crimes."

Judge Lankershim nodded, glanced curiously at Mason, who seemed to be taking but very little interest in the entire procedure.

"I will now call Thomas Lunk," Hamilton Burger announced with something of a flourish.

Lunk came shuffling forward. He seemed reluctant to testify, and Burger had to draw his story from him a bit at a time, frequently using leading questions, occasionally cross-examining his own witness, a procedure which Judge Lankershim allowed because of the apparent hostility of the witness.

Pieced together, Lunk's story made a convincing and dramatic climax to the case the district attorney had been building up. He told of how he had gone home from work that night, of how Helen Kendal had brought the kitten to his house where it was left for safekeeping, told of how he had listened to the radio, read a magazine, and while he was in the midst of reading this magazine, he had heard steps on the porch, knocking at the door. He had opened the door, and then drawn back in surprise as he recognized the features of his former employer.

He mentioned but briefly that they had "talked for a while" and then he had given Shore the bed in his spare bedroom. He had waited until he felt certain his visitor was asleep, then had quietly slipped out of the front door, taken a late street car, got off at a point nearest the Shore residence, and started hurriedly for the house; that the defendant had intercepted him, asked him if he wanted to see Mrs. Shore, and, on being assured that he did, had taken him in an automobile, stating that she would take him to Mrs. Shore; that thereafter she had, as he reluctantly admitted, "stalled around" until Perry Mason had appeared on the scene, whereupon they had gone to a hospital, and Mason had told him Mrs. Shore was virtually in the custody of the police; that thereafter Mason had taken him to the Maple Leaf Hotel, had secured a room for him under the name of Thomas Trimmer; that he had gone to his room. After he had started to undress, there had been a knock at the door. Police radio officers had taken him into custody. He had no idea how they had found out where he was.

"What was the condition of Mr. Shore so far as his clothing was concerned when you left the house?"

"He was in bed, if that's what you mean."

"And undressed?"

"Yes."

"And you felt that he was asleep?"

"Never mind what the witness felt," Mason said. "What did he see? What did he hear?"

"Very well," Burger conceded with poor grace, "I will reframe the question. Was there anything in his appearance which you saw or heard which indicated whether he was asleep or awake?"

"Well, he was snoring," Lunk reluctantly admitted.

"And you, at that time, were fully dressed? You hadn't been to bed?"

"No, sir."

"And you left the house?"

"Yes, sir."

"Did you try to leave quietly?"

"Well, yes, I did."

"And you walked to the car line?"

"Yes, sir."

"How far?"

"A block."

"How long did you have to wait for a car?"

"There was a car coming when I got to the corner. I hopped aboard."

"How long were you on this street car?"

"Not over ten minutes."

"And how long from the time you left the street car until the defendant in this case accosted you and picked you up?"

"Oh, not very long."

"How long?"

"I don't know."

"Was it a minute, two minutes, five minutes, or twenty minutes?"

"Oh, a minute," Lunk said.

Hamilton Burger said, "I submit, Your Honor, that it's unreasonable to suppose this man who was sleeping peacefully in this bed aroused, investigated to find that Mr. Lunk had left, dressed himself, and left the house within that short space of time. I think it is a reasonable inference for the jury to draw that Mr. Shore was in that bed in that house at the very time Miss Street picked up this witness."

"That's an argument counsel can make to the jury," Mason said. "He has no right making it now. If he wants to argue the case now, I'll say that . . ."

Judge Lankershim stopped him. "The jury will pay no attention to the arguments of counsel at the present time," he admonished the jury. "They are directed exclusively to the Court. Proceed with your examination of the witness, Mr. Burger."

"After the defendant in this case picked you up and took you in her automobile, Mr. Perry Mason joined you, did he not?"

"Yes."

"And thereafter Mr. Mason took you to this hotel?"

"Yes."

"Now was Miss Street, the defendant, with you all of that time?"

"No."

"When did she leave you?"

"I don't know."

"Do you know about what time it was?"

"No."

"Where did she leave you?"

"I don't remember."

"It was in front of a hotel, was it not?"

"I wouldn't want to say."

"But it was at some point where she took a taxicab, was it not?"

"I think there was a taxicab there."

"And afterwards Mr. Mason remained with you for some time, getting some flowers, sending them to Mrs. Shore in the hospital, going out to your house to inspect it, and then driving you to this hotel?"

The witness hesitated for several seconds, then gave a sullen, monosyllabic answer. "Yes."

Burger said, "You may cross-examine, Mr. Mason," and there was a smirk of triumph in his voice as he said it.

Mason looked at the witness. "Mr. Lunk, I want you to answer my questions frankly. Do you understand?"

"Yes."

"After Miss Street left us, we went to your house, did we not?"

"Yes."

"We arrived there about four or four-thirty in the morning?"

"I guess so, yes."

"It was cold?"

"Yes, sir."

"There was no fire going in the house?"

"No, sir."

"You lit a gas heater after we arrived?"

"That's right."

"When you first left the house, you had left the door between the *front* bedroom and the bathroom closed?"

"Yes."

"And when we arrived there, that door was open."

"Yes."

"And the contents of the dresser drawers had been dumped out and clothes taken from the closet?"

"That's right."

"Was anything missing?"

"Yes. Some money had been taken from where I'd been keeping it hid—in a pocket of my best suit."

"That suit had been left hanging in the closet?"

"Yes, sir."

"How much was missing?"

"Objected to," Burger said, "as incompetent, irrelevant, and immaterial. It's not proper cross-examination. It has nothing whatever to do with the facts of this case."

"Overruled," the Judge said. "The defendant is entitled to show the condition of the premises and anything which would reasonably make it appear the departure of Franklin Shore might have been prior to the time the prosecution claims that departure took place."

"Around three hundred dollars was missing," Lunk said.

"The door to the pantry was closed?"

"Yes, sir."

"Now, when you had been cooking, you had taken flour from a can in the pantry?"

"Yes, sir."

"And some of that flour had been spilled on the floor around the can?"

"Yes, sir."

"When we arrived, there was a kitten in the house?"

"That's right."

"This was a kitten which had previously been left with you by Helen Kendal?"

"Yes."

"And, I believe, I called your attention to the fact that the kitten had evidently run through this sprinkling of flour which surrounded the can, and then had run across the kitchen, through the door of the kitchen, and into the back bedroom?"

"That's right."

"There were tracks showing that this had happened?"

"Yes. It ain't far from the pantry to the door of the back bedroom, only three or four feet, I guess."

"And not more than four or five feet from the bedroom door to the back bed?"

"Yes."

"And by the side of that bed I called your attention to a place where the tracks showed the kitten's paws had been bunched together as though it had jumped up on the bed?"

"Yes."

"The kitten was curled up in a little ball in the center of the bed in the *front* room when we got there? Is that right?"

"That's right."

"But you remember distinctly that the pantry door was closed?"

"Yes."

"On a table in the sitting room was an ash tray, and a. visiting card bearing the name George Alber, some writing on this card, and an ash tray which held the stub of a cold cigar?"

"Yes. The cigar was left by Franklin Shore. I found the card stuck in the door when I went out."

"When you went *out*?"

"Yes."

"You didn't hear any knocking at the door or ringing of the doorbell while you were there?"

"No. That's why the card bothered me. Alber must have tried to ring the bell, and it didn't work. Sometimes it gets out of order."

The district attorney said to Mason, "May I withdraw this witness temporarily to put on two other witnesses who are anxious to get away? Then this witness can return to the stand."

Mason bowed grave assent. "No objection."

Burger called in rapid succession the taxi driver who told of taking Della Street to the neighborhood, of the length of time she was absent from his cab, and of then driving her to her apartment. Tragg, recalled to the stand, testified as to finding the kitten in Della Street's apartment, and Helen Kendal, recalled, identified the kitten as the one which had been poisoned and which she had left with Thomas Lunk on the evening of the thirteenth.

Mason apparently paid not the slightest attention to any of these other witnesses. He did not bother with interposing any objections, nor did he use his right of cross-examination.

Then Lunk was recalled for further cross-examination.

Mason studied the witness for several seconds until the silence focused the attention of everyone in the courtroom upon the importance of what he was about to say.

"When was the last time you remember opening that can of flour in the pantry?"

"The morning of the thirteenth. I made some pancakes for breakfast."

"And, since I called your attention to the rather large amount of flour which was sprinkled around the base of the can, you haven't taken the lid off the flour container?"

"No, sir. I haven't had any chance. The police took me from the hotel and have held me ever since."

"As a material witness," Hamilton Burger hastened to explain.

Lunk turned to him with some show of temper and said "I don't care *why* you did it, but you sure did it!"

Judge Lankershim said, "The witness will confine himself to answering questions."

Mason looked up at Judge Lankershim. "If Your Honor will take a recess for half an hour, I don't think it will be necessary to ask any more questions."

"Just what is the object of such a continuance?"

Mason was smiling now. "I couldn't help observing, Your Honor, that the moment I began this last phase of the cross-examination, Lieutenant Tragg rather hurriedly left the courtroom. I think that thirty minutes will give him ample opportunity to get out to the house, search the flour can, and return."

"It is your contention that the cover was removed from that flour can sometime during the evening of the thirteenth, or the morning of the fourteenth by some person other than the witness Thomas Lunk?" Judge Lankershim asked.

Mason's smile broadened. "I think, Your Honor, Lieutenant Tragg will make a very interesting discovery. Your Honor appreciates my position. I am only interested in establishing the innocence of this defendant. Therefore, I don't care to make any statement as to what may be discovered, nor as to its evidentiary value."

Judge Lankershim said, "Very well, the Court will take a thirty-minute recess."

As the people shuffled out of the courtroom to congregate in the hallways, George Alber came pushing forward, a somewhat sheepish grin on his face.

"Sorry if that card mixed things up any," he said. "As it happens, I was driving by Lunk's place after the theater. Thought I'd stop and see if a light was on. One was, so I went up and pushed the bell. No one answered, so I left the card—thought Helen might appreciate my thinking of the kitten—and I *was* a bit worried.

"To tell you the truth, it never occurred to me the bell might be out of order."

"A light was on?" Mason asked.

"Yes. I could see a light through the shades. I just didn't knock, because I thought the bell was ringing."

"What time was this?"

"Oh, right around midnight."

Mason pursed his lips, said, "You might casually mention it to the district attorney."

"I have. He says he knows the bell was out of order, so it's unimportant."

Mason said, "I guess it is, then."

22

WHEN COURT reconvened, Hamilton Burger showed very plainly that he was laboring under great excitement. "If the Court please," he said, "a very startling situation has developed in this case. I ask permission to withdraw the witness Lunk from the stand and re-call Lieutenant Tragg."

"No objection," Mason said.

"Very well," Judge Lankershim ruled. "Lieutenant Tragg will once more take the stand. You have already been sworn, Lieu-tenant."

Tragg nodded and walked to the witness stand.

Burger asked, "Have you recently made a trip to the residence of the witness Lunk?"

"Yes, sir."

"That was within the last thirty minutes?"

"Yes, sir."

"What did you do?"

"I went into the pantry and took the lid off the tin of flour."

"Then what did you do?"

"I reached down inside the flour."

"What did you find?"

Tragg couldn't keep his voice from being nervously rapid. "I found a .38 caliber, double-action Smith & Wesson revolver."

"You may tell us what you did with reference to that revolver."

"I rushed it to the criminal laboratory to see if fingerprints could be developed. I took the number and, while I have traced that number to *my* satisfaction, I haven't as yet secured the necessary witnesses to appear and testify. I think I can have a witness here by tomorrow morning."

"Cross-examine," Burger said.

Mason said urbanely, "But you have satisfied yourself, Lieutenant, as to what the sales record will show?"

"I have. We have recently compiled statistics so that the sales of any guns within the county, over a period of fifteen years, can be instantly determined—that is, so far as the police are concerned. Of course, those records aren't anything we can take to court as evidence. We will have to get the original record from the dealer who made the sale."

Mason said, "I understand, Lieutenant. But those records do give you, for police use, the information which is contained on the dealers' registers of firearm sales?"

"Yes, sir."

Mason said, "I will waive all objections as to whether this is or is not the *best* evidence, and ask you if the police records don't show this revolver was purchased by Franklin B. Shore sometime prior to January, 1932?"

Tragg's eyes showed that Mason's question caught him by surprise, but he answered after a moment, "Yes, sir. That gun, according to our records, was purchased by Franklin B. Shore in October of 1931."

"And what do you deduce from all this, Lieutenant?" Mason asked.

Judge Lankershim frowned at Mason. "That question, counselor, calls for something which could hardly be binding upon the defendant, nor, of course, would it be permissible, if asked by the prosecution."

"I understand," Mason said, "but I take it there is no objection from the prosecution."

"None whatever," Burger said, with a triumphant leer at the jury. "I would like nothing better than to have Lieutenant Tragg answer that question."

Judge Lankershim still hesitated, then said, "There is only one theory upon which this would be admissible as cross-examination, and that would be to show the bias of the witness. In view of the fact that the question *may* be permissible upon that ground, since there is no objection on the part of the prosecution, I will permit it to be answered. The Court cannot, of course, tell what counsel for the defense has in mind. But the Court does feel that, so far as the proceedings against this defendant are concerned, the constitutional guarantees must be observed. Therefore, the Court will limit the consideration which the jury may give to the answer, as relating to and showing a possible bias on the part of the witness. Under those circumstances, the witness may answer the question."

Tragg said, "There is no question in my mind but what Franklin B. Shore got up after Thomas Lunk left the house, went to the pantry and concealed this gun in the can of flour; that this kitten followed him into the pantry, jumped in the flour, and that Mr. Shore pushed the kitten out, and the kitten thereupon ran into the bedroom and jumped in the bed which Mr. Shore had just vacated. I may state further that this simply goes to indicate how vitally important a witness Franklin Shore is and was, and emphasizes the gravity of any attempt which might have been made to spirit him away."

Mason smiled. "It also indicates that Franklin Shore was, very shortly after the shooting of Jerry Templar, in possession of the revolver with which the shooting was perpetrated, and of the same revolver which, in all probability, fired the fatal bullet into the body of Henry Leech, does it not?"

Burger said, "I'm going to object to that question, Your Honor, upon the ground that it is argumentative, and not proper cross-examination."

Judge Lankershim said, "It is highly irregular. It is far afield from the ordinary course of examination. It indicates what happens when a police witness is permitted to give his opinion and deductions under the guise of evidence. However, by failing to object to that other question, the prosecution has opened the door to this entire line of cross-examination. Only, however, for the purpose of showing the bias of the witness. If this witness is once permitted to give his deductions as to what the facts indicate, counsel for the defense should be permitted to point out to the witness a possible fallacy in his reasoning. I think I see the point counsel is driving at, and I think I appreciate what his next question will be—a question which might very seriously affect the case of the prosecution. By permitting the door to be opened at all, the district attorney has given counsel an opportunity to open it all the way. I am going to let the witness answer this question as well as the question which I feel certain will follow."

Tragg said cautiously, "I don't know that it's the same gun with which the crimes were committed. It is a gun of the same caliber and the same description. There were three discharged shells in the cylinder of that gun, and the remaining three cylinders were loaded with shells and bullets of the same general character as those recovered from the body of Henry Leech, from the woodwork at the Shore house, and from Jerry Templar at the time he was operated on."

Mason looked at Hamilton Burger and winked. He turned to

the jury and smiled triumphantly. "And now, Lieutenant," he said to the witness, "I will ask you if it isn't equally fair to assume, if this weapon *should* prove to be the murder weapon, that Franklin Shore, having concealed that weapon in the residence of Thomas Lunk, *would then have been most anxious to make his escape?*"

"Objected to," Hamilton Burger shouted, "upon the ground that this is taking the witness far afield into the realm of conjecture. That is a matter which counsel can argue to the jury. It is not a question to be asked of this witness."

Judge Lankershim said, "It is precisely the question which I *thought* counsel would ask next. The objection is overruled. The witness will answer it—but remember, the answer is admissible only to show possible bias."

Tragg said, "I don't know. It is, of course, a possibility."

Judge Lankershim turned to the jury. "The jurors will understand that these last few questions have been permitted only for the purpose of showing the attitude of the witness. In other words, the possible bias of the witness, meaning by that any prejudice which he might entertain against the defendant. The questions and answers can have no evidentiary value except for that single purpose. You will consider them only for that purpose."

Mason settled back in his chair and said to Lieutenant Tragg, "Now when you found that gun in the flour, Lieutenant, you were somewhat excited, were you not?"

"Not exactly."

"You were in a hurry to get back to court and hand that gun to the police laboratory?"

"Yes."

"In so much of a hurry," Mason said, "that I take it you didn't search the can of flour to see what else it might have contained."

The expression of sudden consternation upon Tragg's face foreshadowed his answer. "I . . . I didn't make any further search of the can. But I did bring that can along with me and give it to the police laboratory to search for fingerprints."

Mason glanced at Judge Lankershim and said, "I submit, Your Honor, that the case having gone this far, the witness should be permitted to . . ."

There was a commotion in the back of the courtroom. The dour Scotchman who presided over the criminal laboratory of the police came pushing his way through the spectators who had gathered around the door.

Mason said, "However, Your Honor, I think that Angus MacIntosh is about to supply that information. We are perfectly willing to let Lieutenant Tragg step down and Mr. MacIntosh, who has already been sworn as a witness, take the stand."

Hamilton Burger said, cautiously, "I don't know what counsel is getting at. If the Court will pardon me a moment, I would like to talk with Mr. MacIntosh."

Burger arose hastily and stepped over to the rail which separated the counsel table from the spectators. He engaged in a whispered conference with Angus MacIntosh, then looked at Perry Mason with a puzzled frown, following which he said abruptly to Judge Lankershim, "If the Court please, we would like to have a recess until tomorrow morning."

"Any objection?" Judge Lankershim asked Perry Mason.

"Yes, Your Honor. If the district attorney won't put Angus MacIntosh on the stand, I want to call him as a witness for the defense."

Hamilton Burger said testily, "The prosecution has not yet concluded its evidence. The defense will have ample opportunity to call its own witnesses when the prosecution rests."

Judge Lankershim said acidly, "The request for a continuance is denied. Proceed with your cross-examination of Lieutenant Tragg, Mr. Mason."

Mason said, "I have no further questions, Your Honor. Nor have I any further questions of the witness Lunk whose cross-examination was interrupted to permit Lieutenant Tragg to be once more placed on the witness stand."

Hamilton Burger said quickly, "Under those circumstances, I have some more questions to ask the witness Lunk on redirect examination."

Judge Lankershim's voice showed his impatience. "Very well. You may stand down, Lieutenant, and the witness Lunk will again take the stand. But, kindly don't waste time, Mr. District Attorney."

When Lunk had once more resumed his position in the witness chair, Hamilton Burger said, "Mr. Lunk, did you at any time after the morning of the thirteenth open that can of flour in your pantry?"

"Objected to as already asked and answered," Mason said.

"It *has* been asked and answered, but under the circumstances, I will permit it to be asked again," Judge Lankershim said. "The witness will answer the question."

Lunk said, "No. After I made the pancakes on the morning of the thirteenth, I didn't take the lid off the flour can again."

"Did you use that flour can for any other purpose than storing flour—in other words, did you keep or did you put anything other than flour in that can at any time?"

"No, sir."

Burger hesitated, then said, "That is all."

"No questions," Mason said.

Judge Lankershim looked at the clock, then at the district attorney. "Call your next witness."

Hamilton Burger said, with somewhat poor grace, "Angus MacIntosh will take the stand. Mr. MacIntosh has already been sworn and has testified to his position in the police laboratories."

MacIntosh returned to the witness stand.

"You were given a can of flour a few minutes ago by Lieutenant Tragg?" Hamilton Burger asked.

"Yes, sir."

"What did you do with that can of flour?"

"I wanted to photograph the can and develop latent finger-prints on it, so I dumped out the flour."

"What did you find?" Burger asked.

"I found currency in bills of fifty and one hundred dollars, making a total of $23,555."

There was a stir of excitement in the jury box.

"Where are those bills now?"

"In the police laboratory."

"Cross-examine," Hamilton Burger snapped.

"No questions," Mason retorted promptly, and then smiling at the judge, said, "And now, Your Honor, the defense has no objection whatever to consenting to the continuance which the prosecution has requested."

"The prosecution doesn't want it now," Burger said shortly. "The prosecution rests."

"The defense rests," Mason said promptly. "It is four-thirty. I will stipulate that, so far as the defense is concerned, arguments on each side may be limited to ten minutes."

"I'm not prepared to argue the case at this time, or in that short a time," Hamilton Burger said. "The recent startling developments have been such that I would like more time to correlate the various matters which have been discovered."

"Then why," Judge Lankershim asked, "did you object to an adjournment when the defense suggested it?"

Burger said nothing.

"Apparently," Judge Lankershim went on, "you wanted to see what the evidence of the defense would be. Counsel consented to a continuance, and you rejected it."

"But, Your Honor," Hamilton Burger protested, "I felt that I was in a position to go ahead with the case so far as the cross-examination of the defendant's witnesses were concerned, but that I was not prepared to argue the case."

Judge Lankershim shook his head. "Court will adjourn at five o'clock. You may proceed with your argument. The Court will limit the argument to twenty minutes to each side."

Hamilton Burger accepted the ruling of the Court, marched up to a position in front of the jurors and said, "In view of the limitation which has been placed on the argument, and the unexpected developments in this case, I am not prepared to make an extensive opening argument. I will conserve my time so as to make a longer closing argument. I will state, however, that the circumstantial evidence shows conclusively the defendant in this case and her employer, Perry Mason, were engaged in activities which included spiriting away material witnesses. What was done with the witness Lunk is virtually uncontradicted. The defendant is not on trial for that, but her willingness to spirit away a witness is shown by the manner in which she and her employer got the witness Lunk away from the police and endeavored to keep him in concealment.

"We are asking for a conviction of the defendant upon the evidence as it now stands. Regardless of what Franklin Shore may have done, I don't think any person on this jury doubts that Della Street's purpose in going to the residence of Thomas Lunk in the small hours of the morning of the fourteenth was to spirit Franklin Shore away. The Court will instruct you that it is not necessary that the attempt be successful in order to constitute a crime under sections 136 and 136½ of our Penal Code. The spiriting away of a witness, *with the intent of preventing him from testifying at a proper legal proceeding or an investigation, constitutes a crime.*

"That, ladies and gentlemen, is the contention of the prosecution. If the defendant wishes to adopt the position that Franklin

Shore had already left the premises before Della Street's arrival, it is incumbent upon the defense to assume the burden of proving that fact.

"I will not consume any more time now, but will reserve such time as I have left for my closing argument."

Burger, glancing triumphantly at the clock, and realizing that he had jockeyed Perry Mason into the position of completing his opening argument prior to the evening adjournment, leaving the prosecution in the advantageous position of being able to sleep over the developments, before making its closing argument, marched back to his chair and sat down.

Mason slowly got to his feet, walked deliberately over to the jury box and smiled at the puzzled jurors.

He opened quietly. "The prosecution can't shift the burden of proof to the defendant until it has first proven the defendant guilty beyond all reasonable doubt.

"I submit to you, ladies and gentlemen, that Franklin Shore was not present at Lunk's residence when Della Street arrived there. The reason I have introduced no testimony is that the evidence of the prosecution proves my point conclusively.

"I will not comment on the evidence of the flour. I will comment only on the actions of the kitten. Someone opened the flour can. Some object was placed in that can, perhaps the gun, perhaps the currency, perhaps both. The kitten, a playful, careless, fearless animal, attracted by the motion of the hands over the can of flour, jumped into the flour can and was promptly tossed out. The kitten thereupon ran through the partially opened door, into the back bedroom and jumped upon the bed.

"It must be perfectly obvious that the bed was then vacant, equally obvious that the kitten forthwith jumped down on the other side of the bed and went directly through the bathroom to jump on the bed in the front bedroom.

"Ladies and gentlemen, I will ask the prosecution, since this is a case of circumstantial evidence, to explain one thing to you—and preparatory to that, let me remind you that inasmuch as this is a case of circumstantial evidence, the law is that you must acquit the defendant unless the evidence not only indicates beyond all reasonable doubt the guilt of the defendant, but cannot be explained upon any *reasonable* hypothesis other than that of her guilt. Therefore, ladies and gentlemen, *why* did the kitten, after getting in the flour and after jumping on the bed of Franklin B. Shore, leave that bed to go into the front bedroom and curl up on the bed in there?

"Having relied upon circumstantial evidence, it is up to the district attorney to explain every bit of it. Therefore, in the morning, let the district attorney answer that interesting question as to the conduct of the kitten. And some of you, who are quite probably familiar with cats, their psychology, their habits, will doubtless have an answer of your own.

"And that, ladies and gentlemen, concludes my argument."

Several of the jurors looked puzzled, but two of the feminine members were nodding and smiling as though they had already grasped the point which was causing Hamilton Burger to scowl blackly.

Judge Lankershim himself seemed also to have some knowledge of kittens, for there was a smile playing about the corners of his lips, and a twinkle in his eyes as he admonished the jurors not to form any opinion as to the merits of the case, not to discuss it among themselves, or permit it to be discussed in their presence, and adjourned court until the next day at ten o'clock, remarking that the defendant was on bail and would be released upon that same bail until the next morning at ten o'clock.

23

As soon as court had adjourned and the Judge had left the bench, Hamilton Burger came pushing his way across to Mason.

"Mason, what the devil does this mean?"

Mason smiled affably. "I'm sure I couldn't say, Burger. All *I'm* doing is defending Miss Street against a criminal charge. I don't think the jury will convict her, do you?"

Burger said, "To hell with that. We all have a duty to perform—apprehending a murderer. Did Franklin Shore do it?"

"I'm sure I couldn't tell you."

Lunk came through the rail which separated the counsel tables from the spectators. "I want to talk with the district attorney."

"What is it?" Burger asked, turning to him.

Lunk said, "Franklin Shore may have put that gun in the flour, but I don't think he did. And I know darn well he didn't put the money in there."

"How do you know that?" Mason asked.

"Because Shore was trying to get me to give him some money," Lunk said.

"You didn't do it?"

"No."

"Why?" Mason asked.

228

"Because I wanted him to stay where he was until I'd had a chance to talk with Mrs. Shore."

"And why was he so anxious to get money and get away?" Mason asked. "Come on, Lunk. You told me that you might let me know what it was Shore really told you. Now, you've done a lot of covering up. Suppose you come clean now."

"I reckon I better," Lunk said. "Shore came to the house. He was nervous. He said that he'd had some trouble with a man and had shot him. He said he had to get away quick, that he'd had to shoot to keep the other guy from shooting him, but he was afraid the police might think it was murder. He said Matilda wouldn't like anything better than to get him in a spot. I told him I thought he'd better talk with her anyway before he left, and he didn't want to, so I told him that he could hide at my place, but that as soon as I could get in touch with Mrs. Shore the next morning, I'd try and get an advance on my salary and give him a stake so he could get out. After I told him that, he went to bed and to sleep. That's when I went out to see Mrs. Shore. I wanted to tell her I'd seen her husband. I wanted to see whether she wanted to stake him or whether she didn't."

"If she hadn't," Mason asked, "would you have surrendered Shore to the police?"

"I don't know, Mr. Mason. Shore had used me pretty square. Understand, I didn't intend to tell Mrs. Shore that he was staying at my house. I was going to tell her that I'd seen him. I was trying to give them both a square deal."

Mason said, "Go ahead, Lunk, tell the district attorney the whole truth. You've got to do it now. Tell him what Shore told you about where he'd been."

"He didn't . . . we didn't talk much."

"At least as long as it took him to smoke a cigar," Mason said. "Tell Mr. Burger what he said."

Lunk hesitated, then blurted, "Well, he ran away with that woman."

"Where and why?" Mason asked.

"It was like I told you," Lunk said. "When Franklin Shore was down in Florida people began to mistake him for another man. Shore looked this man up. They might have been twins. So they had a joke and had their pictures taken, and Shore started joshing his wife that he was going to tell this man all about the people he knew and have the guy be at the bridge parties as his stooge.

"Then Shore fell in love with this younger woman, so he got the idea that he maybe could disappear, take this dame with him, and go to Florida, and start training this other guy to be his double, telling him all about his business affairs and the people he was dealing with.

"Then after six months, when this man had everything all down pat, he would show up and claim he was Shore. He'd say his mind had suddenly gone blank, and even after his memory got back he was still shaky.

"Well, Shore did it. Things went fine. Inside of six months his double was all ready, so Shore sent a postal card to his niece from Miami. He figured police would come and find this double, apparently still in sort of a daze, but claiming to be Shore. And his memory would come back a little at a time. Of course, he'd be too sick to be very active in business, but he'd draw plenty of dough from his investments and he'd send the real Shore a cut out of it, and Franklin Shore would take the other guy's name, and marry this dame and it would be okay. Then the night Franklin Shore sent the postal, this guy was killed in an auto accident. Well, there was Shore with his bridges all burned up, holding the sack."

"How about Leech?" Mason asked.

"Leech had got the boss sold on his mine. So the boss had given Leech some dough in cash to put in the mine, saying it wasn't from

him, but from a guy in Florida—and Leech, thinking the Florida
guy was a sucker, froze him out when he struck it rich. . . . Of
course, the boss guy's name, and marry this dame and it would be
okay. Then the night Franklin Shore sent the postal, this guy was
killed in an auto accident. Well, there was Shore with his bridges
all burned up, holding the sack."

"How about Leech?" Mason asked.

"Leech had got the boss sold on his mine. So the boss had given
Leech some dough in cash to put in the mine, saying it wasn't from
him, but from a guy in Florida—and Leech, thinking the Florida
guy was a sucker, froze him out when he struck it rich. . . . Of
course, the boss was the real Florida guy. He'd just given Leech a
phoney name.

"Lately Shore got to needing money. He went to Leech. Leech
was to have given him the dough, but he was stony broke by this
time. . . . So Shore had to come back. The dame left him a couple of
years ago and Shore was flat broke. And that's everything I know
about it. That's the whole story the way the boss gave it to me there
in the shack."

Hamilton Burger said, "The thing's incredible! That's the
damnedest story I ever heard."

Lunk said in the flat, emotionless voice of a man who isn't trying to convince anyone, "It sounded all right to me. Maybe hearing
it from the boss's own lips made it seem more convincin', but that's
the story he told me."

Mason said to the district attorney, "Suppose it's all true—up
to the point where the auto accident took place, Burger. Then suppose it was Shore who was killed. This double had been training
to take Shore's place. He knew intimate things that Shore had told
him, and he'd written them down and memorized them. A fortune
was waiting for him if he could impersonate Franklin Shore and
make it stick."

"Then why didn't he show up sooner?" Burger asked.

"One possible explanation is that Mrs. Shore knew about this double her husband had dug up," Mason replied. "Remember, Shore had started it as a joke, and his wife knew all about it. But if Mrs. Shore should die, then the double could show up as the missing husband and claim the whole estate."

Burger gave a low whistle—then said, "Damn," explosively. "And *that* would explain the poison."

Mason lit a cigarette.

Lunk said, "This wasn't no double that came to my place. It was the boss."

"How do you know?" Mason asked.

"Because he told me some things only the boss knew."

Mason smiled at Hamilton Burger.

Lunk frowned, then said suddenly, "Well, no matter *who* this was, he was broke. Why should he steal the few hundred I kept hid in my clothes and then leave a fortune in my flour can?"

Burger looked at Mason for an answer.

"No comment," Mason said, smiling.

"Do *you* think the man who called on Lunk was the double, or Shore himself?" Burger asked Mason.

Mason said, "I don't know, Burger. I didn't see him. After all, you know you've said you'd prefer I minded my own business and let the police solve their murders. Suppose *you* wrestle with that problem?"

"Damn it, it *could* have been either one!" Burger exclaimed.

Mason seemed completely disinterested. "Well, I think my clients are in the clear, both Della Street and Gerald Shore."

Hamilton Burger's voice showed exasperation. "This is the *damnedest* case!"

Mason stretched and yawned. "I don't find it so," he said. "However, *I'm* not interested in anything except getting Miss Street acquitted."

"What the devil is that business about cat psychology you're talking about, and what does *it* have to do with the case?" Burger asked.

Mason said, "I'm afraid if I told you, Burger, you'd accuse me of trying to outwit the police. I've been thinking over what you said to me there in your office. I think there's a great deal to be said in favor of your position. You think an attorney has no business going out trying to solve murders, that he should confine himself to handling his own law practice, and I'm forced to agree with you. I'm representing Gerald Shore, and I'm representing Della Street. I have no interest in solving murders as such."

"But you want to get Gerald Shore entirely out in the clear, don't you?"

"Yes."

"There's no better way to do it than by showing us who committed the murders."

"No," Mason said, "that isn't the law. It's what you were objecting to about my methods, Burger. You see, it's up to you to prove that my clients committed some crime. As long as I confine myself to representing those clients, I'm practicing law in a staid, conventional manner. The minute I go out and try to 'outwit the police,' as you called it, I'm guilty of that unconventional conduct which has proven so irritating to you. In fact, Mr. District Attorney, I've decided to let you solve your own mysteries—and that's the last word I was telling you I was going to have.

"Come on, Della. Let's leave Lieutenant Tragg and the district attorney to work out their little picture puzzle. After all, it's no skin off our noses."

Burger said, "Look here, Mason, you can't do that! I'm satisfied you know a lot more about this case than we do."

"No, I don't," Mason said. "You have every essential fact that I have."

"Well, perhaps you've applied the knowledge we all have to better advantage."

Mason bowed. "Thank you, counselor."

"All right, you owe it to us to tell us what conclusion you've reached."

Mason said, "I'll tell you what I'll do, Burger. I'll put you on an equal footing with me. There's one thing I know that you don't. Lunk told me that he was satisfied Komo, the houseboy, had been experimenting with poison, that he'd first started experimenting about ten years ago, that shortly before Franklin Shore's disappearance, Lunk's brother died, and Lunk has always been under the impression the houseboy poisoned him."

"Is that right?" Burger asked Lunk.

Lunk said, "That's right. I don't think that damn Jap had anything against my brother in particular, but I think he was experimenting with poison—just the way he started experimenting on the kitten."

Lieutenant Tragg, who had just come up to join the group, said, "There were four bottles of stout in the icebox. Every one of them had been loaded with strychnine. Do you think the houseboy did that?"

"I know damn well he did it," Lunk said vehemently.

"How do you know?"

"Well, just from putting two and two together, the same as you know anything."

Burger said to Tragg, "There's some new and startling evidence here, Lieutenant. I want to talk with you."

Mason smiled and said, "What Lunk means, Lieutenant, is that he feels very positively Komo is the poisoner. You'll remember, Lieutenant, that you told me you thought the evidence would show the bullets had all been fired from the same gun, and that would mean that one person had been guilty of both crimes. Now, follow that reasoning out. Matilda Shore has a perfect alibi. She was in the hospital when the second crime was committed. Gerald Shore has an alibi. You probably know what it is, but I'm not going to stick my neck out by telling you that because I don't want to be a witness. And you can eliminate Helen Kendal and Jerry Templar. You can eliminate darn near everyone under that theory except three or four people. There you are, Lieutenant. Pay your money and take your choice. But if I were you, I really *would* investigate the death of Lunk's brother, and see if it isn't possible that the death was due to poison rather than natural causes.

"And now if you gentlemen will excuse me, I have a dinner date with the defendant."

24

THE DANCE orchestra was perfect. The lights were dim and on the floor only a few couples were dancing so that they were neither crowded nor conspicuous.

Without either having spoken for a long time, Perry Mason and Della Street were drifting through the strains of an Island song. As the orchestra swung into the chorus, Della Street began to sing the words very softly. Suddenly she stopped with an involuntary choke.

"S'matter? Swallow a fly?" he demanded. "Go on, do some more. I like it."

She shook her head.

"Something wrong?" he asked more seriously.

"No. I guess not. I've eaten, I've drunken, I've been merry, so I guess I'm all set for tomorrow."

The music stopped at that moment. Mason, with his arm still around her waist, swung her away so that he could look at her. His eyes were puzzled for an instant. Then they cleared. "I didn't get you. I see—tomorrow you die. Have you been worrying about that damn silly case?"

She laughed nervously. "Well—I suppose every nice girl has to go through this sort of thing sooner or later."

"But you haven't committed any crime."

236

"I wish you'd remember to tell Hamilton Burger when you see him. It seems ridiculous not to clear up this little misunderstanding, when all you have to do is say, 'Listen, Ham, old fellow, this little girl is . . .' Oh, hell's bells, let's sit down."

Perry followed her to their table.

"I thought *you* were worried," Della went on, "when you brought the kitten out to me and found that Franklin Shore wasn't there."

"I was," Mason admitted. "If I'd used my head, though, I needn't have been."

"I don't get it," she said, lighting a cigarette.

"You should—if you know kittens."

"You mean the kitten jumping in the flour?"

"No, not that . . . What is it?" he asked, noticing that she was staring over his shoulder.

"Paul Drake."

"How did he find us here?" Mason asked, frowning.

Drake was close enough to hear Mason's remark. He pulled out a chair and sat down.

"As you well know, I can find anybody, any time, any place. Here's my card. Aren't you going to order me a drink?"

"Cops and private dicks shouldn't drink when they're on duty."

"Paul Drake, the fellow I work for, is broad-minded. He's a swell guy. He's a prince. You ought to meet him."

Mason summoned a waiter. "Three Scotch and sodas."

"Five Scotches," Drake corrected. "But only three of 'em in my glass. I never could stand strong highballs."

The waiter hesitated, then deftly withdrew.

"You know, Perry, I didn't just drop in here to buy you and Della Scotch and sodas. There's something worrying me."

"Have *you* been arrested, too?" Della cried.

Paul Drake ignored her comment to look steadily at the lawyer. "Perry," he said, "you weren't by any chance planning some especially dramatic blowoff for tomorrow, were you—using your friend, Tom Lunk?"

"Perhaps. Why?"

"You're not going to do it now," Drake said.

"Why not?"

"Lunk's dead, found at a road intersection a couple of blocks from his house, a hit-and-run car. A witness saw it happen and chased the car for half a dozen blocks, but couldn't even get close enough to see the license number. The car swung around the corner just after Lunk got off the street car he rides home on."

Mason drummed on the tablecloth with his fingers. "Burger was a damn fool to release him," he said.

"Apparently, he thought Lunk had told 'em everything he knew and there was no reason for holding him any longer."

Mason frowned.

"What were you intending to spring on Lunk?" Della asked.

"Quite a few things. Has it ever seemed curious to you, Della, that after I had taken all the precautions to get Lunk registered in a hotel under the name of Thomas Trimmer, the police should have picked him up so easily?"

"Someone must have followed you," Drake said.

Mason shook his head. "Don't kid yourself, Paul. When I don't want to be followed, no one follows me."

"Then who tipped them off? It couldn't have been the hotel clerk."

"No," Mason said. "And you can follow that process of elimination right on through. There's only one person who could have done it."

"Who?"

"Lunk."

Drake looked incredulous. "You mean that he telephoned the police himself?"

"Yes."

"But that was a goofy, crazy thing to do. Why would he do anything like that?"

Mason said, "That fact gives you the key to the whole business."

"But why?" Della Street asked.

Mason said, "There's only one reason I can think of."

"What's that?"

"He wanted to be arrested," Mason said dryly.

"You mean that he felt he was in danger?"

Mason shrugged his shoulders.

The waiter brought the drinks. Drake raised his glass to Della. "Here's to jail," he grinned. "Well, Perry, what do you do now?"

Mason said, "Nothing, absolutely nothing. Hamilton Burger is going to have to crack this nut by himself. That jury will never convict Della—not as long as there are two women on it who know something about cats."

Della Street put her glass down firmly. "If you don't explain what you mean by that, I will be convicted of a crime, and it will be murder."

"No prosecutor in this state would charge you with murder for killing Perry Mason," Drake pointed out. "You'd get a reward! But what *did* the kitten do that's so significant?"

Mason grinned. "It was a cold night," he said. "The kitten jumped into the flour when someone was hiding the gun in the can. Naturally, the kitten got thrown out, probably with a cuff on the ear. Now, that kitten had had a lot of kind treatment and didn't like the rough stuff. It ran out of the kitchen and into the back bedroom, and jumped up on the bed. It didn't stay there, though. It jumped off that bed and went to the other bed."

"Why?" Drake asked.

Della Street gave a sudden, quick gasp. "Oh," she cried, "*I* know why! Anyone would, if he stopped to think about it."

Drake shook his head and got up.

"Where are you going, Paul?" Della demanded.

"I'm going out to buy a cat so I can study him and learn about some of the important facts of life."

"You would, at that, you know," Mason told him seriously.

"Good night," Drake muttered lugubriously.

With Paul Drake gone, Mason turned to Della. "You know, Della, this has been more of a strain on you than I realized. As soon as the jury brings in its verdict tomorrow, what do you say we take a run out to the desert—around Palm Springs or Indio. We'll do some horseback riding, lie in the sun—"

"Perry, I may be convicted tomorrow."

Mason grinned. "You forget those two women on the jury who know cats."

"Aren't you going to explain any more to the jury?"

"Not a bit."

"Why?"

"Because if I did, I'd be explaining to Hamilton Burger. I'm going to let him fry in his own grease."

"What will Lieutenant Tragg do?"

"Eventually," Mason said, "Lieutenant Tragg will solve the case."

"But won't it take the jury a long while to get the whole idea through its head?"

Mason said, "Now that's something that would be a sporting bet. I'll bet you five dollars that jury will be out for at least three hours. It'll come in with a verdict of not guilty, but it'll be a dazed sort of jury, with two triumphant women smiling at you, and the men scowling. Then we'll start out for the desert, and Hamilton Burger will start talking with the jurors, trying to find out what it was about the kitten that broke the case. Then he'll try to get in touch with me, and we'll be out in the desert somewhere. Let's forget it and dance."

25

THE BIG car purred smoothly out through the velvety darkness. As only in the desert, the stars, stretching in a vast, arching sweep, were no less brilliant over the clear horizon than they were directly overhead.

Mason said abruptly, "Let's pull off to the side of the road and soak it up, Della. It's an incomprehensible spectacle—makes you forget this strange human biped who commits murder."

They came to a wide place in the road. Mason pulled off, switched off his ignition, cut off the headlights, settled down into the cushions.

"I love the desert," Mason said after a little while.

Della Street snuggled close. "We supposed to be working on this trip?" she asked.

"Uh huh. I've brought that brief along with me. We won't go back to the office until we've finished it."

She said, "Well, I owe you five dollars. It took that jury three hours and ten minutes to the dot. Chief, *I* know about the kitten, but what else happened?"

Mason said, "The kitten jumped up on the bed which was supposed to have been occupied by Franklin Shore; then it jumped down and went into the other bedroom and curled up in the middle of the bed which was supposed *not* to have been occupied by Tom Lunk. The kitten proves Lunk was a liar. The bed in the back bedroom hadn't been slept in, and was cold. The bed in the front bedroom had been occupied and was warm.

"I don't know whether you've ever thought about it, Della, but if a man has some hiding place which he thinks is safe, he naturally hides everything there. For some time Lunk had been putting the money he'd collected for playing his part in the game into the flour can—a typical hiding place for a crusty old bachelor. Then when he had to hide the gun quickly, he naturally hid it in the same place."

"Why did he have to hide the gun?"

"Because, dope, after he got to bed, Mrs. Shore telephoned him from the hospital and told him to rush out to the house, crawl in through the window, and get the gun out of the desk. She suddenly realized police were going to search the place. It's a wonder they hadn't found it when they made the first search, but at that time Tragg was concentrating on the medicine cabinet and looking for poison."

"I wish you'd tell me the whole story."

Mason said, "Somebody poisoned the kitten. It was an inside job. The kitten hadn't been out of the house. Komo *might* have done it, but he had no motive. The reason suggested by Lunk that he was trying out the poison was cockeyed because the kitten had been given such a large dose.

"You can figure out what happened. Mrs. Shore had a telephone call in the afternoon. After that call, she decided the time had come to commit the murder she'd planned so long and so carefully. She was tired of paying blackmail. She had to get Helen out of the house for some length of time, so Helen wouldn't know she was away from home. She knew that if she could poison the cat, Helen would dash madly to a veterinary hospital. Gerald came in unexpectedly, but he went along with Helen, of course. Then she sent Komo out to get some stout. With the coast clear, she took Franklin Shore's old gun, got into the car, and went up to the reservoir above Hollywood where Leech was waiting by appointment to collect another installment of blackmail. She paid the last installment with a .38 caliber bullet, came back, put the gun in the desk. She realized that suspicion *might* attach itself to her, so she poisoned the stout in the icebox, pretended she had symptoms of poisoning, and was rushed to a hospital. That helped direct suspicion even more toward Franklin Shore. It didn't occur to her until after Tragg showed up that police would make a thorough search of the house. She realized then they'd find the gun. Police had her sewed up in the hospital, so she rushed through a telephone call to Lunk, and told him to go out and get the gun.

"Lunk was her accomplice. She'd groomed and trained him carefully in the details of what he had to do. All she had to do that afternoon was call him up after she heard from Leech and tell him to go ahead."

Della objected, "But I thought Franklin Shore hadn't told Matilda or anyone about Helen's getting tight on the punch or rescuing the—"

Mason laughed. "Lunk, pretending to be Franklin Shore on the telephone, told Helen he hadn't said anything to Matilda."

Della said, "Well, I'll be— So Lunk came up to the house to get the gun—and shot to keep from being caught doing it."

"Yes. He crawled through the window, upset a night stand, and thinking fast—no fool, Lunk—tried to cover up by making sounds as though Mrs. Shore were walking across the room. He hobbled over to the desk, got the gun, and was just getting over toward the window when Jerry Templar opened the door and started to turn on the light. He fired a couple of shots, dropped to the ground, and then beat it back to his shack, probably in his car.

"Lunk was lying about not having gone to bed. He had been in bed when Matilda telephoned. When he went back to the shack, he hid the gun in the flour. Then he turned down the bed in the back bedroom, lay in it long enough to wrinkle the sheets, planted the cigar butt, then dumped the things out of the bureau drawer, and out of the closet. He took a street car to go back to the Shore house, hoping the police would pick him up and question him. Reluctantly he'd tell the story Matilda had cooked up about Franklin Shore turning up at his shack. The police would high tail it over there, and find all the planted evidence that Shore *had* been there but flown the coop after robbing Lunk. Of course, Lunk never expected they'd search the flour can. That was his own, particular secret hiding place . . . and they wouldn't have searched it either if it hadn't been for me."

"How do you *know* all this?" she asked.

"The kitten's actions show conclusively that the bed in the front room was warm. The one in the back room wasn't. That is the key clue to the whole business. Lunk got up out of bed. The bed was warm. The kitten climbed in that bed. Lunk came back to hide the gun and the kitten got in the flour, was chased out, went to the bed in the back bedroom, jumped up on it, found it was cold, remembered the warm bed in the front room where it had previously been lying, and went back there to crawl up and go to sleep. Lunk went out with his carefully prepared story for the police, expecting to run into them at the Shore residence. You picked him up instead. He wasn't particularly anxious to tell his story to us because he wanted to tell it to the police; yet he had to *pretend* that he didn't want to have anything to do with the police. He was afraid I wouldn't pass it on to the police fast enough, so the minute he was free to do so, he gave an anonymous tip to Lieutenant Tragg over the telephone which resulted in his being picked up.

"Matilda had it planned out to kill a lot of birds with that one .38 slug by making it appear her husband was still alive and had done the job. Incidentally, his being alive—and of course the police would never be able to find him—would keep Gerald Shore and Helen from probating the estate, keep Helen from becoming financially independent, and save forty thousand dollars in legacies."

"But why did she have Lunk telephone *Helen?*"

"Don't you see? That's the significant part of the whole business. Helen was the only one who really couldn't have recognized Franklin Shore's voice. She was only fourteen when he left. There's a great difference between fourteen and twenty-four. Lunk could deceive her, where his voice probably would not have deceived Gerald."

"What about Franklin's personal belongings in the car beside Leech?"

"Matilda got out some of her husband's old things and wrapped them up in one of his handkerchiefs and took them out with her. The laundry mark was a giveaway. Franklin Shore *wouldn't have carried the same handkerchief for ten years.* The fact that the watch was wound up at around four-thirty shows that that was when Matilda got things ready to go out on her little hunting trip. People don't wind watches at four in the afternoon. It's so plain it stands out like a sore thumb.

"You know, Della, she might have got away with it if it hadn't been for Amber Eyes. It was shrewdly worked out. She did one stupid thing, though."

"What?"

"That note, supposedly from Leech, directing us out to the reservoir that she mailed on the way back from the murder. She wrote it as a Jap would, trying to pull Komo in as a red herring to confuse the trail. That wasn't very smart."

"But why was Leech blackmailing her?"

"He found out the truth."

"What truth?"

"Remember the body that was found at about the time Franklin Shore disappeared—the unidentified body?"

"You mean that was Franklin Shore? Why, Chief, that's impossible. That . . ."

"No, it wasn't Franklin Shore. It was Phil Lunk."

"Phil Lunk?" Della gasped.

"You see, Matilda Shore didn't love her husband. What's more he was about to ruin the man she did love. If Matilda could get Franklin out of the way, she would inherit his fortune and be in a position to indulge her lust for power; she could save Stephen Alber financially, and, later on, marry him. Our friend Lunk was her man Friday from the beginning. His brother was dying. They knew that his death was only a matter of days—perhaps hours. Matilda laid her plans with that in mind. When he died, the doctor who had been in attendance came in response to Tom Lunk's call, and quite properly filled out a death certificate. But the body the undertaker picked up was that of Franklin Shore who had previously been given a dose of quick-acting poison. His body was waiting—probably outside in Lunk's car, all ready for a quick switch. After disposing of his brother's body, Lunk whisked Shore's body off to the East to bury in place of his brother, and later lied about the time he'd left, saying it was *before* Shore's disappearance."

"But he had a mother in the East. Wouldn't she have known it wasn't the brother Phil?"

Mason grinned. "You're still believing everything Lunk told you! I'll bet you that five bucks I won from you today that when Tragg investigates, he'll find Lunk never had lived in the place to which the body was taken for burial. Now here's another clue. George Alber went to Lunk's shack about midnight. Lights were on, but there was no sound from the inside. Lunk says he was listening to the radio before Franklin Shore came. If that had been true, Alber would have heard either voices or the radio."

"But how about that post card from Florida?"

"That post card is really as much of a giveaway as what the kitten did," Mason said.

"How?"

"Don't you see? Because it was written in the winter of 1931, not the spring of 1932."

"How can you tell?"

"He said he was enjoying the mild climate," Mason said. "Florida has a good summer climate; but people don't talk about enjoying a *mild* climate except in winter. Then he says, 'believe it or not,' he's enjoying the swimming. He certainly wouldn't have said that if he'd been writing from Florida in the summer, because then there wouldn't have been any '*believe it or not*' about enjoying the swimming."

"But the card was postmarked in June of 1932."

"Sure, it was," Mason said. "But there was no date on the card, only on the postmark. People seldom date picture post cards. Don't you see? There's only one explanation. It was a card he'd written Helen when he and Matilda Shore had been visiting there the winter before. He'd probably slipped it in the pocket of one of his suits and had forgotten to mail it. Matilda found it when she was cleaning out his closet soon after his disappearance. It gave her a chance to ring in an artistic touch to the whole case. So six months after the 'disappearance' Helen gets a card mailed from Florida. I don't know how Matilda got it mailed, but it could have been done in any number of ways. Too, that gave her a chance to concoct this story of the mysterious double, which would confuse the police even more when she wanted to arrange for a 'reappearance' and make it seem Franklin Shore had really killed Leech." Mason sucked in a prodigious yawn. "I'm getting sleepy."

Della Street said, "I think you're the most baffling and the most exasperating individual I've ever known."

"What's wrong now?"

She said, "All these clues are so plain once you explain them. That's what makes it so particularly exasperating. They're so *very, very* plain. The answer is obvious, once you really look at them properly arranged. But somehow I can't ever arrange them and interpret them."

Mason said, "But it's all there. The kitten jumping onto the warm bed, the handkerchief with a laundry mark ten years old, the watch that was wound at four o'clock in the afternoon—a time when no person would normally wind a watch. The post card sent in summer, but obviously written in winter . . ."

"And you're not going to help Hamilton Burger figure this out?"

"Not a bit of it. Let him fry."

"Are you going to let her get away with this, and . . ."

"She won't get away with it," Mason said. "Tragg will eventually figure it out. He probably has the kitten angle straight already. He'll go digging up the body of Phil Lunk, and find it's really that of Franklin Shore. He'll begin to wonder who could have driven the car that struck down Tom Lunk, and will reason it out that it must have been the person who had killed Leech, trying to silence the lips of a man who might talk too much. And you have to hand it to Lunk. He played that most deadly efficient of all parts—that of a witness who is smart, but pretends to be stupid. His lying about Franklin Shore's visit was a masterpiece. But that, of course, is one of the things an investigator has to remember. A murderer will naturally lie, and a person who is clever enough to work out an ingenious murder plan will be clever enough to work out an ingenious lie. Matilda had, of course, helped him. They'd worked that all out in detail. But if it hadn't been for that kitten, they'd have fooled us—for a while, anyway.

"And believe me, darling, the next time I get in on a case, Hamilton Burger and Tragg won't tell me the proper place for me is in my office waiting for clues to turn up. They're going to be in a hot, hot spot for some time now, and when they finally do get it solved, they'll realize I had the answers all along."

Della Street confessed, "Well, I'll tell you one thing. You had *me* scared."

"Afraid you were going to get convicted?"

"I . . . I didn't know. It seemed so darn hopeless when I saw all that circumstantial evidence piling up."

Mason took one hand from the steering wheel to slip around her shoulders. "My dear, you should always have confidence in your lawyer," he told her gravely.

AMERICAN
MYSTERY
CLASSICS

from

*Available now
in hardcover and paperback:*